THE *seduction* OF KINLEY FOSTER

A WHAT HAPPENS IN VEGAS STORY

LISA WELLS

Phil,
To one of my favorite guys from high school.!
Lisa Wells

This book is a work of fiction. Names, characters, places, and incidents are the product of the author's imagination or are used fictitiously. Any resemblance to actual events, locales, or persons, living or dead, is coincidental.

Copyright © 2016 by Lisa Wells. All rights reserved, including the right to reproduce, distribute, or transmit in any form or by any means. For information regarding subsidiary rights, please contact the Publisher.

Entangled Publishing, LLC
2614 South Timberline Road
Suite 109
Fort Collins, CO 80525
Visit our website at www.entangledpublishing.com.

Lovestruck is an imprint of Entangled Publishing, LLC.

Edited by Vanessa Mitchell
Cover design by Heather Howland
Cover art from Deposit Photos

Manufactured in the United States of America

First Edition June 2016

Chapter One

Kinley Foster side-stepped down the airplane's crowded aisle juggling her carry-on, her Mac, and her neck pillow featuring head shots of Jimmy Fallon and Adam Kaufman. Her *Trust No Bro* T-shirt, stained a horrid hue of orange from her breakfast Slurpee, summed up the type of morning she'd endured. *Ugh.*

The chatter of excited women filled the small cabin of the chartered plane. Not her chartered plane. She was the green banana in their veggie bin. Dropped in when her plane was grounded due to a minor mechanical malfunction. *Minor, my library card. If it grounds a plane, it's major.*

She was heading to Vegas for five glorious days with 2,200 other romance writers, romance readers, romance models, romance…

Those who made a living out of selling love.

And if her nerves didn't combust and kill her, she would pitch her manuscript to an agent. The mere thought gave her hives. More hives than *The Rockettes* have pasties. But what was a little scratching when it came to chasing your dreams?

"Did anyone else see the ass on our pilot before he

disappeared into the cockpit?" said a young brunette with boobs that would make a Playmate proud.

"Are we going to have to talk about asses the whole trip?" one of the few men on the plane asked.

Since when do men not want to talk about asses?

Kinley passed row after row of boobs, bling, and babes in all shapes and sizes. Talking. Giggling. Texting. Drinking.

"I hear they are having a strip—"

An eruption of laughter from those sitting in row ten—seats a, b, and c—kept Kinley from picking-out the last part of the comment. Spotting her empty window seat in row twenty, she stopped. A handsome middle-aged black man, sitting in the aisle seat, stood and helped her stuff her suitcase in the overhead bin.

"Thanks." Chivalry wasn't dead.

"My pleasure." He stepped aside so she could do the awkward dance of crossing over the middle passenger: a full-figured woman who reminded Kinley of Vanessa Williams. Or what Vanessa would look like if she had a Jersey-Housewives' makeover.

A loudly spoken *oye* told her the dance lacked perfect choreography.

"Sorry." Kinley shuffle-stepped too quickly for her grace-level. Her feet twisted like crossed fingers. She lost her precarious balance…and ended up with her ass in the face of "Vanessa."

Before her brain could tell her backside to move, a pair of hands planted on her butt. Static electricity ensued. The widespread palms clutching each ass cheek gave an unexpected shove. Already off balance, Kinley went face first into the window. Obviously, Vanessa wasn't a butt-in-the-face-between-strangers type of gal. "Ouch."

"Oh… My Lord," the lady said in a southern drawl, the volume too loud to be considered lady-like. "I grabbed your tushy and caused sparks."

The gentleman sitting in the aisle seat chuckled. "Darling, you can't just grab a person's tushy without their permission." He sounded like he was joking.

But Kinley couldn't see his face, couldn't be sure.

"Hush yourself. You know I didn't touch her tushy on purpose."

Kinley twirled and faced the woman. She checked her head for a lump.

"I am so sorry," the ass-grabber said, fanning herself with her hand, which had bling rings on every finger.

"It's okay." What else could she say? *That's the most action I've seen in a year.*

"I'm Charlie." The lady pulled out a lavender silk hankie and delicately dabbed at her brow. "The Shemar Moore look-alike is my husband. Dan. His sense of humor is fractured." She moved the seat belt out of Kinley's way and patted the cushion for Kinley to sit.

"Thanks." Kinley sat and quickly jammed her purse and Mac under the seat in front of her. "I'm McKinley, but my family calls me Kinley." Her words came out rapidly and practically overlapped.

"What an unusual girl's name."

Kinley stiffened. "I'm named after my dad. He died before I popped out of my mom. In a freakish plane crash." She wiped her palms on her jeans. "I didn't pop out of my mom in a freak plane crash. My dad died in one."

Charlie's eyes rounded. "Bless your momma's heart. So lovely of her to name you after your daddy."

Kinley nodded. Remained silent. Some people didn't like to make small talk in a plane. And truly her desire to chatter was all nerves and not friendliness. "She says I'm just like him." *Shut. Up.*

Charlie smiled understandingly at Kinley, her eyes

crinkling at the corners like the grooves in ruffled potato chips. "You must be one of the passengers from the grounded Spirit Airway's plane?"

Dan placed his hand on top of Charlie's as if to inconspicuously quiet a child. "Did you say your dad died in a plane crash?"

"Rushing home to see my brother play in his first little league baseball game." Her brother carried that guilt on his shoulders to this day. He was always trying to be both a brother and a father to Kinley. Overprotective to a fault. "This is my first time flying. You could say I have a phobia when it comes to the friendly skies."

"Well don't you worry one little bit," Charlie said, pulling her hand out from under Dan's grasp and patting Kinley's knee. "This plane is sturdy. I know the pilot, and it's not going to go down over the Grand Canyon like his last one did."

Kinley's spine straightened, and her heart banged out several hard-rock beats. "What?" *What?* How had she gone from—

Charlie giggled. "Gotcha. Dan says my sense of humor puts the fun in funny."

Kinley took a breath that struggled to get past her closed off throat. She pointed a shaking finger at Charlie. "We'll see how fun your funny is when I write you as an out-of-work, cross-dressing prostitute in my next book."

"You're a writer?" Charlie clapped her hands causing the gold charm bracelets on her wrist to clickety-clack and their tiny charms to chime against one another. She nudged Dan. "Aren't we the lucky ones she's sitting with us?"

"Damn straight," Dan said, not looking up from his issue of Sports Illustrated.

"Do you write the good stuff?" Charlie asked in a stage whisper. Staged as in someone standing on a stage in New York could be heard by those sitting in the balcony of a theater in California. "You know, hunks and sex?"

"Is there anything else?" Kinley tucked a loose strand of hair behind her ear. "I'm going to Vegas for the eighteenth annual Romance Lovers Convention. It's my first time attending."

"I've heard of that. I hear it's a huge party."

"Complete with romance cover models." The perfect place for Kinley to enjoy a scorching affair. Something she was greatly in need of after a one-year hiatus from the dating scene.

"Have you been writing long?"

"Since middle school. My dad was a writer." *Stop rattling. She won't care that your New Year's resolution is to do whatever it takes to be successful or to get laid at least once every three months. How sad is it that I had to make a New Year's resolution to get laid? Like I have to work at that like I have to work at getting to the gym or eating more greens. You might be a loser if...* "I write semi-steamy. Not E.L. James... but close."

"I don't know the names of a lot of authors, but I recognize E.L. James," Dan said, putting his magazine away.

"Of course you do, dear," Charlie said, kissing her husband on the cheek and then buckling her seat belt. She glanced at Kinley and placed a finger to her lips as if about to whisper a secret. "E.L. James has done a lot for Passion Parties, Inc."

The whisper wasn't a whisper.

"She brought orgasms out of the bedroom," someone said a few seats ahead.

"Are we talking orgasms?" asked someone else.

"I had a singularly pleasant one this morning with our latest product," chimed in another.

Kinley clicked her seat belt and tugged on the strap to make sure the connection worked. Was she really sitting on a plane listening to women openly talk about orgasms?

What exactly was Passion Parties? What was their link with sexual satisfaction? "How has—" The plane lurched, taxied backward. Stopped. Kinley grasped the chair's handles.

Panic descended upon her like a tornado, twisting the breath out of her. She squeezed her eyes shut and started counting. *One, I'm not going to die. Two, what are the odds I'll die today? Three, son-of-a-bitch I'm going to die.*

"Bless your heart. You're nervous." Charlie laid a hand over Kinley's and squeezed. "Your hand is ice cold."

Kinley didn't respond. She continued to count. *Four... Guardian angels, where the hell are you? Five...* She turned her head into her neck pillow and envisioned the face there. Adam Kaufman with eyes the same color as—

"Love...that pillow," Charlie said loudly, causing Kinley to nearly jump out of her seat. The seat belt kept her in place.

Kinley pried open one eye and glanced at Charlie. "Thanks." The word came out muffled and low. Probably because her lips were plastered to Adam's.

"What does it look like?" the lady in the seat in front of them asked.

"It's a travel pillow with Adam Kaufman's face on the left side of the pillow and," Charlie struggled to lean across Kinley to see the face on the other side, "Jimmy Fallon's on the right. When she turns her face into the pillow, it looks like she's making out with them."

"That little Jimmy Fallon can climb into my bed any night," said someone in the plane.

"You can have Jimmy. I'll take Adam. He's got foreplay eyes and an after-sex voice."

The plane jerked. Kinley searched the backseat pocket for a barf bag. "Tell me about Passion Parties. What do you se—"

The plane lurched again.

Kinley's heart wobbled, cutting her question short. She

swallowed. Tried again. "Sell?"

"She wants to know what we sell at Passion Parties," Charlie shouted.

"Sex," everyone responded. Even Dan.

Chapter Two

The flight from Kansas City, Missouri to Las Vegas, Nevada took less than three hours. By the time the wheels touched solid ground, Kinley knew enough about Passion Parties, Inc. to be a representative.

They sold sex toys. Mostly at house parties. But when the occasion presented itself, they sold them on chartered planes heading to Vegas. Drinking often involved.

"Good luck with your agent pitch," Charlie said, before stepping into the aisle in front of her husband to exit the plane. "And don't stress."

"I wish I could tell you I won't. But I will." Kinley stuffed her newly purchased sex toys into her purse. Along with the We-Vibe 4, a dandy little vibrator with a remote control, she also possessed a toy called the Lipstick Vibe. A vibrator disguised as a tube of lipstick. Plus, she'd won a couple of mystery gifts that she'd yet to open.

Gadgets for today's woman…add a man to the mix—optional.

On the ground, an attendant told her how to find baggage

claim.

She squeezed into the crowd and watched for her hot pink suitcase. With its hand-painted tropical flowers, spotting her case was the easiest part of her day. She leaned forward and grabbed for the handle.

"Here, let me," a man said from behind her.

Kinley took a step back and bumped into a solid form. For an airport luggage boy, he smelled really nice. Sort of like a spring thunderstorm. "Sorry," she mumbled, twisting and sliding out of the gazillions of bodies. How nice of someone to grab her bag for her. She fumbled in her pocket for a dollar and found a five.

"Thank you," she said, handing him the money, while reaching for her suitcase.

He didn't let go of the handle...or take her money.

Wasn't five enough in Vegas? "I'm not giving you more money." She tugged on her suitcase.

He tugged back.

What the hell? She looked up and stared him in the eyes.

Incredible cornflower blue eyes stared back at her.

She blinked. Scowled. Refused to believe what she saw. She'd only ever known two guys with eyes that shade of blue and one of them was on the travel pillow hooked around her neck. The other—a jackass.

Him.

The moment she allowed the thought to take root, it must have shown on her face, because he gave her a slow, you-got-it-babe grin.

Her jaws clenched. Sonofabitch. It couldn't be. *Him.*

She stepped into his space. The toes of her purple Chucks touched the toes of his fancy-ass dress shoes. She reached up, way up, and fingered the lock of thick dark hair falling over his forehead.

He jutted his chin as if daring her to look.

She'd never been one to back down from a dare. She lifted the hair. "Damn." There it was. Still. The last piece of evidence to know her eyes weren't playing a trick on her. She stepped back. "I thought by now you'd be dead." Killed by a jealous husband or fiancé.

He looked the same but different. Ten years ago he had been crazy cute and sizzling sexy, but now, dressed in a tailored business suit cut to hug his broad shoulders and long legs, his face defined with new character lines, he was an advertisement for power. Rugged. A man's man.

A man who'd taught her not to trust.

"And in my mind, you're always buck-toothed and adorably chubby." His tone was serious. Not teasing. Freaking serious.

Kinley huffed. "I haven't been buck-toothed since I was twelve, and you know it." Chubby was in the eye of the beholder.

His eyes did a slow survey of her.

She stood rigid. Tried to imagine herself through his eyes. Crazy, curly brown hair pulled back in an I-don't-care messy bun. A sensible sweater for warmth. Jeans too tight from too many late night glasses of wine. Shoes made for comfort—not seduction.

Finally, his gaze travelled back up to meet hers.

Did he like what he saw? "Well?" The one word question sprung out of her mouth despite her brain telling it not to.

The last day they'd seen one another, she'd been a sassy sixteen, and he'd been an insufferable twenty-two. She'd wanted to give him her virginity. He'd wanted nothing to do with her. Then, before she could escape his apartment, her brother's fiancée walked naked out of his bedroom carrying an array of condoms and wearing an amused smile.

What in the hell was Ian Thompson doing in Vegas?

Ian touched her scar and grimaced. "The only thing that

hasn't changed about you is your sass." He turned and walked toward the exit with her suitcase. "Come on." The comment was said in a casual tone. As if they were friends.

The movement and demand shattered her this-can't-be-real state of mind. "Hey, stop." She grabbed her carry-on and followed. Her brother may have accepted Ian's explanation for that scene in the apartment, but not her. No sir.

Ian's stride was long, and she had to hustle to catch him. "I said stop," she shouted, making people stare. What was it with trust-fund babies that made them think they could always do what they wanted?

He was hailing a cab when she caught up with him. At six foot four, he looked ridiculous standing on the sidewalk with her hot pink suitcase.

"Are you kidnapping my suitcase for a reason?" She dropped her carry-on on his feet. "Or is the rumor true that you came out of the closet, and now your feminine side wants my girly luggage for yourself?"

She'd never believed the rumor about her old high school's star quarterback. Mostly because she started it.

But she wasn't above needling the jerk. He probably still believed he was every girl's lose-your-virginity-to dream man.

His lips twitched. "I told your brother I'd make sure you made it to the hotel, get you settled into your room, and keep an eye on you while you're at the conference."

She sucked in a breath of outrage. "*What?*" Her heartbeat shattered its old mad-to-furious acceleration record. A record set ten years ago in *his* apartment. *Ass*. "When?" A desire to knock Ian and her brother's heads together and then push them into a lane of fast-moving semi-truck traffic swept through her. "How?" Why her brother stayed in touch with Ian after he'd been the cause of his marriage never taking place was beyond her comprehension. The guy deserved to be elbowed into a snake pit, not forgiven.

Kinley pulled out her phone. If what Ian was saying was true, she was going to—

"Who are you calling?" Ian asked, giving her a lazy, seductive look.

The words he spoke barely registered. Probably because the way they sounded coming out of his mouth short-circuited her brain and super-charged her girly-parts.

His deep rumbly voice left her feeling naughty. Like scandal and sin were dancing on her soul.

Confused with her body's betrayal, she glowered. "None of your business."

"Calling your brother?"

She shrugged. Maybe she was calling her boyfriend. He didn't know she didn't have one. Unless her brother told him. "Maybe?"

Disappointment darkened his eyes. "I see you're still a snitch." He handed the suitcase to the driver, who stored it in the trunk, and opened the passenger door.

Her determination wavered. Damn him. Why should he be disappointed in her? "Whatever." He was the bad guy. Not her. She dropped her phone in her purse.

"Thank you," he said, in a voice that sounded sincere.

She rolled her eyes, not caring that the gesture was childish.

He motioned toward the open door to the backseat. "After you."

Halfway in, she felt the sharp sting of his hand on her ass.

She inhaled sharply, scrambled the rest of the way in, and turned on him. "How dare you. You can't just slap a woman's ass. Especially one who despises you. What the hell—"

The sound of his laughter cut off her tirade, and she grimaced. Damn it. She'd reacted exactly the way he wanted. Just like when he used to pull her ponytail and she'd yelp.

Growing up, he'd been a master at riling her emotions.

Not anymore. She was a grown woman, and her buttons were no longer so easily pushed.

He stuck his head in, an amused glint in his smug eyes. "You'll find I dare a lot. And the swat was for insinuating I'm gay. And so what if I was?" He slid in beside her, scooting much closer than necessary. His shoulder touched her arm; his presence invaded her space.

Grown up Kinley resisted the urge to thump him. Besides, if she did, the dramatic action would be more for show. And she prided herself on not being a drama queen.

Truth was, she was semi-turned on by the alpha-male ass-slap.

It wasn't because it was Ian that she was feeling aroused. Surely, it was because she'd done a ton of research on spanking in relationships for her current manuscript. And quite possibly the two chocolate martinis she'd drained on the plane were to blame. And...or...the sex toys burning a hole in her purse, saying, *hurry, get to the hotel and try me out.*

Realizing she was sitting in the middle of the seat, she scooted toward the window, away from him so they weren't touching. Even across the seat, his presence affected her. She pushed her glasses up her nose. "Why would my brother ask you to keep an eye on me when he knows damn well I can't stand you?"

God, I can't believe I'm in a cab with Ian Thompson. After all these years.

Ian stretched one arm out along the back of the seat. His fingers touched her shoulder. "Are you sure about that? According to him you ask about me all of the time."

She knocked his hand away. "I do not. He didn't say that." She might occasionally mention him, but it was always in a what-has-the-asshole-been-doing-lately way. To say her brother was too easy to forgive was like saying water is wet. Or love is a myth. Both true, but no way would her brother ask Ian to keep an eye on her. No way would he do that to her. Family loyalty trumps all other loyalty.

The driver got in the yellow taxi. "Where to?"

"The Masquerade Hotel and Casino," Ian said, before Kinley could reply.

"How do you know which hotel?" Could he see the thump of her heart against her chest? Hear the underlying emotions in her voice? Crud. Why wasn't she better at playing it cool?

"Your brother. It was nice to hear from him. I'm afraid we're guilty of letting life get in the way of our friendship." He once again rested his arm along the back of the seat.

She lifted her eyebrows. "Don't you mean your dick got in the way of your friendship?"

His lips tightened and then quickly relaxed. "You're not ever going to let that go, are you?"

"I can't imagine why I would." According to her brother, Ian never gave him a reason as to why his fiancée came out of his bedroom naked. Just played the trust-your-best-friend card, and her brother allowed it.

Who gives that kind of trust so freely? Not her. Not then. Not now. If she ever had to choose between her gut and her vision, she was going with what she saw. Eyes don't lie. Guts, on the other hand, tend to be in cahoots with one's emotions.

"Asking you to keep an eye on me is the most ridiculous thing I've heard all day. And trust me, I've heard some bizarre things today." Kinley caught an image of herself in the driver's rearview mirror and realized she still had her travel pillow around her neck. She yanked it off.

"And yet it's true." He slashed an eyebrow. One of his signature moves. A move that used to turn her knees wobbly. A move that prompted her to start reading romances at the age of twelve, hoping they'd teach her how to get him to slash that move on her.

He never did.

And, my god, after *sooo* many years, she shouldn't even remember that signature move let alone react to the sight of a simple raised brow. She pulled her phone out of her purse. "I told my brother I'd call and tell him I landed safely."

"I called him when your plane landed. He knows you're safe."

Kinley frowned and once again put her phone away. She stared out the window. "Do you live in Vegas?" The guy's social media presence was all protected from casual observers. And he had a picture of his yacht as his avatar. The only thing she knew about him were the bits and pieces she slyly pulled out of her brother.

"New York."

She could feel his eyes on her, but she didn't turn to make eye contact. "Please tell me you didn't drop everything and fly to Vegas just to take care of me."

He chuckled, a sound of condescension. A sound she'd heard before. And, damn it, these memories shouldn't be so clear. It was like she'd rewound the last decade and could recall every frickin' detail about him. Ugh. "If I had, getting to see grown-up Kinley Foster would have been worth the effort."

"Gag." She turned to see his reaction to her use of the old go-to expression she used to say whenever he said something she thought was disgusting. Did he miss the way they used to spar with one another?

"You've grown-up quite nicely, little Kinley. I almost didn't recognize you. Good thing your brother told me about your dreadful suitcase."

She tried not to look pleased. A near compliment. From Ian. The guy she fell in love with at the age of eight when he agreed to take her for a sled ride down the monster hill. Didn't matter that they'd crashed. Or that they'd ended up with scars on their foreheads. Her love had been freely given that day, because he'd told her "yes" when everyone else told her "no." And then the love blossomed when he dried her tears and told her that when two people have matching scars, they have magic powers. "Well, you're even uglier than you used to be."

He placed a hand across his heart. "That hurts. When did your tongue get so clever?"

"Bite me."

He reached out and touched her hair. Twirled a strand between his fingers. "What if one bite isn't enough? What if I want a five-course meal of bites?"

She smacked his hand away. "You always were greedy." Was he flirting with her?

His eyes flashed with promise. And then it was gone. Gone so quickly she wondered if she'd imagined the male version of a come hither look. He raised his hand and trailed a finger down the side of her face. "In all seriousness, I'd like to talk with you."

"Why?" she asked, pushing his hand away again. Her brother had mentioned a couple of times since the blow-up that Ian wanted to speak with her. She'd always refused.

In the beginning, she'd been too hurt and too angry to want to listen. Then, as the years passed, it had been more about not wanting to face her own humiliation. To not relive that awful moment when he'd taken her hopes and dreams— her heart—and shattered her.

Was her anger and bitterness toward him a decade later perhaps a wee bit over the top? Would a normal woman handle this situation with decidedly more panache, a bit more of a water-under-the-bridge attitude? Probably. But then she'd always considered panache to be overrated. And Ian always had a way of unnerving her. Time, it seemed, did nothing to lessen the effect. *Gag*, indeed, to the nth degree.

The laughter in his eyes disappeared. "Because there's something I've been wanting to tell you for a long time. And this gives me a chance."

She narrowed her eyes. Ignored her gut telling her she didn't want to hear what he had to say. Pulled up her big girl panties. "I'm listening."

Ten years was a long time to wait for an explanation.

Chapter Three

Ian Thompson sat in the backseat of a taxi with Kinley Foster, his tongue tied in knots. He'd been flustered since her brother had called and asked for a favor.

Ian wasn't accustomed to being flustered. He preferred compartmentalizing his emotions and only calling upon the ones that suited his needs. "I'm sorry," he blurted, like an inexperienced teenage boy who'd just been shot down for copping a feel.

Kinley jerked like he'd decked her with an uppercut, and he swallowed the rest of his apology.

"Sorrrrrry?" The word came out of her sounding like a snake's hiss.

Like he was her fallen hero. Which he was. Not that he'd ever wanted her to see him as a hero. He'd teased her like crazy when she was growing up, trying to kill the puppy-love adoration.

When he'd finally managed to get the job done, he'd really done it. She'd gone from hero-worship to hate with the blink of an eye. And it stuck.

Still.

He would never be forgiven by her. Even though what he'd done—

"My brother may be the forgiving type, but I'm not." Her tone was fierce, full of loyalty toward her brother and loathing toward him.

He sighed. "You used to think I could do no wrong." It'd been so long, he'd thought, surely after all this time…

She closed her eyes for a few uncomfortable heartbeats.

Which scene was she replaying in her brain?

The one where he turned down what she was offering him? Or the one where her brother's fiancée came strutting into his living room wearing nothing but a tan?

She opened her eyes. "I have no idea what you're talking about." Her voice held no signs of distress. No signs of hidden emotions. But her eyes held a winter-storm warning.

"Liar." It wasn't a word he used lightly. But damn it, she knew exactly what he was talking about.

She glanced out the car window. "Aside from some inane request of my brother's—which you can bet I'm going to verify—why are you in Vegas?"

He picked up her pillow and glanced at it. Scowled. Were these her new heroes? The ones she thought could do no wrong? "You really don't know?" Her brother told him she didn't. Told him he'd started to tell her once, but she cut him off. Said she could care less what 'the ass' did for a living. But he'd figured she'd simply found out from another source and was putting on an act for her brother.

She glanced back at him. "Sorry to burst your ego, but I don't know."

He ran his hand down his jaw. Was she deliberately trying to annoy him? "My pride's wounded." Sure he used an assumed identity, but she was smart enough to figure it out if she wanted to. "You haven't dug deep into Google to find out what I do for a living?" The brat had morphed into a curvy bombshell. One that could blow-up his easygoing lifestyle if he let his guard down.

She laughed. Not a happy laugh. A bitter laugh. "Why on earth would I do that? Have *you* dug deep into Google to learn all about me?" There it was…in her voice. The truth. In her world, he didn't exist in any depth.

Which meant her anger didn't stem from any part of her that maybe still thought about him or had an inkling of feeling for him. Damn it.

Her brother was wrong. He'd called with a two-fold plan. The first plan intrigued Ian the most. Her brother hoped that they could patch things up so Kinley could move forward in her love life without her puppy love of Ian holding her back. When pushed for details, her brother clammed up.

Part of Ian had been hopeful that things could be repaired between them.

Nope. That wasn't going to happen. He didn't know what happened to end her last relationship, but it had nothing to do with her pining after him. All the good kind of emotion she'd ever had for him was extinct.

That meant her anger…was purely that. Loathing and disgust for the past that she refused to see beyond.

The realization sliced at more than just his ego.

Hell. While she wasn't thinking about him, he'd been busy wondering whom the lucky boy was that did get her virginity. Who the lucky guys were she dated in college? Who the lucky men were she dated now? Did she work with them? Were they educators? "I loved that tiny red bikini you wore in your Cayman vacation pictures at the beach last summer." He'd had more than one fantasy of peeling if off of her.

Kinley flushed—a beautiful spotlight to her rounded cheekbones.

"Why are you really here?" Her tone ripped him back

to the moment. "There's no way my brother asked you to fly from New York to Las Vegas to babysit me."

This is where he should tell her the truth. The whole truth. He settled for a partial. The second half of her brother's plan. "Work."

She glanced away— "Did my brother tell you why I'm in Vegas?" —and slid her hands under her legs.

He smiled. How many times had he witnessed her crossing her fingers and hiding them under her legs while growing up? Her theory? If you cross your fingers before telling a lie, the lie doesn't count. "Why don't you tell me why you're in Vegas?"

She stared solemnly back at him with her beautiful eyes. A sultry brown. He remembered once hypothetically wondering what color eyes their children would have.

"Va—"

"We're here," the driver said, opening the door on her side, cutting off their conversation. Cutting off her lie.

Ian cursed under his breath. He wasn't ready for the two of them to be in a sea of thousands. He wanted more alone time with her.

Kinley jumped out. "Wow. This place is crazy awesome." She juggled all of her stuff under one arm and grabbed her suitcase from the driver. "Be a doll and pay the fare," she said to Ian in a faux haughty tone. Underneath, he could hear all of the same confusion he was feeling.

Before he could respond, she rushed toward the hotel's entrance, her swaying ass mocking him as if to say "sucker." He chuckled. Did she really think he was going to let her get away? That he wasn't going to chase her?

That he didn't know why she was in Vegas?

• • •

Kinley scurried into the hotel's lobby juggling her luggage

and laptop. People were everywhere. Mostly women. She took a steadying breath.

What little she'd taken in of the outside of the hotel had overwhelmed her. A little bit of jester, a little bit of international kitsch, and a whole lot of Bourbon Street. The inside besieged her eyes with exploding colors. Golds, purples, greens, and silvers. Excess appeared to be the hotel's motif.

Would Ian follow her inside the hotel? Or had he fulfilled his promise to her brother by getting her here? Just in case there was more to the plan the two of them hatched to keep her *safe*, she whipped around a group of five women and three men and stood very still in an attempt to blend in with the crowd.

If Ian made an attempt to find her, he wouldn't, and then he'd go away.

A voice behind her said, "Hey, what's the rush?" Then a hand landed on her shoulder causing her to jump.

"Damn it." She pivoted and glared up at Ian. "Can't you take a hint?" The people around her gave them a funny look, so she stepped away from the group.

Ian gave her a smile that reminded her of the teenager he used to be when he'd hang out at her house after football practice with her brother. Of the boy who pulled her hair and teased her excessively.

But mostly, the smile reminded her of the boy who'd spent the evening watching movies with her when he found her crying because the cool girls didn't invite her to the middle school end-of-year party.

He picked up her suitcase. "Shall we get you checked in for the Romance Lovers Convention?"

The breath she was about to expel tumbled back down her throat. She coughed. *Wait. What?* Her brother was *sooooo* dead for telling Ian about her dreams of being an author. Why would he do that? Why?

"This young lady needs to check-in," Ian said smoothly to the attendant behind the desk. He stepped aside, and Kinley stepped up to the counter.

"Hi, I have a reservation under Kinley Foster." Once she got to her room, she'd ditch Ian. Ditch the memories his presence stirred, both past and present. Then she'd call her brother and unleash her inner sister-bitch. This was the last time he'd ever interfere with her life. She was a grown woman. With a career. And her own apartment. She paid her own bills. She didn't need a babysitter.

"Welcome," the perky blonde said as she pushed buttons on the computer. Her smile dropped into a frown. She glanced at Kinley. "We don't show you having a room for tonight. Your reservation starts in two nights."

Kinley's smile didn't waver. "I have two confirmation numbers. One for the first two nights, and one for the conference nights." During the nights of the conference, rooms had to be booked through RLC. Kinley had added two additional nights under a separate reservation so she could keep her writing expenses separate from her personal expenses.

She set her purse on the counter and searched for her confirmation number for the first two nights. She handed the computer printout to the lady behind the desk.

The woman plugged in the numbers. "You're right. You're supposed to be booked for tonight and tomorrow night, but you booked through a third party for those two nights and sometimes, unfortunately, they overbook us."

Kinley placed her Mac on the counter. "What does that mean? I have a confirmation. I'm guaranteed a room. Don't you have to give me a key?"

The lady shook her head. "I'm really sorry. I hate when these companies do this. I can offer you a room in a nearby hotel." She started punching keys again.

"But, I'm here for a conference. I don't want to go to another hotel. I might miss an opportunity to visit with an agent or editor."

The attendant glanced up. "I'm sorry. It's the best I can do."

Kinley slid her glasses down her nose. "Please check again for a room at this hotel."

"We're sold out. We've been booked solid all week. We have a Tool Man's conference in town."

Kinley pushed her glasses back in place. Took a deep calming breath before the cloud of tadpoles in her stomach could become a knot of toads. First Ian and now this. What other surprises were in store for her in Vegas? "What is the name of the hotel you can get me in to?" Did the universe want her to go home? Was it trying to tell her if she stayed, her plane going home was going to crash?

"The Irish. It's in the older part of Vegas. You should be perfectly safe...as long as you don't go out at night by yourself."

Kinley placed a hand on her stomach. The toads were frolicking. She ignored the voice in her head telling her to go home. "I can't believe you don't have to give me a room when I have a confirmation number." She resisted the urge to stomp her foot like kindergarteners did when she told them their books were due, and they didn't want to give them up.

"If you'd booked directly with us, you'd be right. But as it is, this is the best I can do."

"May I speak to your manager?" Kinley hated being *that* customer. The one who thought if they just go over your head, they'll get their way. But what choice did she have?

The attendee pointed at her name badge. "I am the manager. I'll tell you what. For the inconvenience, we'll comp your room for two nights."

Kinley sighed a sigh that didn't nearly express the true

emotions inside of her. This wasn't how she wanted to start her first conference. No telling how many opportunities she'd miss by being in a different hotel. Everyone knew once a conference started, editors and agents were bombarded with *pick-me, pick-me* requests from authors. The trick was to catch the gatekeepers of publishing prior to the mad-zoo marathon they are about to run. When they are fresh and eager to say yes.

Ian placed a hand in the small of her back and leaned against the counter. He gave the blonde a dazzling smile causing the lights in the foyer to flicker. Or maybe it was something in Kinley that flickered to life. "Are you sure there isn't something else you can do? Surely you have a few rooms saved back for minor glitches like this."

Kinley watched him as he leaned across and whispered something to the attendant that caused her to giggle and touch her face.

"I really wish I could help you," the manager said to Ian in a different tone of voice than she'd used on Kinley.

Kinley resisted the urge to make a gagging noise. She laid a hand on Ian's shoulder to get his attention—not claim her territory. "Do you have a room here tonight and tomorrow night?"

Her touch didn't draw his attention away from the attendant. But she did feel him stiffen. "Of course. I always book directly." His voice was low and cautious.

The woman nodded approvingly.

Kinley argued with herself over the half-formed idea stirring her tired brain cells. It was a bad idea. A really bad idea. But staying in a hotel across town didn't exactly meet her list of great idea requirements.

Next to them, a woman stepped up to speak to a different attendant. She gave her name. Liz Pelletier.

Kinley's mouth went sidewalk-chalk-in-the-mouth dry.

She knew that name. She was an editor for Entangled. She was in the market to acquire authors who wrote steamy romance. Was Kinley really willing to let a computer glitch keep her from achieving what she came to Vegas to achieve? "Does your room have a couch?" she asked Ian in a no-nonsense tone.

He straightened. Glanced at her with a hooded look. "I don't recall."

She could practically see the wheels turning in his head. *How can I get rid of her? I've done my good deed.*

Too bad. He shouldn't have plotted with her brother to "watch after her." And it wasn't like he'd never seen her in her pajamas. He'd practically lived at their house for eighteen years. She gave him a crinkly nose smile.

He opened his mouth. The "no" formed on his lips.

She jumped in first. "That settles this mess. I'm going to stay with you." She glanced at the attendee. Gave her a triumphant smile. "Please give him another key to his room."

Kinley picked up her laptop and walked to an empty corner in the hotel and stopped. She tapped her foot and waited for Ian to choose helping her over the drinks and sex with the manager he'd probably been hoping for.

After another brief conversation with the blonde that ended in the handing off of a key card, and if Kinley wasn't mistaken, Ian's business card, he strolled over to her.

Kinley held out her hand. "Key."

"Still a bossy pants."

She couldn't help but smile at the reminder of his childhood nickname for her. Grown-ass adults simply didn't say "bossy pants." "Yep. Hand it over."

He pulled at his collar. "This is a bad idea."

She placed her hands on her hips. "I agree. Although I doubt our reasons are the same." She glanced back at the attendant who was staring at them.

"I'd say you might be right."

A tiny part of her wanted them to be talking about the same thing. But that would be tantamount to becoming a traitor to herself. Something she'd never do.

He jerked his gaze back to her. "Your mom and brother won't approve of us shacking up."

"Then we won't tell them." And if they did find out, they would understand. The alternative was for her to stay on the seedier side of Vegas. Their fear for her safety would trump their desire to protect her good-girl reputation. And *shacking up*? Surely he didn't mean that the way it sounded.

Ian reached out and tilted her chin up with his finger. "Aren't you afraid I'll take advantage of you?"

Oh shit. Yes, he had. She shivered at the sexy tone in his low voice and wrenched her chin away from his touch. "Considering you don't have a stellar reputation for keeping your hands off property that doesn't belong to you, I'd say you make a valid point." She took a step back. "Am I safe in a room with you for a couple of nights?"

His nostrils flared. "Still trying to get me into your bed?"

Her nostrils flared.

Before she could wither him with another reply, her stomach growled sounding like an awakening bear.

His expression became concerned. "You must be tired and hungry. Your brother said you were afraid to fly. Let's take your things to my suite, and then I'll feed you, and then you can take a nap."

She shook her head in dismay. "I'm not a dog. You don't need to feed me. I can feed myself." She held out her hand. "The key please." A nap sounded lovely. Not that she'd let him take credit for the idea.

He held the key card high, out of her reach. "If I'm going to let you stay in my room, there's one stipulation."

She crossed her arms across her chest and widened her

stance. She refused to jump for the key. "If there's a necktie on the doorknob, I know enough not to come in. I'm not a moron."

He blinked. "Well—there is that."

"Of course, if there's a pair of panties that means you stay out."

He narrowed his eyes. "I was going to say, you're not allowed to call your brother until after you and I have had a chance to talk."

She chewed on the inside of her cheek. Why did he care if she talked to her brother? Was there more to this than she knew about? "I can't imagine what you have to say that I'm going to be interested in hearing."

He waved at someone in the midst of a crowd of people.

Kinley didn't know anyone in the group. She probably should. No doubt, there were agents and editors all around, and she didn't recognize their faces. She needed to research the agents who were taking pitches at the conference. Put names and mugshots together. She'd been putting this task off until her manuscript was finished so she wouldn't be tempted to submit before her story was ready—a common error with new writers.

Ian tapped her nose with the room key. "Oh, you'd be surprised how the things I could come up with to talk to you about."

Chapter Four

Ian sat across from Kinley at a quaint table in Café Mascarade, a French café inside the hotel. The decor reminded him of sidewalk seating in Paris—a decadent city he'd visited once and would like to return to someday on his honeymoon.

He'd requested a booth as far away from the bustle as possible. They'd gotten a tiny table for two. Which wasn't nearly secluded enough. He should have insisted on room service so they could talk in private.

Kinley bugged her eyes at him. "You're staring," she said in an accusing tone.

He lifted a brow. "Do you object to a man being left speechless by your beauty?"

She had changed into a tan dress she'd cinched at her small waist with a wide leather belt. The top half of her dress fit snug and the lower half flared.

She gave him a what-the-Hades look. "Save it for someone who doesn't know you. I'm impervious to your lackluster charm."

He smiled. He wasn't feeding her a line of shit. But it was

just as well she thought he was. Truth was, the new Kinley really took some getting used to. "Impervious is a big word for such a petite thing."

"Is that your way of saying you don't know what such a big word means?"

Gone was the pig-tailed imp he remembered.

"I see you still have a smart mouth." Damn, she'd changed—in a good way. Pig-tailed Kinley Foster had been easy to resist. But she'd morphed into Killer Kinley with long legs and a curvy ass. This Kinley wasn't nearly as easy to ignore.

She leaned forward, placed her elbows on the table, and propped her chin on her laced hands.

He groaned, glancing pointedly at her cleavage. "You're killing me, Foster." Any man with a validated dude card couldn't help but notice her tits were threatening to spill out of her V-neck dress. When had she grown those? They hadn't been so noticeable ten years ago.

She glanced down, blushed, and sat up straight. "Enough with the suspense, what is it we're supposed to talk about?" She picked up her drink, awkwardly stirred her lemontini with a rock candy swizzle stick, and then sucked the drink off the stick.

She had to be doing that on purpose. No way was she that naive. "I can't think straight when you're sucking on that." His honesty surprised him and caused her to jump.

The stick dropped out of her mouth and bounced off the table. She ducked down and then popped up with the sex prop in hand. Rolling it between her fingers, she said, "Your room is fabulous." Her cheeks were bright red. "It must be nice to be an endowment brat and be able to afford a suite in a hotel like this."

Ian studied her face. He resisted the urge to ask her if she'd ever given a guy a blowjob. Not because he didn't want to continue to shock her, but because if she said yes, he had a strange feeling he might want to strangle the recipient. "Usually when women mention my endowment, it's not my bank account they're referring to."

Her elbows slid off the table and she made an awkward movement of grabbing the table to keep her balance, snapping her swizzle stick in the process, sending one end flying at him and the other hitting her in the chin. "I see you're still as crass as ever," she said.

He bit back the laughter filling his throat.

She leaned back in her chair, her eyes warning him to choose his next words carefully.

"Tell me, Kinley Foster, what do you do for a living when you're not chasing a fantasy of becoming an author?" He knew the answer—elementary school librarian in the town they grew up in—but he asked anyway.

She shook her head, causing her dangly gold hoop earrings to swing. "Enough. We're not friends chatting over drinks. Let's start with you answering my question."

He'd always liked how straightforward she was. Even when she'd been shy, and wearing orthodontic headgear, she'd always said what was on her mind when she was around him. "Okay. When I graduated from college, I decided not to go into the family business."

"I heard your parents disinherited you after the fiasco with my brother."

He leaned back, stretching his legs out under the table. "I heard that rumor as well. And I also heard you started it."

She gave him a serene smile. One as fake as most of the eyelashes he'd seen today. "I didn't, but only because I didn't think to start that one."

He believed her. "The truth is I wanted a career the family name couldn't buy me a position into."

She gave a bored sigh. "And what did that end up looking

like?" She glanced at her pale, square nails. "Wait. Don't tell me. You're racing yachts for a living." She picked up her drink and took a sip. "Am I right? That's why you have that as your avatar."

"I don't race yachts. But I find it interesting that you know what my Facebook avatar is. I thought you never looked me up…"

She sputtered. "D-don't get too puffed up. I only know because you commented on one of my brother's posts. That does not count as looking you up. So if not a yacht racer, what?"

He scooted his chair around the table so that they sat side by side. He wanted to see her reaction when he told her. "I became a literary agent."

Kinley choked on her drink, spewing it on him. She grabbed her napkin and dabbed at his chest, managing to spill more of her drink down his slacks. "Sorry." She headed south with the napkin.

He captured her hand, stopping her. The last thing he needed was for her to realize he had a hard-on with her name on it. "I'm fine." He took the napkin and cleaned up the mess, watching her as he did.

The blush from earlier traveled down her neck, drawing attention once again to her creamy cleavage. "I've ruined your suit," her voice cracked. She fanned herself with her hand.

"If you were any other woman, I'd think you did it on purpose to get me out of my clothes." He loosened his silk tie and slipped it off, stuffing it in his pocket. "Why does my being a literary agent cause you to get all hot and spewy?"

"I'm…" She stared at him for a long moment. "I just don't see you as a reader." Her voice was full of genuine shock. It deflated his ego like a pin to a balloon. "You honest to God read books other than Playboy?"

"Voraciously." Why was that so hard for her to believe?

His love of reading started when he tried asking his dad what girls wanted, and the only advice he gave Ian was that every girl had a certain laugh to be leery of. A laugh that signals she's about to hand you your balls on a silver platter. A platter you unknowingly gave her.

End of advice.

He hadn't even been able to give him an example of what *the laugh* sounds like. Just *learn it early and never forget it.*

The conversation with his father prompted Ian to steal several of Kinley's romance books to read and try to figure out what girls wanted, and what the laugh his father told him to tattoo to his memory was all about. And wonder if any girl had ever given him that laugh and he'd missed recognizing it.

The waitress came and set their meals down. "Is there anything else I can get you?"

"We'd like another round of drinks," Ian said.

"And some ketchup," Kinley added, glancing at her salmon.

The waitress left.

"I forgot your terrible habit of eating ketchup on everything," he murmured before taking a bite of his eggplant napoleon.

"I forgot everything about you," she said, forking a piece of salmon. "So you're telling me you have authors who let you represent them?"

"They do."

Her brows furrowed. "Romance writers?" She took the ketchup from the waitress and dumped half the bottle on her plate.

"Mostly writers of thrillers and espionage, but I also have romance authors on my list."

She slapped her palms down on the table. "Shut…up."

He took a sip of his drink. Smiled at two women walking by their table.

She leaned back, crossing her arms under her breasts, once again drawing his gaze to where it didn't belong. "I don't believe you."

He glanced up. His lips tightened. "That seems to be our pattern. I tell you something, you call me a liar."

She grabbed her purse and pulled out the conference agenda. "You're not in here. I'm sure of it. I would have noticed if your name had been on the list of agents attending the conference." She thumbed through to a chart showing which agents were taking pitches and what they were searching for.

"Are you sure about that?" he asked, leaning back in his chair.

She glanced up at him. "Of course, I'm sure. I wouldn't have come to a conference you were attending." He refrained from telling her that the only reason he'd decided to attend was because her brother had mentioned in an email that she was attending. Then he'd casually replied he was attending the same conference. That's when her brother called him, and they'd hatched their scheme for Ian to earn her forgiveness. Finally.

He pointed at a name. One that was highlighted in pink. "This must be an agent you really want to meet."

She jerked the agenda away from his view. "Not necessarily. He's just one who is taking pitches at the conference. Why haven't I heard of you?"

He glanced around the room. Was anyone listening to their conversation? He lowered his voice. "I don't agent under my real name. Like I said, I wanted to be successful on my own."

She stilled like a child who's just seen the boogeyman. Her eyes widened. She glanced down at her chart. "What name do you use?"

"I. Hartley. My mom's maiden name."

"You're—"

He placed a finger on her lips. "Yes."

She moved his finger. "You're this I. Hartley?" she whispered.

He nodded. Leaned in. "So you have heard of me? I'm not just another agent taking pitches at this conference?"

She stared at him. "My brother told me on the way to the airport I should try to pitch to you. That you are the agent of his favorite author."

"That's not a lie. He told me the same thing." The waitress set their drinks down and left.

"So my brother knows you are I. Hartley." The whisper was gone, in its place a cold, hard accusatory tone. As if someone's head was about to be chopped off.

He nodded and then sipped his drink.

"I can't believe you guys are still friends. Still scheming up ways to annoy me. If I were him, I would have, at the very least, made you do something hideous before I would even contemplate forgiving you."

Her words cut deep, but he smiled like they didn't. "Vengeful wench."

"I didn't used to be."

His pride told him not to even try. She wasn't the forgiving sort. And he wasn't the explaining sort—especially if never asked. And, unlike her brother, she'd never asked. "Tell me about your book. Pitch it to me now." Kinley had taken Stacy's version as gospel and never asked him for his. At least her brother trusted him enough to know there was more to the story. Although he hadn't told her brother the whole truth. He couldn't. The truth would have hurt Kinley.

Kinley gulped half of her drink. "I'm not ready."

He took a sip of his, enjoying the burning sensation as it went down. "You've written it, haven't you?"

"Why would I pitch a book I haven't finished?"

"Then tell me in a conversation what your book's about."

She folded her hands neatly in her lap. "Why? So you can pretend you're interested and then tell me no, because I just told you that's the sort of thing I'd do to you?"

He sighed. "I don't have a reason to hate you. I wouldn't do something so petty. Tell me about your book."

"I'm not petty. Just loyal to my brother. And damn it, you hurt him. You hurt my family. You hurt…us."

He rubbed his jaw. "I have a confession."

"This should be interesting. Are you going to finally admit that the truth is you stole his fiancée from him because you were jealous and not whatever bullshit you told him that night to make him break off his engagement and take your side of things?"

"That's not what I'm talking about."

"If not that, then what big confession do you have?"

"I've read your book. Your brother sent it to me."

Her eyes widened. Her face went white. "What? Why?" She looked like she might faint.

Ian's stomach lurched. He didn't want to continue this conversation. It was going to get harder before it got easier. He did anyway. "Your brother asked me to read your book and to keep an open mind about becoming your agent."

"You read my manuscript? He sent it to you? Tell me he's not trying to mend the broken fences between us by having you become my agent?"

"Yes, I've read your manuscript. I won't tell you he's trying to mend our friendship. And I'm free to reject your manuscript."

"You're free to reject my manuscript?" She nibbled her bottom lip. "He's not twisting your arm?"

"He thinks you're perfect. Nothing's changed there. But yes, I can reject you. As I explained to him, I have very high standards. I've only added one new author to my list in the past two years."

"And?"

He took another sip of his drink. "And what?" He braced himself for the next question. Wishing like hell he didn't have to answer.

"You said you read my manuscript. Are you rejecting me?"

Tension snaked around his gut. "Not you. Your manuscript. And not outright."

"What does that mean?" Her words were stiff as if they were weighted down with concrete bricks. Like she was trying to hold down her emotions so they didn't attach themselves to the words coming out of her mouth.

He really hated rejecting authors. He knew how hard they tried and how much they wanted the elusive "yes" from an agent. "It means you're a damn good writer. Except for one thing."

"What's that?"

He placed a hand on her arm and then withdrew it when she jerked away. "Don't take this personally, but you suck at sexual chemistry on the page."

Chapter Five

Kinley sat in the café with Ian Thompson—aka I. Hartley.

"Excuse me?" she said in a remarkably calm voice.

He sighed. "I don't mean to be blunt, but I can only help an author if they can handle the truth."

She breathed in the fragrant aroma of freshly baked croissants and told her heartbeat to slow the hell down. "What do you mean I suck at sexual chemistry?" She prayed the salmon she'd just consumed didn't come back up.

"There's no sexual chemistry between your characters. When they do finally hookup, the sex is bland. My dick didn't twitch once when I was reading your sex scenes."

She clenched her hands into fists. Inhaled and exhaled a turbulent breath. "I didn't write it so your dick would twitch."

"Maybe not. But no man is going to get laid as a result of his woman reading your book. And if you're going to write sexy contemporary, then that is your ultimate end desire."

Were his eyes laughing at her? They were.

"Well, I didn't ask you to read it. It's not even ready yet." She wished her drink wasn't empty. She'd throw it at him. How could her brother place her in this humiliating situation? If he were here, she'd throw a drink at him as well.

Damn it, what was wrong with her? She was an adult. An accomplished professional. She didn't whine or throw tantrums—or throw drinks at people. Or even entertain such immature thoughts. It was like Ian was her personal time warp, sucking her mind and body back to adolescence and rendering her a veritable teenager all over again.

"This is a brutal business. If you're going to be an author, you have to learn how to handle constructive criticism."

Her stomach rolled. How dare he lecture her? "Constructive? Constructive? You're not being constructive. You're being a jackass."

Ian checked his watch.

Was he anxious to get away from her? Was he meeting the check-in attendant somewhere?

He looked at her. "And you're responding like a teenager. All defensive. Just like the time I told you you couldn't flirt your way off a paper plate."

She ignored the part of her brain telling her he was right. "You were an ass then, and you're still an ass. And for your information, if I was behaving like a teenager, I'd do this." She kicked at him under the table as hard as she could. The toe of her boot made contact.

He grimaced.

It was like all of the emotions she'd felt that fateful afternoon ten years ago were in control of her. "I'll have you know, I'm behaving like a woman who was scorned by you once. And I'm not going to sit here and let you scorn me again." She grabbed her purse and pushed her chair back.

"Still running away from things that make you nervous," he drawled in a tone that irritated the hell out of her. Full of supreme superiority. Of a maturity sadly missing from her current arsenal of defense.

"I'm walking away because I think I've had all the 'blunt truth' I can handle from you for one day." Actually, this last humiliation should last her the rest of the century.

"Let's recall that first offense where I—" he made air quotes— "scorned you. The situation called for it. You were a minor, Kinley, asking an adult to make a woman out of you."

Heat flamed through her body, and his words halted her exit. "Lucky for me you said no, and I found someone better to give my virginity to." She told herself to stand up and walk away. But she couldn't. She wanted to see his response. Wanted to know if she hit a nerve. Wanted to know if he cared even a little that he hadn't been *the one*.

God knew she'd cared at the time. And maybe, just maybe, still did.

He scowled. A vein bulged by his right eye. "If the quality of your sex scenes are anything to go by, he didn't teach you much."

She slammed her palms on the table, causing their glasses to shake. "Damn you, Ian Thompson. How dare you reject me twice!"

She pushed into a standing position, prepared to make an exit worthy of a Regency heroine.

"Sit down." He spoke in an authoritative tone. A tone a teacher uses with an unruly student.

"Go to hell."

His lips tightened. "Are you really going to walk away from this conversation?"

She turned her foot toward the exit. She wasn't done. But she didn't trust herself to stay. She'd long since moved past the mistakes of her youth, but that didn't mean that ripping the scab off this particular wound wouldn't hurt. A lot. "I'm done talking, Ian."

"I'm not." There was a plea in his tone.

They stared at each other for long seconds. Seconds that

felt like eons.

She huffed and took a seat. "What else do you want to say?" She had no idea why she allowed him to boss her around.

"I'm not rejecting you. I'm rejecting your manuscript."

"Well…praise the Lord. I feel so much better now." Why did she let him sucker her into thinking he was going to say something nice?

"Great. Glad to hear it. And while you're taking my advice so well, I suggest you hit all of the workshops this week and seriously consider switching over to writing Amish romances or something that allows you to close the door on sex scenes."

She jerked back, his comment catching her on the chin. The back of her eyes burned. "Why do you have to be so hateful?" She'd worked really hard on the manuscript he'd read.

"Hateful?" He ran a hand through his hair, messing it up.

But not nearly as messed up as his words left her self-confidence. "You heard me."

He exhaled harshly. "Believe it or not, I see a great writer in your manuscript. You just can't write sex. It comes across as a nun trying to write spanking romance."

"And that's your idea of not being mean?" She glanced away. No way in hell would she cry in front of him.

"You're right. That was uncalled for." He reached out and touched her hand. "Sorry."

She yanked her hand away. "I can't unhear your comment just because you say you're sorry."

"You're right. I'll tell you what, if you learn how to write sex, you can query me with the manuscript again."

She rolled her eyes—a bad habit she'd picked up from working with fifth grade girls who desperately want to appear in control of all situations. "No, thanks."

"You have a raw talent that needs cultivating. My offer is

sincere."

No matter how sincere the offer was, the condescending raw-talent comment struck a nerve. "You have a raw talent for being an asshole. No cultivating needed." She grabbed her purse, once again ready to bolt. Yet…she didn't move. It was like her brain and body weren't on the same page. Or even in the same state. "And my insult is sincere."

"I have an idea." He said the words so softly she almost didn't hear them.

"What?" Why did he have to be an agent? Why did her brother have to send him her manuscript?

"Since you're spending the next two nights in my suite, if you like, we can talk about the craft of writing. I can give you some concrete ways you can turn your manuscript into something an agent can sell."

What was it about him that made her want to say yes? "Forget it."

"Don't let your pride get in the way of this opportunity. Didn't you say you came to this conference to find an agent? Well, I'm offering you two one-on-one evenings with me."

He was right. And she hated that. She wanted to say no, but her New Year's resolution demanded she didn't. "Fine. I'll spend a couple of evenings with you letting you teach me about writing." She waited for his gloating response.

He motioned to the waitress. "We'll have another round."

"I'll take a water," Kinley said to the waitress.

"Tell me, Kinley Foster," Ian said once the waitress walked away. "Are you the type who only has meaningful sex? Or do you do one-night stands?"

"T—that's none of your business," she sputtered.

"I'm simply trying to decide if your lack of steam on the page is because you've never experienced gut-wrenching sexual tension, or if it's because you're too uptight as a writer to put what you know onto the page."

"And why does that matter to you?"

"Because your answer will make a difference in how I try to teach you what you need to know."

Was he suggesting what she thought he was suggesting? Or was he just fishing, trying to see if she still had a thing for him? "I prefer short-term relationships." "Get in, get out with your sanity intact" was her new motto when it came to relationships. Part of her New Year's resolution. Something she'd planned on putting into practice starting at this conference.

"Me too." She couldn't read the expression in his eyes. Did her response make him happy or angry?

She licked her lips. What would she do if he ever tried to kiss her? He was, after all, her first knight in shining armor. The one she'd never stopped thinking about no matter how much she told herself and her brother otherwise. "I'll sleep better at night knowing that the Great Ian and I have something in common."

He shook his head. "For a moment, I thought the mature Kinley might be able to leave the past in the past for the sake of her future. But you're no more mature now than you were ten years ago."

The fact that he had a point stung. Why did being around him reduce her to such out-of-character behavior? "Would you like to place a friendly wager on that?" The challenge was out before she could suck it back in. Shit.

Chapter Six

Ian opened the door to his suite around seven p.m. and found Kinley, the woman who sarcastically bet she could handle him mentoring her on sex way better than he could handle teaching her about sex—yes, that's right, she'd bet about them and *sex*—dozing on the couch in a pair of flannel pajamas featuring pink elephants in tutus.

He could talk her through the intricacies of passion, give her an understanding of what real chemistry was. This bet was in the bag.

His scrutiny lingered on the sight of her hair splayed across the pillow. One she must have snatched from the suite's king-sized bed. She had one arm thrown across her face as if to shield her eyes from the light of the lamp she hadn't turned off.

A glass of red wine sat on the table beside her with an empty wine bottle next to it. Her laptop stood open on the coffee table. He liked her hair down. All crazy curls and volume. She shifted, and he caught sight of an expanse of bare skin between the gap of her bottoms and her top. His breath hitched.

Damn it. He was going to lose the bet.

He let go of the door and stepped inside the room for a closer look. The door made a clicking noise when it latched, causing her to jump and wake.

"Hi." Her voice sounded drugged, as if she'd been sleeping deeply, and her brain wasn't as awake as her eyes led one to believe. Or maybe she was drunk. She pushed her hair behind her ears, where it fell down the length of her back in a cascade of disheveled silk. Like the sheets he'd slept on last evening.

He grimaced. Not because he'd woken her, but because he'd robbed himself of the opportunity to view her without her pretty little mouth biting at him with its teeth sharpened on pride and anger. "Didn't mean to wake you." The meeting had actually ended over an hour ago, but he'd hit the casino to unwind.

Kinley moistened her lips with the tip of her pink tongue. A move she'd done earlier.

Was it his imagination or was she taking a very long time to wet her extremely kissable lips? Seeing her familiar eyes and soft expression, he was hit in the center of the chest with the realization of just how much he'd missed her. Yeah, Jack Foster had been his best friend growing up, and, even in the wake of Stacy-gate, they'd gotten back to an even keel. But he'd lost Kinley entirely. And what's worse, he hadn't realized back then just how much he'd taken her for granted in his life until she was gone. Seeing her again, in person, after all these years…yeah. It just hit him hard.

She sat up and took a sip of her wine. "I thought maybe you'd decided not to give me tips on writing after all."

Hell. Why was he going all sentimental? She was a frigging knockout. One that had him thinking about sex. Wondering things like what she would taste like if he ran his tongue along her pouty bottom lip. Would she tremor and moan if he lightly bit the flesh?

"How much have you had to drink?" He himself had enough to know his defenses were down. Why else would the sight of her infuse in him a desire to ravage? Boobs or not, she was still bratty Kinley Foster. His friend's little sister. Which in guy speak, meant she was off-limits.

Her cute nose wrinkled. "That's not a polite thing to ask a lady," she said in a prim voice, reminding him of the fact that she was a librarian. A sexy librarian. "Come and have a seat. I have my computer running and a fresh page pulled up to take notes. I'm ready for you to mentor me about sex."

Ian strode to the bar and grabbed a bottle of water. "About that—"

"After all, I did bet you I could handle anything you want to teach me. And I've never been one to go back on my word."

He twisted off the lid and drank the contents of the small container, tossed it, and grabbed another. "I've been thinking. What you need to learn, I can't mentor you for." He hadn't really been thinking that—until now. When he realized they were going to be spending two nights in the same hotel room. And she was of legal age. Now it felt imperative not to engage her in a quest to write sexy.

She glanced up from her computer screen and pulled her glasses down until they were perched on the tip of her nose. "Can't or won't?" Her brows drew together as if warning him there was a right answer and a very wrong answer.

He widened his stance. "Won't."

Their gazes locked.

He sighed but didn't look away. "In order to write sexy, you need to have experienced sexy situations. Your writing needs authenticity. I can't help you get sexual experience."

She still didn't blink.

He glanced at her lips, which were drawn into a tight line, and then back up into her eyes, noticing a smudge of mascara on her cheek as he did. "Are you going to say anything?"

She took her glasses off and held them in one hand, shaking them at him. "Ridiculous male response." Her pissed-off voice punctuated each word a little heavier than necessary.

He stood mute.

She shook her head as if to rid herself of the ridiculousness of what he'd said and then slid her glasses back on her face. "That's like saying I need to kill someone if I want to be a decent murder mystery author."

He opened the new bottle of water and took a seat on the arm of the chair across from where she sat. "Killing someone *would* be the best way to prepare for the life of a murder mystery writer." He held up a finger when she opened her mouth to protest. "But that's not practical. So authors of genres riddled with murders are forced to research in other ways."

She nodded emphatically. "Exactly. And romance authors can do the same." She smiled as if they were in total agreement.

She licked her lips, and he all but groaned aloud at the sight. Did she keep doing that to distract him?

"Absolutely, they can." His voice not quite his own. "And there are two types of romance authors. Those who've experienced love and sex firsthand and write it brilliantly because they understand it, and those who only imagine it and then write it great but less than brilliantly."

She stared at him over the top of her laptop. "Asinine. But...I'm not going to argue with you about it. You are, after all, an agent and should know what it takes to get a book published." She started typing. "Things...I need...to...learn...to write...brilliant...romance... Number...one. Get...sexual...experience."

He watched her fingers fly over the keys and frowned. "Did you just type what you said? Delete that." What in the fuck was she doing? "Are you typing a to-do list?"

"Number two." Her fingers paused, and she glanced up. "I'm going to be your willing mentee. Talk to me. Tell me what else I need."

Jesus, she'd said she'd be a better student than he'd be a teacher—not that he was willing to concede to that. Yet. He yanked off his cufflinks and threw them on the coffee table. Told himself she was just being a brat and trying to get under his skin. She wouldn't really go out and try to get sexual experience just to write a book. He called her bluff. "You also need to broaden your knowledge of writing dialogue. And story structure."

"Learn more about dialogue and story structure." She glanced up. "Next?"

"That's it."

"Okay. I need sex experience and craft knowledge." She stretched her arms over her head and yawned. "Not counting tonight, I've four more nights in Vegas. Surely I can fit four one-night stands in while I'm here." She gave him a smile so bright he blinked. "I bet there're some hunks here for that tool convention."

He bolted upright. "You're not going to have one-night stands while you're at this conference."

Her smile dimmed. "Why? I want to write sexy. It's what I like to read. And, as it happens, one of my New Year's resolutions involves me *dating* more this year."

He threw the bottle in his hand at the trash can. Missed. Marched to the room's sliding glass doors and yanked open the curtains. "You're looking for a man you can *date*?" he asked, while staring out at the lights of Vegas. Her tone left him in no doubt what she meant by dating.

"So?"

He could hear her typing. He exhaled harshly then turned around and leaned against the wall. "So…I'm not going to let you sleep with every Tom, Dick and Harry the Tool Salesman at this conference just because I told you, you can't write sex."

She laughed—a guttural sound. Sexy as hell. "Let's get a couple of things straight. You have zero control over me, and I plan on doing whatever it takes to be a successful writer. Having sex with a hunk in a tool belt would not be a hardship."

She left him with no choice. He took out his phone. How had he lost control of this situation? Her brother was never going to forgive him if he blew this with Kinley. But he'd also never forgive him if he allowed his little sister to become the conference's Girls Gone Wild poster child. "Then you leave me no choice."

"What are you doing?" She walked over to him and reached for his phone.

He held it out of her reach. "I'm calling your brother." When she stretched like that, her pajamas gapped at the buttons. He wouldn't be a man if he didn't enjoy the view.

"Now who's being the tattle-tale?" she said, dropping her arms to her side.

The softly spoken barb pierced a nerve. He stopped scrolling for the contact number. He wasn't a liar, and he wasn't a tattle-tale. "Someone's got to make you see sense."

A thoughtful expression crossed her face. She gave him a thorough look, lingering in places her gaze shouldn't be lingering. "How about a compromise?"

"I'm…listening." He wasn't sure he should be.

She walked back to the couch. Picked up her computer. "You can teach me about sexual tension…and sex," she said in a firm voice. She gave him a smile that she probably thought was casual. It wasn't.

It was freaking sexy. Beckoning.

The phone fell from his grip. "You want me to have sex with you?" Shock made his voice brusquer than it needed to be. Had he heard wrong?

She lifted a shoulder. "Want is a bit strong. It's more like—I'm *willing* to have sex with you for the sake of research. I don't suppose you have a tool belt, do you?"

"I thought you hated me?"

"What does hate have to do with sex? One is an emotion, the other an act. Do you have handcuffs?"

An image of her handcuffed to his bed zipped by his eyes. "You shouldn't have sex with someone you hate."

She raised her eyebrows. "Maybe…I'm tired of hating. Maybe…I want to screw you until all of the hate is gone. Maybe…you shouldn't try to tell me who I should or shouldn't have sex with."

Did she just say she was tired of hating him? He picked up his phone and laid it on the bar. She had to be bluffing. Only she didn't look like she was bluffing. But then, bluffing is all about not looking like you're bluffing. "You're serious, aren't you?" He took his jacket off and tossed it on a chair.

"I am…unless…you know…you've got a tiny little—"

"You're asking me to have sex with you? Like you did on your sixteenth birthday?"

She clamped her lips shut and stared at him with a look so sharp he felt sliced. "It would appear I am," she said calmly.

God, he was a bastard. He walked across the room, headed to the bedroom. Away from her. He needed to think beyond the reaction his dick was having to her suggestion. He needed to put a stop to the insanity. "I'm not attracted to you in a sexual way." This had to be a trap. She was testing him to see if he really was a pig.

She coughed. "I call bullshit."

"Your brother is my friend. I can't have sex with his little sister."

A harsh laugh erupted from deep inside of her.

He jerked in surprise.

She got up and cut him off at the door, separating the

living space from the bedroom. She leaned against the frame. "You can have sex with his fiancée but not me."

"I'm not debating—"

"Before you tell me no, you should know, I've been told I give a hell of a blowjob." She blew her hair out of her eyes as if giving weight to the word "blow."

His mouth fell open. How did she know he'd been thinking of her and blowjobs? Images of her lips wrapped around his dick tortured him. He searched for his resolve. "The fact remains, I'm not attracted to you." He forced the words out, hoping he was doing a better job of convincing her than he was himself.

She arched her back against the frame of the door. "I can see you're trying to do the right thing. Be a good friend. I'll make you another wager, Ian Thompson."

"I'm not being a...what kind of wager?" God, how did she pull off sexy wearing those pajamas?

"If I can seduce you, you have to spend the nights of the conference teaching me about sex and sexual tension."

He rubbed a hand down his face. "Cut the crap, Kinley. Why me? Is this a test of my character? Are you pushing me to see if I'm worthy of your brother's friendship? If I'm worthy of your forgiveness?"

She stared him straight in the eyes. "Not everything in life is about you or my brother. And the truth is I'm a little out of practice and could use a practice run with a test dummy."

He'd give anything to be able to read her mind right now. "A practice run? With a test dummy? Meaning me?"

"Sure. Who better to strike that kind of deal with than the devil? Isn't there a saying about the devil you know being better than the devil you don't?"

He reached out and plucked at the string on her pajama bottoms. Not enough to untie the cute little bow. Just enough to cause her to react.

She flattened her back against the door. Out of his reach.

He sighed. "Damn it, Kinley. You don't have the personality to write steamy sex. You need to try your hand at something tamer."

She unbuttoned the top button of her top. "I don't want to try something tamer." She unbuttoned the second button. "I want to do some role playing." He thought he heard her murmur something about a New Year's resolution.

"Forget it." He turned away. "I've been accused of doing the unthinkable to your brother once. I'm not putting myself in a position to have that happen again. Having sex with you isn't going to happen." Hell. Did she want to play out some of the roles in her manuscript?

"Four one-night stands it'll be then," she said airily. She pushed away from the door, walked to the couch, and plopped down.

He glanced back at her. "You're impossible."

She picked up her laptop. "Compromise. My brother doesn't have to know how you helped me, just that you helped me. And I'm willing to concede that you're right. I do lack the necessary experience. But like anything else, I can learn."

He shoved his hands into his pant pockets. No way was he going to make a promise to not tell her brother. "I lied. Your manuscript is full of sexual tension, and your sex scenes gave me a hard-on. I just don't want to be your agent."

She didn't look up at him. "Again with the lying."

The accusation hit him in the gut. He'd been accused of lying once. He'd promised himself he'd never be placed in a position to be called a liar again. Yet, he'd just willingly lied to her. "Okay, you're right. I lied. Your sex scenes sucked. But I can't let you have nameless sex while I've been put in charge of watching out for you."

She gave him a look of surprise. Stared intently at him. "Then we're back to you teaching me."

God, she made his head spin. But that was Kinley. One hundred percent all in, rarely looking before she leaped. It'd been a trait he'd assumed she'd grow out of…obviously not.

He tried again. "This is crazy."

She shrugged. "No doubt."

He groped for a way out of the deal she was bargaining for. There was none. Unless…he fought fire with fire. He'd counter her bet with his own bet. "I'll help you if you can seduce me into the act. But if you can't, you have to do things my way."

She pulled her knees up and rested her chin on them. "What is your definition of my successfully seducing you?"

"You have to make me forget who you are. Make me forget you're off-limits. Get me to sleep with you one time without regretting the decision when it's over. If you can accomplish that, I'll teach you how to feel and then write sexual tension."

"What do you mean without regretting it?"

"Make it so good that I don't care about the consequences. Make it so good, I want to do it again and again and again. Four nights of again." He ignored the voice in his head saying he wanted her to succeed. Maybe a few nights with her would get her out of his brain once and for all. Allow him to have a meaningful relationship without the memory of her standing in his doorway offering up the most beautiful gift any woman had ever offered him interfering with every first time he had with a woman.

"The consequences being my brother's wrath?"

"More like my peace of mind."

"And if I can do that, you'll teach me what uncontrollable sexual tension feels like? Help me with some of the scenes in my book?"

Wow. Were they really having this conversation? Was he really considering saying yes? "I'll mentor you, for the duration of the conference, if you can seduce me. Then you have six months to rewrite your manuscript. Send it to me, if it's any good, I'll send it to another agent with a recommendation they represent you."

"Why not you?"

"Because I don't have sex with my clients. It's not ethical."

A look of admiration flickered in her gaze. "Look at you caring about ethics."

His chest tightened. He'd missed that look. She used to look at him like that all of the time. "If you can't seduce me, though, you have to promise to try your hand at writing sweet romances. I truly think you might be better suited to those."

She jumped up, walked to him, and held out her hand. "Deal."

He shook it.

She turned and went back to the couch. Her ass was freaking cute in her pajamas. "You do have a repertoire beyond vanilla sex—don't you?" she asked, settling onto the couch arm.

"You suffering from *Fifty Shades* curiosity?" His voice was gruff, even for him. She didn't need to know he'd done a ton of his own research into the BDSM lifestyle when he decided to take on his first erotic romance author. Or that while he'd been doing the research, he kept imagining Kinley in different situations with him as the master. He blamed that on stalking her Facebook page and seeing her in one swimsuit too many. He'd never quite been able to get her out of his brain.

She blushed. "It's for research. Not personal taste."

He shook his head. She wasn't going to win. He wouldn't let her win. "Kinley Foster, you're going to fail. And when you do, you're not allowed to accuse me of scorning you for a third time."

Her expression took on a swagger. "Ian Thompson, I'm

going to be the best sex you ever had."

"Or not. Look at you."

"What's wrong with how I look?"

"You're wearing long-sleeve pajamas. Pajamas that cover every inch of your body. You're not a seductress."

"Maybe not if I'm just sitting here. But what if I were to stretch." She stood and raised her hands over her head again and bent from side to side. Then she lowered one hand to the hem of her top and slowly inched it up, showing the creamy expanse of her flat stomach. After what felt like an eternity to him, she slowly lowered her other arm and looked him in the eyes. "Still think I'm not a seductress?"

He ran his finger under his collar. "Kid's stuff."

She rolled her eyes. "You don't stand a chance against what I have in store for you."

He inclined his head. "I like your confidence, but remember the deal. You have to get me to sleep with you one time *without* regretting the decision when it's over. It's going to be hard for you to get me to sleep with you once. To get me to not regret it the next morning will be damn near impossible."

"Why?"

"Because your brother would kill me if I had a casual affair with you."

"I know another female who managed to seduce you despite the fact he'd be furious. I'm thinking my chances are pretty damn good."

"I hope you're wrong."

"Ian Thompson, you better get a good night's sleep, because tomorrow night I'm going to knock your socks off."

"Honey, tomorrow night, it's not my socks you should be focused on getting off."

Chapter Seven

"I have meetings scheduled all day," Ian said, averting his gaze from Kinley, who'd appeared from the suite's bedroom dressed in workout clothes. Somehow she'd commandeered the bed last night and left him sleeping on the pullout couch with a pillow that smelled of her lavender perfume.

She yawned. "Oh right." An impish siren's smile played on her lips. "Considering your age, you might want to try and grab a nap today."

"Why's that?"

"Because I did a little research before falling asleep, and you're going to need your energy tonight." She flounced to the kitchen area of the suite and poured a cup of coffee.

He swallowed the lump in his throat. The lump that hadn't been there until she came out of the bedroom. "So, about that…we'd both been drinking last night…in the light of the day…I think this is a bad idea."

She gave him a look that didn't require words to get its point across. But she used them anyway. "You aren't actually going to go back on your word, are you? I thought you weren't a liar."

He cursed his stupidity. "Of course not. It's just—"

"I'm a grown woman. Completely sober. I've thought about this. Sure, there're some obstacles to what we're doing, mainly me not liking you a lot, but my brother isn't one of our obstacles. He has no right to know anything about my love life. If you have some misguided concern that you can't do this because of him, or that you have to tell him before you sleep with me, you're wrong. If I want him to know, I'll tell him. If we do this, your loyalty lies with me. As in, you can't kiss and tell. Now, I'm telling you that I'm in one hundred percent. The question is—are you?"

When had she gotten so good at arguing? "I'm in—if you can seduce me." The situation with her brother…he wouldn't lie. But they'd cross that bridge if they *ever* reached it. "Tell me something, Kinley. Are you a runner?"

She smiled. A confident woman smile. Leaned against the cabinet. "Only when I'm being chased…or in the right mood." The hot, sexy voice that came out of her lips did things to his ability to think. Did things to his ability to speak.

He took advantage of the opportunity to take in her long bare legs beneath a pair of running shorts. Imagined them wrapped around him. He watched her spoon several helpings of sugar into her coffee. "I take it you're in the right mood to be chased."

"Oh I am. Shall we meet back here at say six o'clock this evening?"

He walked over and poured himself a cup of coffee, nudging her out of the way with his hip. All too aware of the length of her legs. "I may be in, but I'm not letting you seduce me that easily."

She nudged back. "What does that mean?"

He put some space between them. "First, you have to pick me up. Then you have to talk me into coming back to the hotel with you."

She twirled and pinned him with an arched brow. "Pick you up?" Her hair was pulled back in a ponytail. Her face bare of makeup, and she had on an antitrust T-shirt with a lime green jog bra showing through underneath. "Beg you to come back to the hotel with me?"

"I didn't say beg. But now that you did, I'm digging the idea of you begging."

She thumped her coffee cup down, causing some to splash out. "I don't beg."

He took a sip of his coffee. "If you're any good, you won't have to beg." Damn, she looked good.

As in a good girl. Like the Catholic schoolgirl she once was.

"Please tell me you know how to pick-up a guy?" He didn't know why he was teasing her. Or why there was a sensation of excitement tightening his gut.

"Of course I know how to bring a guy home from a bar with me." Her voice jumped several notes.

Ian continued in a blasé tone he hoped annoyed the hell out of her. "Great. Tonight you have to flirt. Make me laugh. Make me want to come back to your room with you. Make me feel macho." Okay, now he was laying it on extra thick.

Her somber inspection slid smoothly over him. She tapped her lips with her finger. "Are you insecure in certain areas of your manhood? Is that why you need a woman to make you feel macho?"

He grinned. She'd always had witty comebacks when they were arguing. "I guess you'll have to successfully seduce me to find out." And if he wasn't mistaken, this was the second time she'd made a reference to the size of his cock. The lady was prying. How long had this curiosity about him been stashed in her brain?

She sat down at the table and tucked her legs underneath

her. Her smile fell away. Determination filled her eyes. "Where exactly am I going to find you to flirt with you?" She raised her hands over her head and did a series of side stretches.

He couldn't force his gaze away. Where was the tomboy of years gone by? The one who'd shown up to his apartment to seduce him wearing sneakers and a baseball cap and her school uniform? "Mmmm." The easiest place would be in the bar down stairs.

Except tonight she would fail to seduce him. Success wasn't an option. No matter what she said, one didn't accept the task of "watching out" for a sister and then fall into bed with said sister. And he didn't want her to fail in front of other writers, agents, and editors. "I'll tell you what. I'll be at Club Uno by nine o'clock tonight. You can show me what you've got there."

She dropped her hands to her sides and frowned. "I heard that's impossible to get into if you don't know someone."

"You know someone."

"Who?"

"I'll have your name on the guest list. Go to the front, you'll be able to skip the line."

"Make it eight o'clock." She placed her left foot on the chair and tied her shoestrings.

"Anxious?" Did she know he could see up her shorts when she did that? Was she doing it on purpose? He glanced away and focused on the potted plant in the corner of the room.

"I'd like to have you seduced and asleep by ten. The conference starts tomorrow, and I want to be fresh for it."

He glanced back at her.

She swapped feet and tied the other shoe.

"Kinley, when the time comes, you can say no." At this rate, she wasn't going to have any problem getting him to say yes. He better get his priorities straight before tonight.

"And in the morning, if I've wowed you with my abilities, you'll spend the next three nights wowing me with yours?"

He reluctantly nodded. "Yes."

She dropped her foot to the floor. "Are you going to think less of me for doing this?" She nibbled her thumb.

He shook his head. "This has nothing to do with my feelings for you one way or another."

Chapter Eight

Kinley sat at the blackjack table with Charlie, glad her new airplane friend agreed to spend the day plotting with her. Not book plotting. Seduction plotting. All Kinley had to do was promise to play some blackjack with her first.

They'd been playing about an hour, and Kinley was up twenty dollars. "Hit me," she said to the dealer.

The dealer laid a seven on Kinley's cards.

She waved her hand over them. "Stay." You couldn't just tell the dealer you wanted to stay on your cards, you had to make the hand movement for the cameras to pick up.

The dealer moved on to the next person at the table.

The Pit Boss came to their table. His name was McGill. Black, bald, and a man of few words.

"Hi McGill," Kinley said, giving him her best flirtatious smile. "Have I bet enough yet to be comped some buffets for my friend and me?"

McGill picked up her card and swiped it in a machine he held in his hand. "Not yet," he said, lying it back down on the table.

Kinley sighed in a dramatic fashion. "I'll make you a deal. You give us two buffets, and I'll give you a starring role in my next book. And I'll be very generous with your measurements."

McGill's lips twitched, but he didn't smile. "You're going to have to keep an eye on this one," he said to their dealer.

"Doubling down on a bust card," said a dealer at the table beside them.

McGill walked away and went to that table.

"I would have never pegged you to be such a flirt," Charlie said. She was sitting at first base.

After a year hiatus from men, Kinley was having a hard time holding her flirting back. It was like a vital part of her had been released from jail, and she was enjoying the hell out of the freedom. "You know what they say, still waters run deep."

Charlie gave her a quizzical look. "Obviously so."

Kinley glanced around. She didn't even know the chairs at a blackjack table had names until Charlie made them search for a table with first base open. According to Charlie, she didn't want newbies messing up the cards for her. She always sat at the far most right chair at the table.

"Are you sure you want to seduce him?" Charlie asked, bringing Kinley's attention back to her cards.

"McGill?" Kinley shook her head. Why would she want to seduce McGill?

"Ian."

Oh. "No. Yes. I don't know," Kinley said. "I could probably use some practice in the seduction scene. And he's as safe as any man is going to be. I mean, if I say no at the last minute, he'll honor my desire."

The dealer flipped up a ten, giving him sixteen. He took a hit, which was another ten. "Dealer busts," he said.

The table cheered.

"You're the Tom Sawyer to my Huck Finn," Kinley said

to him. He'd been busting more than winning. She pushed a chip toward him as a tip.

He took it, tapped it on the tip jar and then dropped it in.

Charlie gathered up her chips. "Let's get out of here. We've got things to do."

"But I'm winning," Kinley said. "Unlike McGill, Tom Sawyer's being good to me," she said, speaking loudly so McGill could hear.

McGill lifted a hand in acknowledgement of her reply.

The dealer smiled politely and waited for them to either place their bets or leave the table.

"Come on," Charlie said, standing up.

Kinley gathered her chips. "I guess I'll leave while I'm ahead." She gave Tom Sawyer a wink, and he gave her a professionally bland smile. "You pretend indifference, but I know beneath your polite, this-is-just-a-job smile is a man who likes me."

"How'd you come to be such a flirt?" Charlie asked her as they cashed out their chips. "This side of you changes my whole plan for how tonight is going to play out."

"My mom worked two jobs to pay the bills," Kinley said. "Which left my brother to raise me. He's six years older. I grew up around his friends. If you grow up surrounded by boys who tease you like crazy, you learn how to tease back. Flirting is just teasing with different intent."

Charlie giggled and stuffed her winnings in her billfold. "You've just given me an idea on a sure-fire way for you to seduce Ian into going back to the hotel with you."

"I did?" Kinley took a step to the side.

"First, we need to buy you a seduction outfit."

Kinley glanced around. There were several shops to choose from in the hotel. "Where does one go to buy a seduction outfit?" She spied a couple walking into one of the restaurants. Was that Ian? Who was he with? Why did her heart hitch at the sight?

Charlie grabbed her hand and tugged her out of the casino. "To a store that is owned by a renowned seductress."

Will, one of the hotel's concierges, who looked an awful lot like a young Leonard Nimoy, approached them. "Ladies, may I get you a taxi?"

"Please," Charlie said.

"How does one become a renowned seductress?" Kinley asked, blinking in the bright sunshine that bounced off the immense beads that draped the outside of the hotel.

"I'm not at liberty to say," Charlie said, slipping into the taxi and quickly saying something to the driver.

Kinley crawled in beside her. "Then I shall have to get you drunk later so the secret comes out."

Charlie slipped on her sunglasses. They were the type of sunglasses Hollywood actresses wear when they don't want to be recognized. "Be careful which Pandora's box you try to pry open," she said, with a semi-serious expression.

The taxi pulled away from the curb.

"Something tells me you're more than a sex-toy peddler," Kinley said, staring out her window. They drove by the casino's fountain. A big ass carriage, Cinderella-style, rose from the depths. Kinley blinked. "Oh my God. Look at that."

"Gorgeous, isn't it?"

"Spectacular." Kinley watched all of the sights as they drove slowly by them. Vegas had a lot of unique people walking up and down the Strip. It was like the rich and poor comingled in harmony.

The store they went to was a boutique about a mile from their hotel. A boutique that offered them champagne served in crystal flutes when they entered the unmarked black door.

"Charlie, darling, it's so nice to see you. How may I be of assistance? Are you in need of a new…purchase for Saturday night?"

Kinley looked from one to the other. She wasn't sure what it was, but there was definitely an undertone of something going on between the two women. She took a sip of her drink. The bubbles made her sneeze.

Charlie removed her sunglasses. "This is my friend Kinley."

The woman grabbed Kinley's hands and held her arms out wide and read her T-shirt. "Where did you get this adorable tee?" She had an enchanting English accent. "I'm loving the vibe."

Kinley glanced down at her shirt—black with *Trust No Bro* written in hot pink across the front. And two stick figures. One with a broken heart. The other with a forked tongue. "I sell them at TrustNotTees.com." They were available in five brilliant colors.

"I have a girlfriend who dumped her boyfriend after she caught him with his dick in a chick that wasn't her. She so needs this T-shirt to remind her he's a jerk—because I know her, give her a week, and she'll be right back to him, forgiving and trusting him all over again."

"I know. Right?" Kinley said.

Charlie cleared her throat. "We're on a tight schedule. Kinley needs an outfit that will knock the cum out of this man she has her eyes on."

Kinley blushed. Dear Lord, did Charlie *really* just say that?

"They'll be hooking up at Club Uno tonight," Charlie said.

"Ooo la la. That's a swanky club. Way to go, girlfriend."

Kinley smiled, feeling like she'd been given the best boyfriend ever nod of approval, from an It Girl. Someone who gave out compliments about as often as a sumo-wrestler went on a diet. She had to admit, she was a tiny bit impressed that Ian had the power to get her in without the need to wait in a line.

"What size are you?" the sales lady asked.

Kinley glanced at the ladies over the top of her glass. "A two mostly."

"A two?" the sales lady questioned.

Kinley took a sip. "Sometimes a four. A six feels nice."

The sales lady stared at Kinley with a smile — a smile that didn't grow or falter. Not so much a smile as a comment. Liar, liar, pants on fire.

"Okay I'm an eight, but a small eight, so don't bring me any large eights." Kinley stared into the eyes of the sales lady, daring her to suggest otherwise.

She didn't. But her serene, "I call chubby-girl" smile did.

Kinley folded. "Oh, what the hell, go ahead and throw in a ten. You know…in case they run small."

"Yes. Of course," the sales lady replied, taking the dress off the rack she'd had her hand on throughout the entire size conversation and holding it up for observation.

"That's not quite what we have in mind." Charlie pulled a black dress off a rack and held it up. "We want something that sizzles sex. What do you have that's much sexier than this?"

"Twirl," the lady demanded of Kinley.

Kinley stood on her toes and did what she was told, feeling like a wound-up ballerina perched on a child's jewelry box.

"*Mmm hmmm*. You've got the legs for a mini. Your junk's not fabulous, but it'll do. Unless he's an ass man and then we'll need to get you a fake ass. Will your boobs stand up on their own?"

Kinley stopped twirling. "What?"

"Do you have to wear a bra?" Charlie interpreted.

Kinley glanced down at her boobs. "I guess not. They're perky."

"34 C?" the sales lady asked.

"D," Kinley replied.

Charlie raised an eyebrow.

Kinley sighed. "C."

The sales lady walked to a dressing room, unlocked the door and opened it. "Get undressed, and I'll bring you a few things to try on."

Charlie pushed Kinley toward the door when she didn't move. "She's going to need the works."

"What are the works?" Kinley asked from behind the closed door. Ian Thompson better not have a small penis or she was really going to be pissed to have wasted so much of her conference time on him. She should be researching agents right now.

"Tonight, once you have him back to the hotel room, when you take your clothes off, your body needs to leave him speechless."

"Then she needs a wax and a spray tan. I'll call my guy."

Kinley paused in the middle of unhooking her bra. Anxiety snapped her into action. She opened the door and stuck her head out. "Not doing the wax thing. Been there, done that, ain't happening." She shut the door.

"Nonsense," Charlie said. "Make the appointment for one o'clock. I'll get her liquored up over lunch."

Kinley shuddered. The worst pain she'd ever endured had been for a Brazilian wax. "I'm not getting waxed down there," she stated loudly. She'd rather be featured standing in the nude next to a naked super model in a "who wore their birthday suit better?" photo shoot than wax her privates.

"Trust me, three chocolate martinis in you, and you won't even feel a thing," Charlie replied.

Chapter Nine

Kinley walked into Club Uno a new woman. Her curly hair had been straightened and cascaded down her back like spilled chocolate. Her thick eyebrows had been *oohed* and *aahed* over as the cross-dresser technician plucked them into a hissing-cat arch. Her eye shadow was a clichéd smoky look using colors that enhanced her brown eyes, and her lips were a pale neutral with lots of gloss.

After much discussion between Charlie and the boutique babe, the outfit she wore shouted "do-me, I'm easy." There wasn't anything about the form fitting black dress that gave off an elementary school librarian vibe. The front had a deep *V* that stopped just above her belly button. The back was scooped out so low underwear wasn't possible. Kinley's freshly-waxed playground was going commando.

The grand finale of her attire was a pair of hooker red shoes with toothpick heels that easily added four inches to her height and dropped thirty points from her perceived IQ of those assessing her.

She'd been made to practice runway walking in them

for over an hour after her lunch martinis until Charlie was convinced she could pull them off.

Hours later, she stepped out of the taxi—carefully, mind you, she wasn't about to go all drunken Hollywood Celeb/flash the crowd with her girlie bits—and did the runway strut to the front of the line. "Hi," she purred in her best attempt at a sexy voice. Tonight she planned to be the mysterious woman that others viewed as edgy and ballsy with just a hint of Moscato sweetness.

The bouncer gave her a look that made her want to have a cigarette. Even though she wasn't a smoker.

"I'm—"

"The best looking thing I've seen in years." The bouncer unlatched the cord meant to keep the unsuitables out. He allowed Kinley to enter.

Who needs a man's name when you've got an ass, tits, and heels?

Inside the plush club, she took a deep breath and then smiled like the room was her movie set and she was their porn star. "Show time." She didn't look for Ian. Charlie specifically told her not to. She said to arrive late and casually walk through and find a seat at the bar—then proceed to chat up the bartender and anyone who sat down beside her.

When Kinley fretted about the plan, Charlie assured her Ian would notice her the moment she entered the room, and he would come to her. Getting him to come to her was part of the seduction. He wouldn't want to, but he wouldn't be able to help himself if she did exactly what Charlie told her to do.

"May I buy you a drink?" a man asked, coming up to the bar and standing beside her.

Kinley looked him over. "It depends. What's it going to cost me to let you buy me a drink?" She did an internal sigh. Thank God someone was hitting on her. Just because you dress like you're all that, and just because someone you barely know tells you, you're all that, doesn't mean you're all that. Kinley was more than aware that although her legs might be long, her thighs were too large. And her ass could be perkier. And underneath the makeup was an ordinary woman.

He leaned an elbow on the bar and checked her out. "Not a thing."

"Really?" she sounded as skeptical as she felt.

A sheepish grin lifted his lips. "Okay. I'll be straight with you. My friends think you're going to shoot me down. Let me buy you a drink, and I'm the boss in their eyes."

Kinley resisted the urge to run toward the exit. To call uncle and forget this charade. "How old are you?" she asked the young hunk staring at her. And thus part two of Charlie's plan was in action.

Flirt with members of the opposite sex while you wait for Ian's approach.

"Celebrating my twenty-first birthday," the boy-toy said with a variation of the sheepish grin that made him look about eighteen.

She placed her hand on his arm. "Happy birthday."

"What are you drinking?" he asked.

A woman who drinks bourbon is dangerous. A woman who drinks wine is a housewife. Charlie's words played in Kinley's head.

"Anything with bourbon."

Birthday Boy commandeered the bartender's attention. "We'll take two Boulevardiers with Maker's Mark." He sat down on the barstool next to Kinley. "So what's a beauty like you doing alone in a bar?"

"It's a long story." She smiled like he'd said something incredibly funny. "So have you gotten lucky yet?"

His face turned red, highlighting freckles she hadn't noticed before.

She glanced down at her dress. Had she inadvertently

given him a bald eagle shot? And then it dawned on her what she'd asked him. "Sorry. I was talking about luck at the slots. Not with the ladies." She could feel heat in her cheeks. And this was Vegas. Oh my God, he probably thought she was soliciting him!

"Oh." His shoulders relaxed. "Not yet. If things don't turn around, it's going to be an expensive trip."

Their drinks came.

Kinley held hers up for a toast. "Here's to you having a safe, fun, and luck-infused birthday weekend."

He picked up his glass, clinked hers. "Here's to meeting a beautiful woman on my twenty-first birthday."

She smiled. What a sweet young man. "Thanks for the drink."

Birthday Boy took a sip of his. "If you get lonely, you're welcome to hang with us tonight." He pointed to a group of guys sitting at a table. "We're pretty harmless."

"I'll keep that in mind."

He gave her a smile and then turned to walk away.

"Oh wait," Kinley said, grabbing his arm, remembering Charlie's instruction to lay the flirting on thick. When he glanced at her, she winked at him. "This is for the guys watching. You need bragging rights on your birthday." She leaned in and touched her lips to his—very quickly, but long enough for his friends to see. And long enough for Ian to see if he was indeed watching her from somewhere.

Birthday Boy cleared his throat and touched his lips. "Thanks." He sauntered back to his friends like a cowboy after a successful eight-second bull ride.

Kinley laughed. She could feel Ian's eyes on her. But she hadn't spotted him yet. Not that it mattered if she saw him. Only that he saw her. What would he say when they talked?

Several minutes later, another of the birthday group joined her. Told her it was his birthday. She sent him packing with a pat on his cheek.

Less than five minutes after that, Ian walked up to the bar. "I don't know what you think you're doing, but stop it." The order was made in a pissed-off, gruff voice.

She'd hit a nerve. "Hi," she said, biting back a smile.

"I'll have an Aberfeldy neat with a water back," he said to the bartender. He didn't say anything else to Kinley. He didn't even look at her.

Was this part of the seduction? Did he want her to pretend they didn't know each other? "I see we both have good taste in drinks." She laid a hand on his forearm to get his attention. She felt his pulse beat hard beneath her fingertips.

"Thanks," he said to the bartender who brought him his drink. He took the straw and, eye-dropper style, added four drops of water into his glass. Then he downed the drink and slammed the glass on the counter, still not glancing her way.

Kinley's brows drew in. He seemed mildly livid. A step beyond pissed. "Perhaps you'd like to buy me a drink?" she said, pushing her empty glass next to his hand. There was no way in hell she was buying her own drinks tonight. They cost a small fortune.

"Bring her another, and put her drinks on my tab tonight," he said to the bartender. "And bring me another."

That's better. She slowly uncrossed and re-crossed her legs, willing him to look at her.

He didn't.

"Thanks," she said. Trying to stay in character.

Nothing.

Time to try a new tactic. "Give me your phone," she said in what she hoped was a sexy voice.

He slashed an eyebrow at her, causing her insides to melt into a puddle of dreamy nostalgia. She'd done it. After all these years, Ian Thompson just executed his signature move on her. The one that made all of the middle school girls giggle and the high school girls swoon.

He handed over his phone.

She took it, her hands shaky. "What's your password?"

"Nine, one, nine, two."

She unlocked his phone and punched her name and number into his contacts. "Call me sometime." She handed him his phone back.

"I don't live around here."

"Oh." This is where she should invite him back to her hotel. But Charlie told her under no circumstances should she do that. So she didn't. Was that a mistake?

The bartender brought their drinks.

He picked his up and pushed hers toward her. Then he glanced down at her legs. "Have a great evening," he said, still not looking her in the eyes, and before she could blink, he walked away.

Kinley's smile disappeared. "You too," but he was already too far away to hear her words. What in the hell was that about? *Shit, shit, shit.*

She watched him cross the floor to a table occupied by a woman. When he sat down, the lady leaned in and said something to him that made him throw back his head and laugh.

Kinley felt a shot of some type of emotion. She had no idea what the emotion was, but it wasn't pleasant. Who in the hell was that? How was she supposed to pick Ian up if he was here with some bimbo? Not that the woman looked like a bimbo. Kinley had the market on bimbo for the evening.

She slid off the bar stool and strolled over to the birthday table. "Who wants to dance?" The drinks were beginning to warm her insides and numb her brain.

Four of the guys glanced at one another, and then they all turned their attention to a redheaded young man. A cutie-patootie. "He will."

He stood and led her to the dance floor.

She swayed to the music. A sultry jazz. Reminded herself not to dance like she usually did, although a little voice in her head shouted, "Do the Running Man!" She reined in the impulse. No one would get seduced if she pulled out the Kinley-moves.

"Do you know why it's me you're dancing with and not one of them?" he asked, as they danced.

"Why?"

"Because they're all hot for you."

Kinley stumbled and put her hand on his shoulder to steady herself. Why wasn't he interested in her? Did he see her for what she was? A fraud with fat thighs? "And you're not?" *Kinley Foster, did you just practically ask a guy why he doesn't want you?*

"I'm gay." He wrapped an arm around her waist and swung her around. "You're a horrible dancer."

"I know. Sorry about your foot."

"I probably shouldn't tell you this, but the broody hunk who bought your drink after my friend bought you one…"

Kinley accidentally stepped on his foot again. Broody was a good word for Ian. Especially tonight. "What about him?"

"He walked by our table and told us to stay the hell away from you if we wanted to live."

Kinley giggled. She felt oddly elated by the knowledge. She'd made Ian jealous. "He was teasing. He's got a weird sense of humor like that. Rumor has it he's gay. Would you like his phone number?" Did Ian still have the same cell number? The one her brother gave to her on a Post-it note five years ago with a message from Ian that he would like for her to call him? You'd think she would have forgotten it the moment she wadded up the slip of paper and threw it in the trash. She hadn't. When she'd added her number to his phone, she should've sent a text to herself. Damn it.

Kinley's phone beeped as they were leaving the dance floor. She glanced down at the message.

You've been there long enough. Time to leave. — Charlie.

Kinley texted back. *I don't have him yet.*

Leave anyway. —Charlie.

・・・

Ian watched Kinley walk off the dance floor and back to the table of douches. Fuck. He stood. He was going to have to get into a fight tonight. Where in the hell was the rest of her dress? That couldn't be all of the material that came with it.

He motioned for the waiter. "I'd like to close my tab."

What the hell had he been thinking, inviting her here? No. Stratch that. What the hell had he been thinking throwing down that seduction gauntlet in the first place?

He glanced around impatiently for the waiter and his credit card when Kinley turned and sashayed toward the door. His nostrils flared. Her ass had the room mesmerized. Is that why she was walking like that? To draw the attention of every man in the joint onto her ass? He needed a friggin' blanket.

And where in the hell was she going? Wasn't she supposed to be seducing him?

The guy he'd seen her kiss got up and hurried to catch up with her.

She stopped. They talked and then laughed. Her hand tucked into the crook of his elbow.

Ian settled up his bill in time to see them walk out the doors.

What the fuck? Had she changed her mind about seducing

him? Was she going to find someone else to teach her about sex and sexual tension?

He stormed toward the door. She wasn't going anywhere with another guy on his watch. If she was determined to get laid in the name of research, it was going to be him and not some jackass out for ass.

He exited the building in time to see her sliding into a taxi. Her dress rode up enough to show the outline of her cheeks. The sight had him sucking in a breath and nearly tripping over his own two feet.

The guy with her leaned down to say something.

Ian came up behind them and pushed the guy away. "She's with me," he said. His hands fisted at his sides, daring him to give him a reason to throw a punch. He wanted to hit the guy.

The guy took a step back. "No problem, dude, I was just being a gentleman and making sure she got a cab."

Ian slid into the backseat and shut the door in the would-be-suitor's face. "Take us to the Masquerade," he said to the driver. He turned toward Kinley. "What the hell is going on with you?"

She blinked. Her eyes somewhat glazed. "Nothing. I'm just going back to the hotel."

He swore under his breath. "I thought the whole idea was for you to seduce me into coming back to your hotel with you?"

As the taxi pulled away from the curb, she ran her hand down the side of his face. "You're in my taxi, and we're headed back to the hotel," she said softly. "I'd say I succeeded."

He stared at her for a long moment. Hell. He'd played right into her hands. He threw back his head and laughed. "Well played, Kinley Foster."

Kinley giggled and scooted to the corner of the taxi. The move caused her dress to shimmy up her thighs to the point of nearly being indecent.

Ian's gaze locked onto her legs. "Are you wearing anything under that?" His voice was husky.

She parted her legs slightly. Not enough that he could see anything. Just enough to make him forget to breathe. "What do you think?" she asked.

He reached out and touched her leg at the knee. He slowly ran his hand up her leg until the tips of his fingers were touching the hem of her dress.

"Oh," she said, her eyes half-closing.

He forced himself to remove his hand. She wasn't his for the taking. She was his best friend's little sister. *Best friend's little sister. Best friend's little sister. Best friend's little sister.*

Chapter Ten

Kinley stepped into the hotel in front of Ian and stopped. The elevators stared back at her, and she was swaying *juuuuust* a bit. The two of them were reaching the point of no return. She'd been panting with desire in the taxi. But here in the bright lights, the film of desire was more transparent. It seemed tawdry. She felt like her legs were going to buckle beneath her at any moment.

Was she really going to turn to Ian to help her end her sexual hiatus? To start the ball rolling on her New Year's resolution? She'd be killing two birds with one stone, and all that, but still…

Ian placed a hand on her shoulder and caressed her bare skin. "If you're having second thoughts, we can call off this game."

His words snapped her out of her frenzy. What they were doing wasn't tawdry. It was normal behavior between two consenting adults. He'd like for her to back down. Then he could make fun of her for not having the nerve to finish what she'd started.

Damn it. She wasn't going to be the one who halted their experiment. And yes, by God, she'd be honest with herself about why she was doing this. She wasn't just doing this to get out of her sexual slump. But her other reason wasn't something she wanted to think about right now. She'd think about it later. When the conference was over. Or never.

She licked her lips—a nervous habit that caused her to go through a lot of lip balm. She stepped into his space, placed her hands on his shoulders, and stood on her tiptoes so she could see into his eyes.

Damn, they were a pretty blue. Like a field of cornflower bachelor buttons. She shrugged at her silliness. But, hey, if a romance author can't think of her guy's eyes as cornflower blue, who could? Not that Ian was her guy. Just her stud for a few nights.

And while she was waxing poetic, the pulse pounding in his throat reminded her of the romance heroes she loved to read about.

And the way he was staring back at her shouted *I'm alpha and you're mine.*

She shivered. It was all about the fantasy—and he was quickly fulfilling hers.

She placed her lips against his ear and whispered, "I want to do what you want to do."

He groaned, took her hand, and dragged her toward the elevator. She stumbled as she tried to catch up. High heels were great until you were being dragged behind a horny man and trying to not fall on your face. Then they were a horny fail.

To make things worse, those gathered in the piano bar watched. Some even hooted and hollered like they were still in middle school.

She decided she didn't care. Qualms, anxieties, uncertainties—she didn't care about those either. None of them stood a chance against the desire he'd ignited in her in the cab with nothing more than a blue-eyed glance and the rasping feel of his hand across her upper thigh.

They stepped into the elevator and moved to the back when a group of women got on with them. The elevator stopped on every floor.

Ian's hand slid down her spine, until his thumb was hooked in the low back of the dress, and his hand was resting on the top of her ass.

She wiggled her hips, wanting to feel his hand in other places…like between her legs. She must have made a noise, because one of the women in front of her turned and pursed her lips.

Kinley bit her tongue and stared straight ahead.

Four women got off and three more got on.

Needing his arms around her, she tried to move back into his arms. Into his body.

He held her where she was. Not allowing her the comfort of his warmth. "Do you think they think you're a hooker?" His whisper sounded like a growl in her ear.

The question sobered her, and she wrapped her arms across her middle. Did she look like a hooker? Was he turned on at the idea of her playing the part of a hooker? Of a little *Pretty Woman* action?

At the club, she'd been dressed okay. High heels and little dresses seemed to be the uniform de jour. But in the elevator, she was definitely under-dressed. Or overdressed, in the sense of plunging necklines and stripper heels.

She felt his warm breath against her skin. He was blowing on her neck. Teasing her with what was to come.

When they were the only ones left in the elevator, Ian yanked her back until she was leaning against him. She could feel the hard ridge of his cock pressed into her back. She wiggled.

He hissed.

She basked in the knowledge she'd done that to him. He'd come home with her—Kinley Foster—not the woman from the bar. Whoever she was.

The elevator reached their floor. He pushed gently on her shoulders and the intimate contact was broken. They walked to his room without talking.

He opened the door and softly pushed her inside his swanky hotel suite.

She grabbed the wall for support. Mmmm. Things were wobbly when you drank and wore heels at the same time.

He turned on the light.

She drummed her fingers against the wall. Now what should she do? Was she supposed to seduce him? Was he taking over? Was he going to seduce her?

As if picking up on her uncertainty, he grabbed her hand and led her to the bedroom. At the door, he picked her up, and walked to the bed with her. He laid her down on the fluffy white comforter. "Don't move."

"Okay." There was something very sexy about a man taking charge. She watched as he loosened his tie and slipped it off. Then he unbuttoned the top several buttons of his shirt. She put her lips together to whistle but nothing came out.

Giving up on the whistle, Kinley watched in aroused awe.

He dropped down on the bed beside her and leaned up on an elbow so that he was looking down at her.

She reached out and brushed her fingertips over his scar and down the square line of his jaw. Did he know how much she hated her scar? It reminded her of him. Of—

He traced her scar. "I'm going to kiss you, Kinley. And when I'm done, it's up to you to seduce me into taking this further."

She grinned. Wasn't he just the sweetest thing, telling her what he was going to do?

Ian Thompson, her first crush, was going to kiss her. Something she'd dreamt about so many nights. Her heart executed the whistle her lips hadn't been able to manage. "Why are you doing the kissing? Aren't I the seductress?"

He was wearing a white dress shirt. Open at the collar, rolled up at the cuffs. No jacket. She fought an urge to reach forward and finish unbuttoning his shirt.

"Because it will be our first real kiss. And I want to make sure ours is memorable." His voice wasn't the voice she knew when he was angry at her. Or the voice he used when he teased her. Or the voice he used when he told her she couldn't write sex. Could this be his aroused voice? If so, she liked the thick vibrations of sounds.

Her brain told her to shut up and take what he was offering. Of course, her lips didn't comply. "If I recall right, we already had our first kiss."

He grimaced. "That didn't count. You were sixteen, and I was a jerk. And you threw yourself at me the moment I opened the door."

"It did suck," she said. "But I don't think it had anything to do with me being sixteen, but a whole lot to do with you being a jerk."

He laughed. "It mostly had something to do with me not wanting to go to jail for having sex with a minor." He leaned down—tilted his head. His lips touched hers, skimming against them in a soft, satiny touch.

She could smell his cologne. Something expensive. Something heavenly. Her alcohol-induced fog momentarily cleared. Just long enough to allow in a horrible thought. What if he told her she couldn't kiss again? What if she did it wrong?

His tongue pushed against her closed lips. "Loosen up," he murmured.

She gripped the comforter with her hands and screwed her eyes shut tight, parted her lips.

He pulled back. "What are you doing?"

She opened her eyes. "What do you mean?"

A tiny line appeared between his brows. "Are you afraid of me?"

She could feel her palms sweating. She was disappointing him. "What do you want me to do?"

"Participate in the kiss."

"I'm afraid I'll do it wrong." She wanted to suck the words back in. They made her sound weak. She didn't want Ian to know she had any weak spots.

"You can't do it wrong. Just participate."

She closed her eyes so he couldn't see an emotion there she didn't want him to see. Like pain. Or fear. Or like. "The last time I tried to participate in a kiss with you, you told me it was like kissing your grandma." She'd been crushed to the core. Humiliated and hurt by a man she thought she was in love with. A man she wanted to introduce her to the art of lovemaking.

"God. Did you believe me? I didn't mean it. But damn it, you were my best friend's sister."

She pushed the past to the basement of her brain, but it ran right back up the stairs. "And you had another woman in your bedroom."

He sighed. "This isn't going to work. Yes, you turn me on, but the problem remains of who you are."

If she'd remained in a drunken stupor, what he said wouldn't have mattered. But semi-sober Kinley realized he was turning her down. Again. "Are you backing out?" she asked him quietly.

He rolled on his back. Closed his eyes. "I'm just saying, I don't see a chance in hell of you seducing me tonight."

"Because you think of me as a little sister?" She resisted the urge to do something shocking. Like straddle him. Like...

He opened his eyes and rolled on his side to look at her.

"Trust me. I don't think of you as a little sister. Which means I have to keep reminding myself you *are* my friend's little sister. But that's not the real problem, the real problem is…" He sat up. "What you're wearing is the problem."

She slapped a hand over her mouth to keep a gasp from escaping. This was her at her very best. "You don't like my outfit?"

He grabbed her hand and brought it to him. "My dick likes your outfit. And every other dick in the club liked your outfit."

She yanked her hand away. Not so much because of his blunt words—Ian had never pulled punches with her—but because she didn't understand. "Isn't that a good thing?"

He ran a hand down the side of her face. "Yes. No. I don't know. I just know your outfit pissed me off the moment you walked in. And don't ask me why, because damn if I can explain it. I've never seen a sexier woman."

He thought she was sexy. Wasn't that a good thing? "You're not making sense."

"I know. It's like this: in order to seduce me tonight, you had to get my brain to forget. You didn't succeed."

"Because of my dress?"

"Sure. Let's blame the dress."

She sat up and scooted away from him. There were a lot of things he could have said and she would have walked away with her tail between her legs. But not that. "Fuck you. I spent an entire day being groomed so I could seduce you. Fuck you. Fuck you."

"You had to know it was a long-shot that you could make me forget who your brother is."

Anger exploded inside of her. Burning, dangerous, engulfing anger. Her ears rang from the toxicity of it. She glanced around the room for something to throw at him. The best she could come up with was a pillow. She picked it up and swung as hard as she could at his head. *Thwack*. The momentum caused her to tumble face down into the mattress. "You're impossible," she said, her voice muffled. "My brother has nothing to do with what is going on between us."

One moment she was swinging a pillow, the next she was sprawled across the bed.

A sharp slap on her bottom caused her to screech. "What are you—"

Another slap. The impact stung.

"Stop it," she said. She tried to rise, but he placed his hand on the small of her back.

She felt her dress being shimmied up over her bare ass.

Slap.

"Stop." He wasn't supposed to do this. They hadn't agreed to this. Had they? Well, maybe they had?

"You said you wanted sex. You wanted to learn about non-vanilla sex. That I should forget who your brother is. Well, you've been a very naughty girl dressing so sexy and flirting with men in front of me. You deserve a good spanking." His hand landed on her bottom again. "If you want the truth, that's why I didn't like your dress. I wanted to claim you as my own, and I couldn't because you were supposed to be picking me up."

She rolled as hard as she could away from his reach and managed to get away from him. She jumped up and shimmied her dress down. "Does spanking me turn you on?"

"Your ass turns me on."

"It does?"

He ran his hand through his hair. "When you're being you, you're hard to resist. When you're being this—" he waved his hand in her direction— "you're also hard to resist. You make a guy want...never mind."

"You're talking in riddles."

"I know. Go take a shower. Take off all of that makeup.

Put your good-girl pajamas on. Let's call it a night."

"Are you saying I really lost the bet?" What the hell? To her horror, a tear slipped down her cheek. She turned away so he wouldn't see. She refused to make any sniffling noises.

"It's not you. It's me—" He sounded weary. As if the world was weighing him down.

As if she should feel bad for him.

Well too bad. He should feel weary. Weary of being an ass. She snorted so he would know her depth of disgust. "*It's not you—it's me.* What a line of crap. Of course it's you."

With her back turned, she couldn't see his face. After what seemed like forever, he gave a harsh laugh.

"Yeah. Sure. That's it. We'll talk tomorrow about where we go from here."

• • •

Ian paced the length of his suite. What in the hell had happened to him? He'd spanked Kinley Foster. And he'd liked it. So much that he was concerned his dick would never deflate. That he'd be walking around with a hard-on for the rest of the conference.

He hadn't spanked her hard. Really just a few light swats. But making her glorious ass rosy while she squirmed did something to him. He hated her outfit. Actually, he loved it. But he hated how every cock in the club jumped to attention the moment she strutted through the doors like she owned the world. He hated that other men, besides him, wanted her to give them a view worthy of Upskirt Galleries. Every time she crossed and uncrossed her legs, all eyes were on her crotch. Hoping for a pussy shot. Jesus.

He hated that he wanted a reason to spank her again. Not in the same way he'd spanked other women he'd dated who were into the lifestyle—in a different way. He wanted to lay wall. He hadn't even said he was sorry for not wanting her enough.

She could feel his eyes on her.

When he made no move to leave, or say anything else, she glanced at him. Why wasn't he leaving?

"I'm sorry," he said in a cautious voice.

She caught her breath. Damn him. Did he read her mind? It was easier to keep her emotions at bay if he was an ass. She looked away.

After several more seconds, she heard the click of the bedroom door. "Ass, ass, ass."

She sat staring around the quiet suite. Should she watch TV? Get dressed and try her hand at blackjack again? She thought about writing, but with her thoughts so jumbled she doubted she'd be able to string together a sentence, and she really didn't want to sit and stare at a blank screen. It was early—by Vegas standards, anyway. Maybe she could go downstairs to see if there were any authors or interesting people in the lounge. Under no circumstances would she sit in this room and think about Ian. Nuh-uh. No way.

She grabbed her oversize purse off the floor to rummage for a comb. If she stuck to minimal makeup, she could be out the door in twenty. She unzipped her purse and discovered the boxes that held the items she'd bought from Charlie.

Curiosity took her mind off of Ian. Well, mostly.

She glanced at the front door, to make sure he was gone—it would be just like him to lurk in the hallway—then she dumped the boxes onto the bed.

She didn't need him. She had all of this…stuff.

She picked up the first box and opened it.

A We-Vibe 4. The product was small; it fit in the palm of her hand. It was purple and shaped like a U. A remote control came with it. The product was made to be inserted so that one side of the U shape touched her G-spot and the other her clitoris. The clitoris side vibrated. It had different options to manipulate the speed and strength of the vibrations.

She opened the next box — a silicone sleeve with a vagina opening on one end. A product to be used on a man. One of the mystery prizes she'd won. She poked her finger inside and found it slippery. A man would feel like his cock was pushing into a woman. A man could use it on his own, or a woman could use it to help give him a hand job or a blowjob. That's what the little card inside the box said about the product. *Wow*. Okay.

The next item was a long and skinny stick thingy. The rounded end tilted upward and was the size of a dime. That end vibrated. It was meant to be slipped into a woman to reach her g-spot, where the vibrating head would do the rest of the work.

The final item was a vibrator that looked like a tube of lipstick.

Kinley wanted to lay back and try them all. Of course she wouldn't. Not in Ian's hotel room. He could come back any moment and catch her with her panties down around her ankles. Um, literally.

She stuffed everything back in her purse and pulled out her comb.

She should stick with her plan. Do her hair, get dressed. Leave the room for a while. She was too wound up to sleep. Too depressed to write. But if she went downstairs, she'd probably run into Ian. "Ugh."

She glanced at her boxes of sex toys peeking out of the top of her purse. A quick orgasm would help her relax.

She glanced at the clock. He'd be gone at least an hour. She could gift herself with thirty minutes.

She stood up and padded to the door to make sure Ian wasn't there. He wasn't. The lights were off. She slipped off her panties — started to bring them back to bed with her —

but out of orneriness, hung them on the doorknob outside the bedroom.

She crawled back into bed, lying on the cool sheets. She slipped her headphones on and turned on her favorite music to write love scenes to. Then she picked up the We-Vibe 4.

Reclining on the pillows, she closed her eyes. She tried to call up her normal go-to fantasy. But his face wasn't forming. Instead it was Ian's face she saw. His sexy blue eyes. His hand slapping her bare bottom.

She squirmed. Turned on the vibrator with the remote.

The music played. She slipped the vibrator in.

The steady tap, tap, tap rhythm of the vibrator against her clitoris caused her to squirm. She adjusted it so the vibrator was directly on her happy spot. Then, using the remote, she flipped through the different speeds and intensity.

Her breath caught in her throat when she found a speed that suited her. She laid the remote down and kneaded her breast with one hand while gripping the sheets with her other.

"Ian. Oh God, that feels so great," she whispered into the darkness. She imagined Ian there with her. Imagined him telling her she was being naughty and would have to be punished. She groaned.

"I'll be good, I promise," she whispered. "Don't spank me."

She raised her hips off the bed. The intense buildup edged her toward the cliff, where she would step off and tumble into a mind-numbing oblivion of sexual satisfaction.

"I've been very, very naughty."

She let her legs fall open. "Are you going to spank me?" She imagined Ian's palm landing on her ass. "You should spank me harder. I've been so...so...wicked." She wiggled, cried out, gasped as her imagination took her down the path.

"Stop. Ian. Please. I promise I won't—"

The weight of the bed dipped.

Kinley stilled. A fluttery sensation swept through her. She brought her knees back together.

She inhaled deeply and smelled a springtime thunderstorm. Did her imagination have the ability to conjure up scents? Or was Ian watching her masturbate?

God, this was her worst nightmare/best fantasy rolled into one.

It was only her imagination, her nervousness that would make her think he'd come back. She took a deep breath and focused on the sensations. Only moment's ago, she'd been so close… Her legs parted slightly. She wiggled her hips to get the vibrator just right.

Did watching her turn him on? Would he join her? Would he think she was being very, very naughty? Would he… She squirmed. Her breathing quickened.

Who was she kidding? He was in the room with her. She could feel his presence. And she liked it.

She reached for the cord of her earbuds and muted the music. "You can watch, but you can't touch." She didn't open her eyes. Her voice sounded breathy.

She heard his harsh inhale.

The speed of the vibrations slowed. Ian had the remote.

She groaned. Shook her head from side to side. "Faster. I need faster."

She felt the warmth of his hand on her cheek. He slid it softly across and removed her ear buds.

"Open your eyes." He spoke in a tone filled with awe and desire.

She shook her head. She liked the fantasy. If she looked into his eyes, she'd have to remember. Remember things she didn't want to remember. Feel emotions she didn't want to feel.

"Open them, or I'm going to spank you." His voice rang with command. Total male dominance. A tone she should rebel against—yet didn't.

She couldn't because she was torn between wanting to tell him never to touch her again and wanting his hands all over her body—in every possible way. Her carnal desires won the battle of wills. "Have I been naughty?"

He didn't respond.

Slowly she opened her eyes. It took a moment for them to adjust to the darkness. When they did, she saw him sitting on the bed, naked, his cock in one hand, her panties in the other.

"This is what you do to me," he said, stroking his member—his very, very large member—with her abandoned panties.

"Oh my." Her gaze tilted up to meet his.

Slowly and seductively, his gaze travelled down her body. "You've been a very bad girl."

She removed the vibrator. A dizzying current raced through her. She stroked herself with shaky fingers. "This is what you do to me." She closed her eyes and stroked harder. Her hips bucked as the orgasm she wanted so badly teased her with its proximity but wouldn't happen.

The weight on the bed shifted again.

Ian was above her. His eyes were heavy with desire. "You're the sexiest woman I've ever known."

Kinley resisted an urge to cover her size ten curves with her hands. Of course, he was lying, but it was a beautiful lie. "I doubt that."

His mouth came down on hers. "Trust me on this." He groaned the words against her mouth with such rawness she couldn't help but believe him. Her tongue came out to lick her lips.

He took this as an invitation and his tongue thrust in her mouth, taking far more from her than any man ever had.

• • •

Ian couldn't get enough of her. He wanted to learn all of her curves and tastes. When he teased the corners of her lips, she gasped in pleasure. He traced her lips again and again. The satisfaction of giving her bliss was a heady experience. Every woman that had come before Kin now seemed ordinary. A way to pass the years until she grew up and could be his…Or at least his for tonight.

Then she was kissing him back, nipping at his bottom lip, and he forgot to think.

He held her arms above her head with one hand so he could run kisses from her temple, over her scar, across her cheek, and along the edge of her perfect jaw.

She moaned and struggled against the hand holding her.

He ran his tongue down the elegant line of her neck.

Her back arched, pressing her nipples against his chest, enticing him to hurry.

He'd waited ten years for this moment. There was no way he was going to do anything but take his time. He dipped and stroked the hollow of her collarbone with his tongue, drowning in the little noises of pleasure she made.

"Leave your hands above your head." He released her hands and moved down so his lusting mouth could freely roam over the swell of her beautiful breasts. They were full and peach and begging for his attention. They were perfect. Not too large and not too small. The size a man covets.

A soft hiss coming from Kinley encouraged him to continue with his exploration.

He sucked one taut peak between his lips and bit before laving it with his tongue. He felt her shudder, so he moved to the other to do the same, enjoying her warm, soft flesh as he worried it with his tongue and teeth.

She trembled. The tiny sounds escaping her grew louder.

Ian had imagined this moment many times. Imagined the different ways in which he would claim her for the first time. Slow sex on a beach after he playfully removed that tiny red bikini of hers. Fast sex in a public setting after they'd accidentally bumped into each other in a restaurant and realized they couldn't wait any longer. Rough sex up against a wall, after she'd admitted she'd been wrong to hold him at arm's length for so many years.

But in his fantasies, he'd always been in control. He'd never imagined that when the moment came, he'd feel such an urgency, such a timeworn need to brand her as his.

But when he walked into the bedroom tonight and saw her, saw what she was doing, he'd lost it.

All of his plans evaporated in the face of his need to claim her.

He slowly slid his hand lower. Down past her ribs to grip the curve of her hip. His erection grew even larger as he slid his hand between her thighs.

She surprised him when she squeezed her legs together, capturing his hand. Was she having second thoughts?

He gently opened her legs. "Don't stop me," he murmured. "I just want to touch you." The shakiness in his voice further proof of how off-balance with need he was. "You're so hot."

"Not...stopping you." She bowed her back and opened her legs.

He slid a finger and then two inside. "And wet."

She whimpered and lifted her hips off the bed.

He smiled, moved lower, and positioned himself between her legs.

She stilled. "What are you doing?"

"Let me taste you." This was his ultimate fantasy. The one that kept him awake at night. The one he'd been clinging to for years, in the hope someday it might come true.

"Don't you just want to come up here?" she asked hesitantly.

"Oh, I'm exactly where I want to be at the moment, babe."

Her hands came down and tangled in his hair. Not above her head where he'd told her to keep them. Kinley Foster never had been a rule follower. At the moment, he could care less.

She mumbled something incoherent. He thought he picked out the word *okay*.

Was he the first guy to go down on her? What kind of idiot lovers had she been with? No wonder she couldn't write sex.

Yet the thought that he was the first to teach her about oral sex pleased him intensely.

A desire to tell her that, and to tell her he was about to live out one of his fantasies shuddered through him. But speaking took time, and he was anxious for the fantasy. He touched her with his tongue in one long, slow, upward stroke.

"Oh…oh…OH."

Her reaction impaled him with hunger. He licked her again.

Her hips bucked. Dear God, he was in heaven.

He swirled his tongue along her inner lips and then flicked, and circled, gauging her reaction by her breathing and the grip on his hair. When he began suckling, she squirmed and cursed and said, "Stop. Please. Not yet."

He hissed out a breath. The edge in her voice matched the edge he was unsecurely hanging on to by his nails. "I want to tie you up and fuck you. And then flip you over and do it again."

She sat up on her elbows. "Then come up here and do it."

He laughed. "Give me time, Kin, right now I'm in heaven right where I'm at."

"Are you sure?"

"Hell yes." To emphasize how sure he was, he penetrated her with his tongue. Her pink flesh was so wet for him.

She keened. Fell back into the mattress.

Her admittance pleased him beyond reason. He rubbed her with his thumb as his tongue had his way with her in all the ways he'd been dreaming about for years.

Her nails dug into his shoulders as she wiggled her hips, guiding him in the direction of what pleased her the most. He didn't relinquish his pursuit until her sex pulsed against his tongue.

She inhaled sharply. "Yes…God…please. Oh my God… that was…oh my God, that was fabulous."

His male pride roared. *That's only the beginning, babe. Only the beginning.* "It gets better," he told her, kissing his way back up her torso, spending a considerable amount of time on the soft swell of her stomach. Enjoying the light perfume of sex in the air and the rosy glow of a blush on her skin.

"Come up here," she demanded in a sex-drugged voice.

He chuckled and grabbed the condom he'd laid on the bed after he came back to their room and found her masturbating, calling out his name, her panties hanging on the door like an invitation.

She took the foil package from him. Tore the wrapper open and rolled the rubber down his length.

He jumped and nearly came just feeling her hands touching him.

She laughed like a siren and lightly wrapped the long length of her sexy legs around his waist. "Talk is cheap. Make me feel that again."

"Demanding wench." He ran little biting kisses over her shoulder. He had every intention of taking her back over that edge again. Just not yet. There were so many—

She leaned her head back and rose to push her naked mound against his erection, causing his brain to malfunction. "I'm all yours," she husked.

He raked in a breath as desire ran rampant through him, savaging his ability to do anything but feel. He could no longer resist what she was offering. He succumbed to her charms. "Damn straight you are."

Her hands circled around his back, and she closed her eyes. "Yep."

"Open your eyes," he ordered. He wanted to see her expression. Wanted her thinking of him when he went in deep. Wanted to scorch her brain with the visual memory of this moment.

For once in her life, she obeyed without arguing.

Their lips connected right as he thrust in. He groaned in pleasure at how tightly she sheathed him. Ten years of thinking of this moment washed through him. Nothing he'd imagined compared to how good it actually felt to be inside of Kin. He stilled to enjoy the moment. The sensation.

She pulled back slightly. "I can't keep them open." Her eyes fluttered shut.

He wanted to insist, but she was the most beautiful thing he'd ever seen with her eyes closed, her hair tangled across the pillow, her lips slightly parted and swollen from his kisses.

He leaned down and kissed her scar before giving over to his need to fuck Kinley Foster senseless.

They rocked together. Soft curves against hard muscles. Kin taking as much as she gave. Her hands at times roaming, at others clutching, her nails digging in and then travelling — no doubt leaving marks in their wake. His hands just as frantically explored her curves.

When her fingers dove into his hair, and he felt her inner muscles tighten down over him, he pumped harder, reaching between them and thumbing her clitoris. "Come, baby. I've waited ten years to hear you scream my name while I'm inside you."

She bucked hard against him and then went rigid. "Ian." He drank in the sound of his name on her lips, and the pleasure on her face as she rode out her orgasm. He wished he were an artist so he could recreate the sheer beauty of what he saw. Or a musician so he could write a song. Hell, he was rich. He'd hire someone to paint her and someone to write a song about her.

She opened her eyes and stared into his. "Um…your turn." The words were said softly, almost shyly.

He chuckled. "Sweetheart, I'm just getting started."

She grinned. "I was hoping you'd say that."

He laughed. "You were, were you?" He pulled out and flipped her over on her stomach. Without asking her to, she came up on all fours, and he entered her from behind.

"Is it greedy of me to want another?" she asked, glancing at him from over her shoulder, her hair slightly in her eyes.

He pushed her hair aside so he could see her face. "Not nearly as greedy as it is of me to want to do it again and again and again." With each again, he rocked hard into her. "So many agains you won't be able to walk tomorrow."

She reached between her legs and stroked him. "Do you think you can last that long?" And then her nails scraped lightly against his balls, as she squeezed her inner muscles against him.

The combination took him dangerously close to his own climax. "Damn it, Kinley. Not yet." Hell… Did he really just stop her? He had to, or his ability to please her would be greatly diminished.

She laughed, removed her hand from his jewels and rhythmically pushed her perfect ass into him.

Jesus, he loved this position with her.

He reached around and pinched her nipple, only relenting when she cried out, "Ian, come with me."

He leaned forward and lightly kissed her neck. "I love my name on your lips when they're red and bruised from my kisses."

"What do I have to do to hear my name on your lips?"

She sounded breathless. Like a woman trying to hold on, but losing the battle.

He moved his lips to her ears. "My balls like your hands." He bit her earlobe.

"Ouch." She reached between them. Only this time, instead of playfully scraping, she squeezed.

"Kin—" His breath caught.

"Yes?"

He thrust hard against her until her muscles contracted and tiny sounds of pleasure escaped her lips. Only then did he allow his own release—a release that stopped time. Threatened to change the course of history. "I fucking loved that."

She laughed, gave a sigh of pleasure, and then collapsed. He went down with her, rolling them over until they were spooning. He inhaled the scent of her shampoo—the same scent that had been on the pillow he slept with last night.

She shifted away and rolled onto her back.

He watched as she spiraled back to reality. It started with a slow smile and a soft sigh, followed by the relaxing of her body into the mattress. He wanted to sit up and do a touchdown dance, knowing he caused that reaction in her.

He ran a finger down the side of her cheek, and she rolled so that she was facing him. Did she know she'd just cast a spell over him? One he wasn't sure he could ever break. Wasn't sure he'd ever want to break.

"You are—"

She laid a finger on his lips. "Don't say anything."

He kissed her fingertip. Since when did women not want to talk after sex? "But—"

She sat up and looked down at him. Her eyes hooded. "We can talk in the morning."

Chapter Twelve

Ian woke up pre-dawn with a boner. He was a changed man. Or at least his mind had been changed. Not wanting to wake Kinley, he'd gone to the gym and worked out, stopped by the check-in counter and cancelled her room reservation, showered, and was now lying back in their bed waiting for her to wake up.

He rolled toward her. Listened to her steady breathing. She had the covers pulled up under her chin, but he knew underneath the covers, she was naked. Her silky brown hair framed her beautiful face and splayed across the white pillow she was hugging in her sleep.

She'd won the bet. She'd seduced him. Watching her masturbate had killed his brain cells. To call the experience seductive was like calling heaven pretty. Helping her achieve the orgasm she'd been fantasizing about gave him a paralyzing climax.

God, she'd been imagining him. Being spanked by him. He'd stood there at the foot of the bed, listening to her sex talk as she wiggled her hips and changed the speeds of the vibrator.

When she'd begged to be spanked harder, he'd nearly fallen to his knees.

Shaking away the memory, he glanced at the clock. Eight a.m. Their meetings would start in an hour. He should wake her so they could talk. Make plans for their time together. Supreme satisfaction swept through him, leaving goose bumps on his arms. He rubbed his hands down them. He couldn't remember ever having an actual reaction to the thought of starting a relationship with a woman.

And it wasn't just about having sex with her again, though God knew that was reason enough. But there was something more behind the giddiness he felt. Like he'd discovered a treasure he'd thought lost forever. Like his heart was making room for a new emotion. Like the seduction of Kinley Foster was the beginning of something…

He picked up the remote that operated the curtains and opened them partially. He wanted to wake her slowly. Call him a sap, but he wanted to lie there and watch her wake up. Watch her eyelashes flutter. Watch her lips form into a smile as she remembered the night they'd spent together.

This felt right. Of all the things he'd done in the past that he regretted, this wasn't going to be one of them.

He wanted her, and for the next week, he was going to have her. He was going to teach her about sex—about sexual tension—and somehow manage to make her see he never was the villain she thought him capable of way back then.

Unable to resist the temptation, he caressed the length of her neck. Her skin was satiny smooth.

She smiled and stretched, raising her arms above her head, exposing her breasts.

Desire pulled him considerably closer. "Good morning." He tugged the covers down so he could see the creamy expanse of her stomach. The sight caused his breath to catch in his throat like a baseball in a catcher's mitt. So inviting. He wanted to eat honey off of her stomach…among other places.

She stilled. Yanked the covers back up to her chin and sat up. "Hi." Red spots formed on her neck and cheeks.

She gave him a scowl-y look and muttered something under her breath that sounded like stupid bluff. Or maybe she called him a stupid butt. Or was she calling herself stupid?

None of which made sense.

Okay. So the whole waking up fantasy wasn't panning out like he'd planned. "Did you sleep well?" He laid back, crossed his hands behind his head, and gave her an encouraging smile.

"Close your eyes."

He lifted an eyebrow.

"Please," she said. But not in a particularly nice tenor.

What was he missing? They'd fallen asleep in each other's arms. Happy.

Was she just feeling shy? "Not in this lifetime," he said in a joking tone, trying to put her at ease. No way would he believe she was unaffected by what happened between them last night.

Her scowl got a degree scowlier—if that was even a word. "You are not a gentleman."

His boner agreed with a high-five. "I don't recall you asking for a gentleman in your bed last night." Why was she being so contrary?

She grumbled. And if it was possible, her cheeks turned even redder. She exited the bed, pulling the sheet with her, and haphazardly wrapped the snowy white cover around her body, reminding him of an unraveling mummy.

He couldn't help but smile. "I thought we were going to talk this morning." He wanted her to turn so he could catch a glimpse of her bare backside. The woman's ass could stop hotrods at a race track.

She shuffle-walked to her suitcase. "We had a bad idea."

His stomach tightened. Was this about more than her just feeling shy around him this morning?

She didn't look at him as she pulled out clothes. "End of topic."

The hammer of her sharp tone shattered his ego into more pieces than a beer bottle dropped on concrete. He sat up. "A bad idea?" What the hell did she mean by that?

She turned toward him, her expression guarded. "In between meetings, I'll get checked into my room. It should be available."

He stood, exposing his hard-on. "I thought we had a deal?"

"We did." She glanced at him—at all of him—and quickly averted her eyes.

"And?"

"And…it was a lame idea."

He squeezed the bridge of his nose. "Is it because I spanked you?"

Her mouth fell open. "Shut up. Okay. Just shut up."

"Why, Kinley?" What rabbit hole had they fallen down? None of this made sense.

"Because you're right. I'm better suited to Amish romance." She turned and hurried into the bathroom, firmly shutting the door behind her.

His heart tried to go after her, but his chest blocked its way. "Fuck." What in the hell just happened? What he'd seen as a freaking fantasy, she'd just proclaimed nothing but idiocy.

Damn it. She was wrong, and he was going to prove it to her.

Chapter Thirteen

Kinley stood under the cold, pulsating water coming at her from every direction in a black marble shower the size of her home office, shivering and chastising herself.

The moment she'd became alert, she'd spotted that raised eyebrow. And not the good one. The one he used when he was up to something.

And she'd panicked.

When he'd opened his mouth to speak, she'd gone into full-on self-preservation panic mode.

Sure he was going to tell her that while the sex had been nice, it hadn't been nice enough to make him choose her over his friendship with her brother. *You have to get me to sleep with you one time without regretting the decision when it's over.* He was going to blame last night's seduction on their bet. A bet that hinged on them first having sex, and then what he *felt* about it afterwards. And that raised eyebrow of his was all she needed to see to know he was going to tell her he was full of regret.

"If anyone gets to use the excuse of the bet, it's going to

be me." She forced a laugh. "I did the dumping—not you." Perhaps she was overreacting a tad bit. She did sound a tad manic to her own ears. But in the name of self-preservation, she'd done what she had to do.

She turned the water to warm and squirted soap on her pink scrubby. With more force than necessary, she scrubbed her skin to wash away his DNA.

Sure, they'd had sex.

But not because she made him forget who she was. Who her brother was.

When he discovered her masturbating, his sloshed brain probably shouted, *join the fun. Orgasms up for grabs. She's even done the pregame warm-up.*

She wasn't so vain as to think he walked in and lost the fat head on his shoulders over her. If the do-me-now dress didn't push him over the edge, nothing would.

Where she was concerned, he wasn't interested. Never had been. Never would be. Last night never should have happened. She turned off the three shower heads. "Never, never, never."

Enough with the woe is me. She was a grown woman. She'd saved face. Now it was time to play it cool.

She took a deep breath and stepped out of the shower, then wrapped herself in a fluffy white bath sheet. If he hadn't left yet, she was going to hear him out. And then she'd get dressed and leave. She wasn't sixteen anymore. They could discuss this as adults.

"Life's too short to hide from men who make you nervous," she told her foggy reflection in the mirror.

Besides, today was the first day of the conference—the reason she'd come to Vegas. She wasn't going to let Ian Thompson ruin this trip for her.

She cracked the bathroom door to let the steam out and did a sound check for the presence of human life.

The bedroom was quiet. No television. No voice on a phone.

She peeked out. The lights were off.

He was gone. Was he afraid she would change her mind and try to get him to change his?

She glanced at the bed. The blankets were twisted. On the floor was her abandoned vibrator.

Could sex be better than what they'd experienced last night? Not that she would tell him, but God—just God.

She slipped on the robe provided by the hotel and walked over to the bed, picked up the sex toy, rinsed it off in the sink, and stuffed it into her purse. Sitting down, she pushed images of Ian spanking her out of her brain and instead went through the package of information she'd picked up the day before for the conference.

She put hearts by the conference sessions she wanted to attend.

Then she double-checked what type of manuscripts the agents attending the conference were in the market for. There were ten who were interested in steamy romance. Eleven if she counted Ian. She didn't.

Someday he'd regret not being her agent. When all of her books were being turned into movies, he'd cry into his beer over losing her to another agent.

Out to the side, she printed one more name. Ann Collette—Kinley's girl-crush agent. She was the agent of author Ashley Weaver, Kinley's new favorite author whose debut book—*Murder At The Brightwell*—got Kinley through a lonely New Year's Eve. Ann was the only agent Kinley had done any research on. Ann did a wonderful Twitter thing where she would live tweet as she read queries and say why she did or didn't request them.

Unfortunately, she didn't represent steamy romance. She preferred literary and mysteries and women's fiction. Some authors referred to her as the dragon agent. Kinley thought Ann was a lovely dragon who exhaled pretty pink fire and got mani-pedis.

Ann always responded when Kinley tweeted her a question.

As a result, Kinley would walk through a graveyard, at midnight, during a full-moon to have Ann as her agent.

Satisfied she had a game plan, Kinley dressed. She slipped on an A-Line, long-sleeve red dress with a silver chain belt and silver jewelry, black tights, and knee high boots. She glanced in the mirror long enough to decide to yank her hair back into a low pony-tail. The more somber style gave her a serious writer look. She slipped her glasses on, grabbed her conference material, and hurried downstairs to attend a session on dialogue.

And get her own hotel room.

Chapter Fourteen

By the time Kinley grabbed a bite to eat and found the correct conference room, the place was filling up. She found a seat in the front row and opened her laptop. She laid her purse on the chair beside her to save the spot for elbow room. She didn't like to be crowded at meetings. And she wasn't that good at appropriate chit chat. That's why Charlie knew so much about her by the end of the airplane ride. Lord, the woman even knew she'd been wearing her un-sexy school uniform underneath an un-sexy orange raincoat the day she'd shown up at Ian's offering up her virginity.

A volunteer introduced the speaker—an author whose first book went to auction and sold for big bucks, an event every author hopes happens to them at least once in their career.

"Dialogue should never be on the nose," the speaker said. "On the nose is when the character says exactly what they are feeling. People seldom say exactly what they mean—unless they are with someone they feel safe with. Like a best friend."

Kinley snorted. Obviously, the speaker didn't know even

best friends can't be trusted. Look at Ian and her brother.

"Instead, use subtext. Have characters circle around the truth. This is how we speak in real life," the speaker said.

Was that true?

Kinley's phone vibrated. She pushed her glasses up her nose and read the incoming text message.

Did you use subtext on me this morning? —Ian

Kinley's heart stopped. Her girly parts clenched. She frowned. Was he in the same session? Why was he texting her? He was supposed to be avoiding her so she didn't have to avoid him.

She fanned herself with her hand. Damn. He was older than her. He should know the rule of one-night stands: no further contact. Nada. Zilch. The big fat Uno. It happened. It's over.

What game was he playing? She sat up straight. She refused to turn her head and find him in the crowd. She would ignore him.

She typed what the speaker was saying. Mid-paragraph, her fingers stalled on the keys.

If she didn't respond, would he think it was because she cared? Knowing him, he probably would. No way in hell was she going to let him think she cared. She grabbed her phone.

Using her index finger, she punched out her response.

None of it was subtext. All truth. —Kinley

She wished she could see his face when he read her reply. Was he really so self-absorbed as to think she lied? That she was into him and just didn't want him to know? What an egomaniac.

Maybe I spoke in subtext.

Her brows furrowed. She chewed the inside of her lip. What did that mean? Was that comment subtext for something else? Damn him. Damn her for being curious. Damn. Damn. Damn.

What did you not say?

Why wasn't he out schmoozing with other important people instead of attending a session on the craft of writing? He didn't need to be here.

The speaker segued from subtext to yes/no alternatives. "Never answer a yes/no question with a yes/no answer. Always have them respond in a way that is more interesting. Have your characters respond in a way that makes the reader an active participant in deciphering what the characters are saying."

I enjoyed spanking you. —Ian

Of course he enjoyed spanking her. He enjoyed embarrassing her. He'd always enjoyed embarrassing her.

Because you're an ASS.

She wanted to stand up and shout the words at him, but she settled with texting them in caps. God, this man brought out the worst in her. Five seconds in his presence and she'd reverted back to middle school.

He didn't respond right back. Was he having second thoughts on what he was going to say? Or was he done with their war of words?

Or because you have a fabulous ass, and when it's rosy from my hand it's every man's fantasy.

Kinley could feel the heat of a blush infusing her body. Having him spank her had been so frustrating, but, at the same time, it turned her on. She didn't know why, but—*wowza*. Part of her wanted to push him as hard as she could to see if he would do the deed again. Part of her. Just a small part. The part that was remembering last night's exquisite orgasms.

Of course, she wouldn't allow it to ever happen again. That would be asinine.

Enough of the games, Ian. What do you want?

This time his reply came quickly.

You.

A dizzy feeling swamped her. He wanted her? What did that mean?

What?

Another long pause.

Last night was spectacular. And I want to do it again.

Goose bumps popped like kernels of corn on her arms. She'd won? She'd won the bet? She'd won a bet against Ian. No way. She reread the text. Yep—way.

Kinley wanted to jump and shout JACKPOT!

He hadn't been about to dump her this morning. He hadn't…

She exhaled a breath. This was crazy.

Sure as she was sitting in the front row, this was a joke. Somehow, there was going to be a punch line thrown into all of these texts, and she knew whom the punch line was going to punch.

Ha ha, very funny. Go away.

She didn't have time for this. She dropped her phone in

her purse and listened to what the speaker said. The woman really knew her stuff.

Kinley's phone vibrated in her purse.

She drew in an unsteady breath and ignored the silent pulsing. Ian couldn't harass her if she didn't read his texts. But what if her mom called? To see how things were going? She should check. Just in case. She fished her phone out. Her vibrators tried to tumble out in the process, causing her heartbeat to kick up several notches while grinding through gears and missing a few. *Shit*. She shoved them back down in her purse. Why hadn't she left them in her luggage? She read the text.

If you call me a liar again, I'm going to have to spank you tonight.

A rush of decadent desire flooded Kinley. Or maybe fear. She didn't really want to be spanked. It hurt. The thrill was really just in knowing someone would do it, not the actuality of it happening.

In your dreams.

She pulled at the neckline of her dress and fanned herself, suddenly very hot. Crap, at twenty-six she was having one of her mom's hot flashes. Or maybe it was a guilt flash. Or a "worst sister of the year" flash. Her brother and Ian may have moved past the fiancée incident, but her brother wouldn't move past them becoming sexual partners. Any guy that would sleep with their friend's fiancé sure as hell wasn't going to be good enough for that friend's sister.

The heat intensified.

Was she having a guilt-induced heatstroke?

Could she die of a heatstroke while sitting in a conference room in January with goose bumps coming and going on her arms like ants at a picnic?

She fanned harder.

Or in your fantasies, Kinley.

She uncrossed and re-crossed her legs in the opposite direction. She could feel a pleasant tingle. The kind of tingle that would drive a woman crazy if it stayed there all day. Was his text subtext for saying he'd heard her telling him to spank her in her fantasies? Or was it just a generic saying?

I'm blocking your number.

She fumbled with her phone to find the place to block him. Her finger hovered over the "block this contact" option. A smart woman would block his number. Forget he existed. Just like she'd managed to do over the past ten years. Sort of. Well, not really. But that was beside the point. Another text came through.

Let me teach you kink. You won't regret it.

Then again…she could respond to just one more text.

Liar.

Chapter Fifteen

Ian chuckled, and his palm itched to feel the soft, creamy expanse of Kinley's bare bottom. "Well played, Kinley Foster," he muttered under his breath. "Very well played." He slipped out the back entrance, hoping the speaker didn't see him leave and take it personally. The only reason he'd come was because he'd observed Kinley entering the session and had followed her.

He'd love to make a scene and drag her back to their suite. Make good on his promise to spank her. Unfortunately, he was due to take pitches for the rest of the afternoon. And as a respected agent, he couldn't be seen causing scenes.

Besides...anticipation never killed a man. And Kinley needed time to process the fact that he planned to spank her.

And they would need rules.

"Hi," said a smartly-dressed black lady, interrupting his thoughts as they both stepped into an available elevator and pushed the buttons for their designations.

The door closed and the elevator voice said, "Going down."

The lady laughed. "Sorry. My dirty mind always takes it wrong when I hear his voice saying going down."

Ian chuckled. She was nice looking. Middle-aged. "And now it will strike me as inappropriate every time I hear it." He searched for her name badge. She wasn't wearing one. Which could mean she wasn't a participant of the conference, or it could mean she was an agent or an editor hoping not to be caught in an elevator with an author anxious to pitch to her. He often took his badge off when he wasn't in one of the session rooms. Funny, she didn't look like anyone he normally did business with, and it was a small industry.

She held out her hand. "I'm C. Southern. If I'm not mistaken, you're I. Hartley." She had a nice southern drawl to go with her last name. Her accent reminded him of an author he represented who lived in New Orleans.

He shook her hand. "You're not mistaken." Was she a new editor? He didn't recall seeing her before. "Are you a writer?" He went for the safe question. Of the twenty-four hundred participants at the Romance Lovers Conference, over a thousand of them were writers.

She laughed. A booming noise. "Not exactly. But this week I've found myself branching out. Offering my services to a writer who is trying to broaden her experiences. Bless her heart." She gave Ian a quick look and then stared straight ahead.

Ian had the feeling the woman was up to something. He just couldn't decide what. "I also find myself helping a writer this week."

The woman gave him a sideways look. Ridiculous beads on her eyelashes caught his attention. A tiny smile lifted her lips—a smile that was both mysterious and mischievous.

She was definitely up to something. What?

She rummaged in her purse and pulled out her phone.

The elevator stopped, and the door slid open.

"This is my floor," she said, while pushing buttons on her phone. She gave him another quick glance before placing the phone to her ear. She stepped out the door. "Hi, glad I caught you. You're never going to believe who I rode—"

The door shut.

Ian took a step back and leaned against the wall, chuckling at where C. Southern's phone conversation took his dirty mind. Who did she *ride* last night? He glanced down and noticed a pink card on the floor. She must have dropped it when she pulled out her phone. He bent down to pick up the card. Flipped it over. An invitation.

Fantasy Bashes
By
Charlie & Dan
Must have this card to attend.
RSVP for details.
1800-300-6969

Chapter Sixteen

"Just one moment," Kinley whispered into the phone, stepping out of the session on dialogue and into the hotel's busy hallway. Writers carrying matching conference bags were congregating in small groups, supposedly waiting for the next session to begin. But in actuality, Kinley guessed they were ogling a photo shoot of male models in the adjacent conference room.

Kinley did a little ogling herself.

A male model left the photo shoot. Two women vacated a bench to follow him. Kinley grabbed it. "What's up?" she asked, tugging off a boot and rubbing her toes. What possessed her to bring this particular pair on her trip? They weren't comfortable.

Sexy, but not comfortable.

Oh yeah. She'd brought them to wear while out searching for men to have one-night stands with, all in the name of keeping her New Year's resolution to have sex this year. While her hiatus had given her time to write the book she always wanted to write, she'd missed dating. Missed sex. Had decided to be a woman that dates around. Not settle for one guy at a time. She admired women who went after sex with the same gusto men did. She wanted to be one of those women—a woman with no sexual hang-ups about doing what she wanted.

"You're not going to believe who I rode the elevator with just now," Charlie said. She sounded out of breath. Giddy.

"The Pope?" Kinley searched the hallway for Ian, only half-listening to Charlie. Where had he gone? Had he been serious? Had she? What happened to her grudge against him? Was her hate dissipating? What about her self-preservation?

"Bless your heart. You do try to be funny. I saw your man." Charlie's loud booming voice pulled Kinley back into the conversation.

Kinley's breaths shortened and her stomach tightened like someone had just shoved her body into a pair of Spanx. "My man?" Please let her be misinterpreting the comment.

"Yes. Your man."

"How do you know what my *man* looks like?" She asked the question quietly. Trying not to jump to conclusions. Did she even have a "my man?"

"Ummmm…" There was a short pause as if it dawned on Charlie that Kinley didn't sound peachy. "Dan and I dropped by the Club last night."

Kinley threw an internal conniption. *Son of a—damn it.* "You guys spied on me?" Her tone must have leaked anger, because those around glanced her way. Unable to force a fake smile, she turned her head so they couldn't see her face.

First her brother interfered in her life and now Charlie. Why couldn't people let her be an adult without a shadow guardian? "Why would you do that to me?"

"I thought you might need Dan to hit on you if no one else did."

"Do you know how insulting that is?"

"No."

"Well, it is. You were afraid all your hard work wouldn't be enough for me to get a man's attention."

"Bless your heart. That's not what I thought. I just wanted you to win the bet. I'm sorry if I took my role too far."

Kinley relaxed her grip on the phone. Charlie meant well. Just like her brother. "Fine. Just let me handle things from here on out." She exhaled, letting go of the tension. She was being too sensitive.

"Honey, I don't make promises I might have already broken. Anyhoo…he was really uptight. I couldn't tell if he was wound up in a good way or a bad way. You know what I mean?"

Already broken promises? "What—"

"Whoops. Can't hear you. It's noisier than a swinger's party on Bourbon Street around me. We'll talk later."

The phone went dead. What had Charlie done? And what was that about a swinger's party?

Chapter Seventeen

Three craft sessions later, Kinley's toes were toast. Time for a change of shoes.

She stepped into the crowded elevator. "Fifteen," she said to the designated floor-button pusher, another conference goer.

How did Ian interpret her last text? She'd called him a liar. Did he see that as an invitation to spank her?

Or as a joke. A droll joke.

Like the time she put Nair in his roll-on Icy Hot dispenser his senior year during football season.

In no way had she been trying to solicit…

One of her mom's mom-isms popped into her brain. *If you can't be honest with your own brain and heart, why should anyone else be honest with them?*

Truth was, spanking and kink aroused her curiosity. And who safer to experiment with than Ian?

She scanned her key card in the door, crossed her fingers he wasn't in the room, and opened the door.

No such luck.

"Ian," she said in a strangled voice.

He stood in the entryway wearing a smile. A sexy smile that caused the air to whoosh out of her.

His thick hair was wet from a shower. His chest was bare and beautiful and absilicious—just like she remembered when he and her brother used to peel off their shirts after football practice. A pair of jeans hung low on his hips. "I was wondering when you would show up for your punishment," he said in a voice that scored a twelve out of ten on the sexy radar. Maybe a thirteen.

Shivers and quivers swept and swirled through her, leaving wobbly legs in their wake and a whole lot of sexual awareness toward the blue-eyed rake. She placed a hand on the wall for balance.

He was so freaking handsome. And sexy fearsome.

A blend of stranger-danger and promised wickedness.

"I have no idea what you're talking about." She fought an urge to turn and run. He was Ian. Only Ian.

She swept past him and glided into the living area, lifting her chin in an attempt to appear in control.

"Oh, I think you do." He came up behind her, rested his hands on her shoulders, and lightly massaged.

She sidestepped away. The guy was like a sexual magnetic field to her girly parts. She couldn't reason clearly around him with that going on. "I've done nothing that deserves punishment."

He chuckled, a male sound of confidence. "Are you sure about that?"

She set her purse and conference bag on the table. "I'm afraid you're going to have to tell me what you're talking about." She took a seat on the arm of a wingback chair.

He leaned against the doorway. His head tilted sideways, his cornflower blues caressing her face. "You won the bet." His words sounded thick.

She gave him a wide-eyed look. "You said it wasn't possible for me to win the bet." She was glad her heart was on the inside of her chest and not the outside where its thrashing would be visible.

He swallowed, drawing her attention to his Adam's apple. "I was wrong."

The admission curled her toes with desire. "What do I get for winning?" The tune of *Alice in Wonderland's* "I'm Late" came to mind. *I won, I won, I won, I won, I won. No time to gloat, or say you lost, I won, I won, I won.* She silently sang the revised words.

He sat down on the coffee table across from her and took her hands in his. "You've been taking that dialogue advice from your morning session to heart, I think. Between last night and your comments this morning and in our texts, you've been very fickle, Kinley. So let's try some on the nose dialogue. No more games. I want to have sex with you. The question is, do you still want me to teach you about sex?"

Her throat went dry. "You want to have an affair? Between us—two consenting adults? For the duration of this conference?"

"Yes."

She moistened her lips and looked at her lap. "Okay."

"Okay what?" His voice was raspy.

She bent over and pulled off her boots. "Okay, I want to have sex with you. For research. But I don't need you to help me get an agent. Teach me what you can about sex, and then it will be up to me to incorporate it into my writing. When this conference is over, there won't be a need for us to ever be in contact again." She couldn't quite look him in the eyes when she said the words. Not yet. She needed time to process. And then there was her brother to consider. But she didn't want to think about that now.

There was a long pause. "That's not my preference, but if

it's yours—"

Which part of it wasn't his preference? The part about not needing his help to find an agent? Or the part about not seeing each other again? No doubt both. "It is." She kept her gaze focused on his chin.

"And do you still want to learn about non-vanilla sex?"

In a distant part of her brain, she knew this was a crazy idea, but in the forefront of her brain, things were coming up kisses and orgasms. "Of course."

He hissed out a breath. "Tell me exactly what you want to try."

Chapter Eighteen

Ian forced himself not to grin like a boy whose parents just told him they were leaving him home alone for the weekend. Kinley Foster just agreed to non-vanilla sex for the duration of the conference. "Non-vanilla can mean a lot of things. For instance—whips."

She wiped her hands on her skirt. "No whips. But blind folds, handcuffs, sex toys, and spanking are all good."

That was good to hear. He could never mark her beautiful skin with a whip. "I like your list. Anything else?"

"Maybe. I'll let you know when I'm definite."

Interesting. What did she want that she was afraid to ask for? "I think we need a few rules. About the spanking."

"Like what?" She sat haphazardly on the chair's arm. Like a bird ready to take flight if spooked.

He scooted the coffee table he was sitting on closer so he could have a good look at her face. At her eyes. "Like if you call me a liar, there will be consequences. A spanking. In fact, you've already earned a spanking."

"Already?" She fell off the arm of the chair into its seat

cushion, all arms and legs and monkey grace. "Why? How?"

"Because you called me a liar. I'm not a liar. I don't lie. I will never lie to you. EVER." He leaned in closer. "And you should know, your act of innocent alarm is wasted on me. I know you too well."

"I have no idea what you're inferring." She pulled her glasses down until they perched on the tip of her nose. "I should get a pass on earlier. How was I to know that was grounds for being spanked?"

God, she was sexy. Even when she wasn't trying. He stood and walked to the ceiling-to-floor windows. "I'll take your request under consideration." He didn't see her triumphant smile, but he could feel the heat of it burning his neck. He turned around.

"What are the other rules?" she asked with a neutral expression.

"I'm in charge. For the rest of the conference, I'm the dominant, you're the submissive. You do whatever I tell you to do. I'll keep in mind all of the things you listed that you want to do." When he thought about last night, about her soft body pressed against him, his groin tightened—so he did a few multiplication tables to cool himself off. *Six times six equals thirty-six. Seven times nine equals sixty-three.*

She wrinkled her nose. "And if I don't do what you tell me to do?"

He met her gaze. "There will be consequences."

She ran her tongue over her top teeth. "What kind of consequences?"

"You'll see." He strode toward the bedroom. He was due downstairs and needed to get dressed. "By the way, why did you come back up to the room?"

"For more comfortable shoes." She grabbed her boots and purse and followed. "These hurt my toes." She held up her boots to show him.

"Why did you wear them?" He took a shirt off a hanger and slipped it on.

She set everything down beside her suitcase and peeled off her tights. "Because that's what women do when they come to conferences. They show off their new shoes to one another."

Eight times five equals forty. He did the math while walking toward her.

She took a step back until the wall stopped her retreat.

He reached down and slowly pulled her dress up, his hand caressing her naked thighs during the upward movement. When he reached her center, he ran his finger under the elastic edge of her panties. "Button my shirt." For the life of him he couldn't remember what two times two equaled.

She did, her breasts rising and falling rapidly.

He placed one hand on the wall beside her head and leaned in. "I'm going to enjoy spanking you."

She licked her lips, and her fingers stalled, hovering over the buttons.

"Finish buttoning my shirt," he ordered.

She fumbled her way through the rest of the buttons. "All done." Her words held a soft, breathy quality.

"Where's your vibrator?" he asked.

She gave him a sultry look that set his blood on fire. "Which one? I have three."

He groaned and turned away from her. *Two times two is twelve.* "The one you had last night."

"In my purse."

He picked up her purse and took the vibrator and the remote out.

He glanced at the little purple toy and then handed it to her. "Put it in."

Her thick lashes flew up. "Now?"

He nodded and sat on the edge of the bed. "While I

watch."

She placed one foot on the bed beside his hip. She slowly raised her dress so that her lace panties were on display, then moved her thong out of the way and slowly slipped it in.

Did she always maintain a waxed canvas? Or was that just for the conference? For him? He liked the idea of her doing something just for him. He leaned back on his elbows, held up the remote, and turned it on with the push of a button. *One plus one equals sex.*

She kept her leg on the bed. Her eyes grew heavy.

He increased the speed. "Look at me." In all of his life, he'd never seen anything more beautiful than what he was seeing right now. Nor knew so little about math.

Kinley slowly leaned forward. She reached for the button of his jeans.

"What are you doing?" he asked in a husky voice. "I didn't say you could touch me."

She nibbled her bottom lip. "May I touch you?"

"May I touch you what?" he asked, not allowing himself to yank her down on the bed with him and have his way with her.

"May I touch you, please?"

God, he wanted to say yes. "No."

A sound of disappointment came from her.

He bit down on his tongue until the pain cleared his mind. "There will be time later." *One plus one equals two.* He turned the vibrator off. "Right now, I have appointments in ten minutes."

She blinked.

He sat up, and she lowered her leg.

She made a pouty noise and turned away from him.

"Where are you going?" he asked.

She stopped and glanced over her shoulder at him. "To remove the vibrator." There was an edge of anger to her voice.

"Leave it in," he ordered.

Her eyes closed. "Why?"

"Any future questioning of my orders will result in a spanking."

Chapter Nineteen

Ian stepped into the session on Naughty Words for Nice Writers being presented by author Cara Bristol, a writer of erotic romances.

He sat down next to an older lady, probably in her early seventies, with gray hair and pearls. He wondered if she was published or still trying to get her first contract.

"Some men have nicknames for their penises. I once knew a guy who referred to his as Fred," the speaker said. She was best known for her Rod and Cane Society domestic discipline series.

"Who would call their penis Fred?" the lady sitting beside him asked in a smoker's voice.

He shrugged, trying not to smile. He couldn't tell if she was shocked or tickled.

She elbowed him in the side. "Well…I bet there's a good story behind the nickname."

"I imagine you might be right," he said.

"If you're going to write romance where a man's penis is up for thought or discussion, you're going to need a variety of terms you can use to describe this noble organ," the speaker said.

His elbow partner elbowed him again. "What do you call yours?"

Ian pulled his phone out of his pocket and pretended to have a phone call. "Sorry," he mouthed to the lady. Then he got up and went further back in the room, away from the elderly lady with too many questions, and spotted Kinley. She raised a hand in acknowledgement of him.

He didn't stop. Didn't try to sit in the empty chair next to her.

He'd come to the workshop in hopes of catching the speaker afterward and buying her a drink. He wanted to learn if she was open to mentoring a new author of erotic romance. Of course, he'd pay her. Kinley need never know. He'd agreed to Kinley's term of ending their connection at the end of the week, but there wasn't any way he could just walk away without making sure she had all of the resources she needed to be successful. Cara could help her incorporate her new knowledge into her manuscript in a way the readers found believable.

"Erection, corona, manhood, staff are just a few names you could use to describe a man's cock," the speaker said.

He'd never thought of himself as one who had to be in charge in a relationship, but he'd be lying if he didn't say he was intrigued now that he and Kinley were exploring the lifestyle. Did real Rod and Cane societies exist in New York?

He found a seat several rows back where he could see Kinley. He'd have to ask her what her favorite word was to use when describing a man's cock.

"Just as there are many names for a man's penis, there are also many names for intercourse," the speaker said.

Kinley was taking notes on her laptop. She reminded him of an over-achiever student eager to learn and to please the teacher. How hard would she work to please him in a long-term relationship?

"You can fuck, hump, ravish, surge, just to name a few."

Not that Ian needed to know the answer to that question. Theirs had an expiration date. After this week, she was off-limits. But no wonder her writing was so strong—she obviously loved to learn.

Teaching her about sexual tension very well might be the exquisite death of him. Not taking her this afternoon nearly undid him. But not giving in to the desire to ravish her was part of his job as the dominant one in their relationship. He'd learned that many years ago when he did extensive research into the BDSM lifestyle before he started representing erotic romance authors. And having done the research, he'd discovered aspects of the lifestyle appealed to him. He hadn't progressed to NDA's and red rooms of pain, but he knew his preferences and had no problems finding women whose appetites aligned with his. Thank you again, Miss E.L. James.

"Moving on, let's talk about terms that describe oral sex."

He had to have enough control for both of them. By the end of this week, she would know what sexual tension felt like. She'd be able to write about wanting something so bad you'd kill for it.

"The most famous would be deep throat. But it's also known as giving head, eating, and going down on."

An image of Kinley going down on him caused his cock to harden. He shifted in his seat to adjust himself and felt the presence of the remote to Kinley's vibrator. He pulled it out and turned it on, watching her as he did so.

She jerked and straightened. Lifted her hair off her neck.

He smiled when she shifted in her chair, obviously trying to get the vibrator in the right spot. He changed the vibration, not sure if he was making it harder or softer.

Kinley stood suddenly and sidestepped her way out of

the row she was in while holding her laptop under her arm. She glanced around for him, but he ducked his head so she couldn't spot him.

He watched through lowered lashes as she left the session.

He should feel bad. She obviously wanted to learn from the author. He'd buy the author's book and give it to Kinley.

What she had to learn from him was more important.

• • •

Kinley stepped out of the session and walked quickly away from the conference room. She had to get out of remote control reach. She stopped at the ladies' room and then went to the check-in counter. "I need to cancel a reservation under Kinley Foster."

The attendant punched in her name, glanced up at her, and smiled. "It's already been canceled."

Kinley frowned. Ian must have cancelled her reservation. When did he cancel? Before she told him she was in or after? "May I have a rain check on the two nights you were supposed to comp me for not having a room for me when I arrived?"

"I don't see why not." She pushed some buttons and then printed off a form, signed it, and handed it to Kinley.

"Thanks." Kinley tucked the voucher in her conference bag.

Stepping away from the counter, she got a text and checked it.

Don't remove the vibrator.

Her heart high-jumped a beat. "Too late," she muttered. She'd removed that thing the moment she left the session, and she was only too grateful the bathroom hadn't been crowded, because that particular pleasure device had a long range indeed. And she wasn't putting it back in until it was time to go back to the room.

What Ian didn't know wouldn't hurt him.

Between listening to a speaker instructing writers on how to write hot sex and how to write spanking scenes, and Ian playing loose and ready with the remote to the vibrator she wore, she was about to lose control in more ways than one.

She either had to flee the sublime torture or she was going to be reenacting the *When Harry Met Sally* scene that made the movie famous. Definitely not something a school librarian could pull off in a public place while hoping to keep her day job.

Her phone rang. Without looking to see who it was—figuring it was Ian, making sure she followed his instructions—she answered. "Hello." Hopefully he was going to order her back to their suite for a late afternoon of passion.

"I can't believe you didn't call me back," her brother said, sounding like a pissed-off army sergeant.

"I can't believe you had Ian pick me up at the airport like I'm an idiot who can't make it to the hotel by herself."

Her brother laughed, a noise more annoying than hell springing a leak in August in Dallas, Texas. "That bothered you, did it?" he drawled. "It was time for you two to make up. If I can forgive him, you have no reason to be mad at him. It's been a decade, Kin. Seriously."

"You forgave him because you're a guy, and guys don't know how to stay mad. You punch each other in the face, have a beer together, and get over it. If you knew how to stay mad, you would have never let him off the hook."

"The way I look at it, he saved me from being married to someone who would cheat on me."

She made a face. "It's a male weakness. I'm simply looking after you by making sure he knows that what he did has permanent consequences. The fact that he saved you from Stacy is completely beside the point." She didn't add that part of her anger was based on Ian turning her virginity offer down.

"He did offer you representation, didn't he?"

Kinley paced in a circle. "Why didn't you tell me he was a literary agent?"

"Because out of the gazillion questions you nonchalantly asked me about him, thinking I'm not noticing, not once did you ask what he did for a living."

"And you couldn't have just said, 'hey, by the way, since you're a writer and all, I thought I'd mention that Ian's an agent?'"

"You made me promise never to bring him up in conversation when you were around. All I was allowed was to answer your questions about him. Which was a bit childish to me, but since you are my *baby* sister, I didn't argue."

"Why did you send Ian my book without asking me first?" When her circle walking drew glances, she turned and walked down the Strip.

"Why wouldn't I?" her brother replied in a *well duh* tone. "Your book's freaking awesome. I was doing both of you a favor."

"You should have asked." Kinley knew he meant well, but she stood her ground. There had to be boundaries. "I'm an adult. I don't need either of you interfering in my life the way you did when we were kids. My book wasn't even ready."

"Is that your way of saying 'thank you, big brother, for getting me the best agent in the business'? And it was ready, you're just too much of a perfectionist to let it go."

Kinley stumbled on a crack in the sidewalk. Or that was her story if anyone saw her. "I told him I wasn't interested in being one of his authors."

"Damn it, Kinley." Her brother never—well, almost never—swore. Only when he wanted to knock heads together, which was seldom. "Are you kidding me?"

"Who kids about something like that?" She avoided a

peddler trying to hand her a flyer for a strip club—or maybe it was for a brothel. She avoided the next one by stepping inside a casino.

He made a noise of disgust. "You're cutting off your nose to spite your face." He used another one of their mom's mom-isms.

Tension coiled in her belly like a cottonmouth snake ready to bite her ass. She didn't like it when her brother was mad at her. "He gave me ideas on how to make my manuscript stronger." That was true. *Engage in kinky sex so you know what you're writing about.*

There was a deep sigh. "Like what? What in the hell is wrong with your book?"

She couldn't tell him the truth. What happens in Vegas stays in Vegas. But even if they were in Mayberry, USA, their secrets weren't going anywhere. "Like writer stuff you wouldn't understand. I'm working on the weakness. I love that you want to help me, but you need to step back. I've got this." She weaved her way through slot machines.

"Why can't you two go back to being friends? It's obvious you both miss each other. Why else would you both question me about the other? I used to think you wished he were your big brother instead of me. Then I thought you had a huge girl crush on him."

"Never. And you're the best brother in the world. You've just got to stop trying to take care of me. I'm a grown woman." She stopped at a slot machine and put in a dollar.

"You don't stop worrying about someone just because they grow up. Why do you think mom never remarried? I'll tell you why. You don't stop loving someone just because they're no longer with you."

Was that true? Did love not have an expiration date? Had she ever truly stopped loving Ian? Or had that love remained beneath her shield of indignant anger? Could puppy love survive a winter of hate? Absolutely not. "You do if you're smart. Love is for suckers." She pushed the button again and again lost.

"I think you're afraid to let him represent you. I think you're afraid you might like him."

"God. If I didn't know better, I'd think you're trying to matchmake us. Is that what you're doing?" Was that hope she heard in her voice?

"Hell no. He goes through girlfriends like you go through tissues when you're watching your sappy movies. He's not hitting on you, is he?"

Just how many girlfriends did Ian have?

The answer didn't matter. She wasn't looking for a relationship. Just some fun. "For the last time, my sex life is my business. My life is my business. Don't interfere."

"Your sex life? Are you thinking about having sex with him?"

"Did you hear the part about no interference?"

"Damn right I'm interfering. What kind of big brother would I be if I didn't?"

Chapter Twenty

Kinley sat in the Karaoke Lounge with Kim Killion, owner of Hot Damn Designs, a design and branding company "with an edge," her assistant, Jennifer Jakes, and several babes and hunks who modeled for the romance book covers the company created. The two were known as the dynamic duo in the publishing industry: Kim, a buxom brunette with a ready smile and wicked sense of humor; Jen, a brown-eyed beauty with more attitude than the Joker and Catwoman combined.

Authors sought them out when it came to having covers designed for their books.

"I hope you guys design the cover for my first book," Kinley said, taking a sip of her margarita and glancing around. At nine p.m., the place was packed with loud, laughing customers. Kinley recognized a lot of them from the sessions she'd attended so far at the conference.

"Hope is for those who have given up control of their destiny. If you want one of our covers, have it written into your contract," Jen replied, her brown eyes flashing authority, her smile flashing snark.

The song that was playing ended. A female D.J. tapped the microphone. "I'm going to play one more song, and then it's time to get our karaoke on."

The crowd cheered.

Kinley wasn't among those who were cheering. She couldn't sing. The only reason she'd ventured into the Karaoke Lounge was because it defined hip, and she'd been in the mood to pretend she was hip. And she'd kind of, sort of, thought she'd seen Ian walk into the bar…with a woman.

She'd been wrong. But she'd stayed anyway.

From the outside, the circular walls of the bar looked like a Mardi Gras bead. Thus, when you were sitting inside, you felt like you were incased in a colored glass bead.

Ian, according to the last text she'd received from him, would be busy until late in the evening with clients and editors.

She'd been unwilling to go back to their room and sit and wait on him.

"What type of romance do you write?" Kim asked. She wore a low-cut dress that made the most of her assets.

"Erotic romance," Kinley answered, trying to appear at ease while sitting amongst those who were well established in the industry versus her own beginner status.

How she ended up sitting at the cool table in Vegas's *it* bar, she still didn't quite understand, but wasn't arguing the fact.

Okay. That wasn't true.

She knew how it had happened.

She tripped over her own two feet and fell into their table…into the lap of one of the male models, an enormous man with beautiful black hair pulled back in a ponytail that hung halfway down his back.

The occupants were gracious enough to offer her a seat. Probably because the male model pulled out a chair and plopped her off his lap and down onto it before she could even get an apology out. And because she offered to buy drinks if they'd let her stay.

Conference somebodies kept stopping by their table to say hi and engage them in industry talk.

Kinley tried not to gape, gush, or gawk. She failed on all three accounts. "And I don't give a damn," she said under her breath, taking another sip of her drink. This was fun.

"I love a good, steamy romance," one of the female models at the table said.

Kinley pulled her phone out. "I'm sorry to be such a nerd, but do you mind if I get a picture of you guys?" she asked the two male models, who were wearing kilts.

"Not at all, beautiful," the sexy bald model said.

She raised her phone to snap his picture. She needed to feature him in her next book. He was just as hunky as he could be. Dumber than a box of rocks, but she could smarten him up in a book. Or maybe she'd feature Mr. Ponytail. Because of him, she had a seat at the cool table.

"Wait. You need to be in the picture," Mr. Ponytail chimed in. He had beautiful legs. Like really, really beautiful legs.

"Here, I'll take the picture," one of the female cover models said, her red hair spiraling down her back in perfect ringlets, her wife-beater T-shirt hugging her perky breasts.

The two men stood. The bald one grabbed Kinley's hands and pulled her into his arms, squishing her in a bear hug and pressing his stiff junk into her midriff. *Is that real? Oh, wait, no, that's his fake sword.*

A flash of light indicated the picture had been taken.

The other model grabbed her and bent her backward in a dip causing her glasses to slide off her face. He leaned down as if to kiss her. His lips were inches from hers. Another picture was snapped, probably capturing the surprised look on her face when she caught a glimpse of Baldy's real junk beneath his kilt. Dear God, no wonder he was a romance cover model.

"Have you ever thought about being a cover model?"

Still in the dip, Kinley tore her eyes from the dangling parts and glanced in the direction of the voice.

Kim's eyes were on Kinley.

A blush warmed Kinley's cheeks. "Who, me? No." She couldn't believe the owner of Hot Damn Designs was asking her that. She was ordinary, not novel cover beautiful.

"You should. You have the girl next door thing going for you. The blush is a nice touch."

The model stood her up. "She's right. You've got the perfect figure to do some of her steamier covers." He twirled her around. "With me of course."

Kinley glanced down at her tight-fitting, faded out Lucky brand jeans and deep purple Chucks with no strings. Not so much sexy as comfortable. They were obviously drunk if they thought she was cover model material. "Thanks."

Kim pulled her phone out of the deep *V* of her dress and snapped a picture of Kinley. "I'm serious." She glanced at the picture and nodded. "Are you interested in doing a few practice shots to see how the camera likes you? We're having a shoot tomorrow."

Hell yes. "I—" Before she could finish her reply, a hand landed on her shoulder and squeezed.

"She's busy tomorrow," Ian said in a tone she couldn't decipher.

She twisted to see him. Did he skip his last appointments to be with her?

A smile was on his lips. Too bad his eyes weren't mirroring the happy emotion.

Her brows pulled together. "I…am?" She could miss a session to attend a photo shoot. No big deal.

He gave her a look that reminded her of a bear denied his honey. Not Winnie the Pooh—a humongous, pissed-off grizzly bear. Why was he angry at her? She'd been relatively well behaved today. Hadn't once called him a liar. Did he expect her to be waiting in their room for him?

Those at the table stopped chattering.

He ran a hand down the side of her cheek. "Kinley, did you forget our breakfast engagement with the editor of Random House?" He leaned in and buzzed her other cheek with his lips.

Oh God. Her stomach dipped and twirled and somersaulted. Did he pitch her book to an editor? Was the editor interested? "Are you sure you mentioned the appointment?" Her voice sang with excitement.

He went rigid.

Damn. Did questioning him, constitute calling him a liar?

He studied her eyes. "Perhaps not." He glanced at a table across the room where several men and women were sitting. "She's anxious to meet the new up-and-coming author I've been telling her about."

A woman at the table waved at them.

Wow. Up and coming—Kinley liked those words connected with her name. *Young up-and-coming author hits New York Times with her debut book.* "Is that her?" Kinley asked, waving back. Goose bumps formed on her arms. God. She might actually forgive him all his past sins if he sold her book to Random House.

He glanced at the woman and then at her. "No."

"Oh."

A smile twisted his lips. "She was waving at me. We're meeting for drinks to talk about her manuscript." This time the humor in his smile made it to his eyes. They were practically twinkling. Like lies and darkness could never live in them. Only laughter and truth. And sunshine and rainbows.

Jealousy shot through Kinley, leaving a bad taste in her mouth. "Isn't she the lucky one? I hear you're not easy to get." The jealousy could be heard in her voice, and she hated herself for indulging in the unjustified emotion.

He was at the conference on business. He was in the business of representing authors. If he'd met one who had a book he wanted to represent, of course he was buying her drinks. Schmoozing. No big deal.

"Kinley, is this your agent?" the blond kilt-wearer asked.

"Oooorr your boy toy?" Jen asked, looking him up and down and giving Kinley a thumbs-up.

Kinley didn't know how to answer the question. She needed a third option. Like, he's my lover for the week. Or, if I learn enough about sex and kink, he might—

"Kinley and I go way back," Ian said for her. "Her brother asked me to make sure she stayed out of trouble this week."

"You're failing in your duties," Mr. Ponytail said. "If she's at this table, she's either in trouble or is about to get in trouble. It's a prerequisite."

Ian rubbed a hand down her cheek. It wasn't a soft touch. "So I've been told."

She took a step back, causing his hand to fall away. "I'm a big girl."

"Funny, I don't think of you as a girl anymore," Ian murmured into her ear. "You're all woman in my head."

She trembled. She liked the way his voice sounded when he lowered it to a tone for her ears only—a hefty dollop of sexy admiration with a cupful of bossy possession.

"Are you sure you're not secretly in love with our little Kinley?" the other kilt-wearer asked. "I'm getting this old jealous lover vibe from you. And my lover vibe is never wrong."

Ian chuckled. "Perhaps it's skewed from all of the alcohol you've consumed." He took Kinley's hand and tugged.

Kinley didn't budge. "I'm in good hands. You can drop the big brother act. Go do what you came in here to do. Have a good night." There was a difference between jealousy and not wanting to share your toys. She glanced toward the woman who'd waved at him. If Ian could have other toys, so could she.

His hand slid down her back. "You are still wearing the vibrator, aren't you?" he whispered in her ear.

Kinley shivered. "Go to your table. I'm having fun." Now it was a matter of pride.

He moved his hand, touched the scar on her forehead... frowned. His blue eyes darkened. "I never could tell you no. Even when it was in your best interest."

"Funny how our memories differ. I remember you once, quite eloquently, telling me no."

Frustration flashed across his face, before he schooled his expression into one of sardonic amusement. "Does it help you to know I wanted to say yes?" He turned and walked toward his table.

The redhead beauty sighed. "Wow. That's one hot hunk of he-man."

Kinley shrugged. "He's too bossy for my taste." *Bossy. Boss. Hell.* A full body shudder zipped through her. Ian was the boss. She'd agreed to those terms. She'd just told the boss no. Even if he never discovered she'd removed the vibrator against his wishes, there would still be consequences for not following his demands. Was it too late to get her own hotel room? Had she just earned her first spanking in this game they were playing?

"Oh, I don't know. I think he could boss me any time—any place," Jen said, glancing at her fingernails.

"Anyone want to karaoke with me?" Kim asked, obviously bored with the conversation, tucking her phone back into her boob holster.

"Not me." Kinley slid her phone into her back pocket and wiped her palms on her jeans. There wasn't a lot about death she looked forward to, but singing was one of them. If all went according to plan, and she got the green light to heaven, there she'd be given a new voice, one that could sing. Or that was her hope.

Surely God handed out singing voices to those who entered his blinged-out gates. That and a lifetime supply of red wine and dark chocolate and high heels that didn't squeeze your toes.

"We'll see," the occupants of the table said in unison, replying in faux understanding tones.

"What?" She had an uncomfortable feeling that they were up to something. Did Ian really have an appointment set up for her tomorrow with an editor of Random House? Which editor? She should go back to her room and do some research.

"Shots of tequila for the table," Kim told the waitress in a voice that sounded a little too perky.

"I wish I could sing. I can't," Kinley said, nervously. Wanting to make sure they understood she wasn't joking about her inability to sing. She glanced around for another table to sit at if they tried to pressure her into going up on stage.

"Nonsense. Everyone can sing. You just open your mouth and make a noise," Jen said. "It's like sex. It just happens."

"Not with me. In fact, the guy who just left once told me my voice scares cats and ghosts away."

"That's the beauty of karaoke. The prize is in getting up there. Not if your voice is made for singing," Kim said, her voice still not its normal tone. What was she up too?

Kinley glanced at Ian's table. He was in deep conversation with a female, his arm along the seat behind her back. She was practically sitting on his lap. Why? Their table wasn't that crowded that she needed to sit that close. Kinley stared harder. Was that the speaker from today's spankophile discussion?

Or was it the lady from behind the check in desk on the first day? They had the same blonde bombshell appearance.

Bastard.

The shots came. Jennifer raised hers in the air for a toast. "Here's to never saying never."

They all clicked glasses and downed their shots, including Kinley. Never wasn't one of her favorite words. But, sometimes never is exactly what you needed to say.

Someone ordered another round of shots. Mr. Ponytail held his glass in the air. "Here's to going commando and bringing sexy back."

Kinley downed her shot. She should slip back to their suite, slip off her panties and put some heels on. Why hadn't she dressed up before stepping into the Karaoke Lounge? Her sexy was stuck in the bottom of her suitcase. Luckily the vibrator was still in her purse. She'd get that back in place before she went up to her room.

A third round appeared. Kinley raised her glass in the air. "Here's to being too old to be spanked." Who was she kidding? She was aroused. She liked the game she and Ian were playing.

With their drinks halfway to their lips, those at the table froze. Their heads jerked, and they glanced at her with heavy amounts of curiosity. Knowing eyebrows raised and nods of approval were given.

She shrugged. They could speculate all they wanted. She wasn't going to verify. Hopefully, they couldn't see the blush warming her cheeks.

Jen gave a loud war whoop, causing Kinley to jump and nearly fall out of her chair. Her heart scrambled for cover.

"Hey you," Jen yelled toward Ian's table. When he glanced their way, she raised her glass in his direction, "to you," she shouted, and then they all downed their shots.

Kinley wanted to be invisible. When would she learn not to babble so much? She couldn't even keep her own secrets. Crap.

"Anyone ready to sing?" asked the female model. She was so freaking beautiful you couldn't even hate her. All you could do was stare and wonder how *so much everything* ended up being given to one human. With all that red hair, you'd think she'd have freckles. She didn't. Her skin was flawless.

"Not me," Kinley said. "Not now. Not ever." Perhaps it was time to go back to her room. Not because Ian wanted her there, but because…

"I am," Kim said. "What kind of boss would I be if I didn't lead by example?" She stood and tugged the hem of her skirt, shimmying her ass as she did so. Her boobs looked like they might escape.

Kinley decided she could stay a little longer. She turned her chair so she could see the stage: a tiny platform with a spotlight and a microphone.

The owner of Hot Damn Designs walked up on the stage with a Marilyn Monroe-esque wiggle-step, took the microphone from the D.J., and gave her the name of her song.

The music started and Kim started singing an oldie by Joan Jett and the Blackhearts. "I saw him—"

Her voice was fabulous, and the audience erupted into a cheer.

"I knew he must…"

She fumbled the microphone and bent to pick it up. The movement caused her skirt to ride up, and catcalls rang out. She straightened and found her place in the music. "Singing, I…"

The audience was singing so loud, you could hardly hear Kim.

Kinley settled into her chair. This was fun. And relaxing. Her insides felt like warm brownies. Better than warm brownies. They felt like the middle of warm brownies. Like the middle of warm brownies taken out of the oven a few minutes too early.

When the song ended, Kim held up her hand to stop the applause. "Now, ladies and gentlemen, I have a real treat for you. There's a virgin in the house. At karaoke anyway. So be gentle with her. This is, after all, all about having fun, not about being any good. I'd like to welcome to the stage," she glanced directly at Kinley, "what's your name?"

Kinley's smile froze stiffer than a wet rope left out in the elements in the Antarctic. The ooey gooey happy feeling disappeared. In its place, a lump of solidified Crisco. A lump so large her shots were threatening to come back up.

The spotlight swung to highlight her face.

She turned to look for an exit. The room spun from the quick movement. Or maybe from too much to drink.

"She may need a little encouragement," Kim said into the mic.

The crowd clapped louder.

"Tell them your name," Jen urged.

Kinley opened her mouth. A squeak rolled off her tongue like a tumbleweed in an abandoned town. Only her town wasn't abandoned. It was freaking packed. With people she'd have to attend sessions with tomorrow.

"Kinley," a male said from somewhere in the room. Somewhere far away in the room. Someone with a sexy voice.

"Kin-ley. Kin-ley. Kin-ley," chanted the audience. Those at her table stood as they chanted.

The bald model grabbed her, flung her over his shoulder and brought her to the stage. He set her down gently, took her purse from her, and then left her standing up there. In the million-watt spotlight.

"What song are you going to sing?" the D.J. asked.

Somewhere in the darkest areas of her brain, Kinley realized Ian was the one who gave her name to the audience. Realized she was about to humiliate herself and there wasn't a way out. She searched for his face in the crowd, more for support than anything. He of all people knew just how bad this was going to be.

He was leaning back, his hands behind his head, as if settling in for a laugh at her expense.

For some reason, that pissed her off. Maybe because the blonde was still sitting by him. They were both going to enjoy watching her be humiliated. He wanted to see her fail. The realization pinched at her heart.

"I don't think I can do this," Kinley said. Why did she care if Ian didn't have her back? They weren't a real couple. If the tables were turned, she'd probably sit back and watch him make an idiot of himself.

No probably about it. Of course she would.

The redhead from her table ran up on the stage. Was she coming up to rescue her? Would she sing instead?

Whistles rang out. No doubt every man in the audience had just gotten a hard-on. Kinley tried to hand off the microphone to her savior. She wouldn't take it.

"Here, drink this," she said to Kinley, handing her a shot. "And then sing like no one's listening."

Kinley downed the shot, handed her the glass, and looked at the sound technician. A fuzzy warmth filled her. *What the hell?* What happens in Vegas stays in Vegas. Maybe she wasn't as bad as she thought she was. Maybe she was great. Maybe Ian had lied to her all those years ago. "Do you have any Rolling Stones?"

"Honey, we've got whatever you want."

Kinley walked over to the D.J. and whispered in her ear. She smiled. Nodded.

Kinley unbuttoned the top three buttons of her blouse, exposing the lacy edges and plunging *V* of her red bra. She gave Ian a secretive smile. "This is for you." She reached up and released her hair from its bun. Curls tumbled down and over her shoulders. "Wave hi, Ian." She pointed him out to the crowd and then combed through her hair with her fingers. Two could play at this game.

His smile faltered. Instead of waving, he held his drink in the air. The cool man's wave.

The crowd grew quiet.

"Feel free to talk while I sing. This isn't going to be pretty," Kinley warned them.

If possible, the room grew quieter. So quiet, she could hear her heartbeat in her ears. Damn it. They were going to listen to her sing. These people who seemed so sweet in the conference sessions were liquored up and eager to feed their funny bones on the karaoke virgin.

The music started.

Kinley closed her eyes. Pictured Ian watching her with his smug-ass eyes. She opened her eyes, glanced at the teleprompter, and couldn't read the words. Sweat broke out on her upper lip. Oh God. She wasn't wearing her glasses. The prompter was too close to focus on. What were the words to this song? All she could remember were the ones her college roommate, Adeline Rigby, made-up to go along with the tune after a poor choice in the romance department. Shit. Shit. Shit. She closed her eyes to block out the view.

"I dun dun no—orgasm-action. I dun dun no—orgasm-action. Oh he tried, and he tried—"

On the second try, Mr. Ponytail hollered out, "Hey, your purse is vibrating."

Kinley's eyes flew open, and her gaze swung to Ian. He was standing at the back of the room. Was that the remote to her vibrator in his hand?

Kinley swallowed. "It's my phone. It'll go to voicemail."

She took a breath. Refused to glance at Ian. Damn.

"He can't get me there, he can't get me there," she belted out the words, causing a few sitting at the front tables to jump and wince.

Ian Thompson was a horrible, horrible man. Damn it. What would have happened if she'd still been wearing the vibrator? She would have had an orgasm here in front of everyone. That's what would have happened. And he knew that.

Was this his idea of kinky sex? Getting her aroused in front of an audience?

Kinley managed to hum the next stanza but was unable to actually put a volume to the words.

"He can't get me there…" Somehow she managed to force the made-up song lyrics past the knot in her throat.

Ian pushed away from the wall and took a step in her direction.

Kinley shook her head.

He stopped.

Good. Her singing on stage was enough of a spectacle for one night. He needed to stay the hell away. She glanced at her table. The Box-of-Rocks-for-Brains skirt-wearer gave her two thumbs up.

She hummed the tune. Would the song ever end? And why in the hell were people still not carrying on with their conversations? Leave it to her to debut her karaoke voice in front of a group of well mannered publishing peeps.

Who was she kidding? They weren't well mannered. They were vultures. They were busy taking mental notes of her trainwreck of a performance for future book material.

"Hey honey, I'm sure I can satisfy you," some guy yelled.

Ian frowned and, once again, began walking toward her. Slowly. Purposefully.

"I can't get no…" she sang the words softly, her heart kicking around inside of her like a tantrum-throwing toddler. What was he going to do? Did he lose his brain today?

The crowd noticed his approach.

Why was he drawing attention to himself? He was

supposed to be a professional.

Whispers swept through the karaoke bar.

Kinley couldn't tear her gaze away from his. She wanted to. But she couldn't.

Why did he have that…look on his face?

Ian reached out and took the microphone from her hand. The music faded but continued to play lightly.

"If I'm not mistaken, you've thrown down the gauntlet to all the men in this bar with this song." He spoke into the mic, his voice tight. "And since your big brother, my best friend, asked me to keep an eye on you here at the conference, I'm afraid what I'm about to do is entirely necessary." He leaned down and had Kinley over his shoulder before she knew what was happening.

There was a group gasp and then laughter.

Kinley pummeled his back. How dare he treat her like this? People were watching. Sure, they didn't know her. She was an unknown. But they knew him.

A female from the audience ran up on the stage. She took the mic. "Umm, I'll sing what she sang."

Chapter Twenty-One

Ian carried Kinley off the stage, not giving a damn that people were watching and whispering and videoing. He accepted her purse from that bonehead would-be Highlander and didn't put her down until they were inside an empty elevator.

"Have you lost your ever-loving mind making a spectacle of us out there like that?" Her eyes were spitting poisoned darts at him.

He resisted an urge to smile at her outrage. Maybe his actions had been a little over the top. Then again, his woman for the week had been up on stage asking to be satisfied. And some idiot was ready to take her up on it. "It would appear I have." What in the hell was a man to do if not go all primal? Unable to resist any longer, he grinned. Like a big goofy idiot. He hadn't had this much fun since…since a very long time. "You've been very naughty."

She blinked, shook her head at him, and then twitched her lips. "What are you going to do?" she asked in a suggestive tone.

Was she swaying?

Hell, she was tipsy. He pulled her into his arms to keep her steady. "What do you think I'm going to do?" he whispered against her hair.

She placed both hands on his chest and pushed away enough to be able to look into his eyes. "I hope you're going to give me a man-made orgasm."

He threw back his head and laughed. "Man-made, huh?" He'd turned the vibrator on as payback after he received a phone call from a man she met at the club the other night whom she'd given Ian's phone number. He'd wanted to know if Ian would like to hookup.

She tapped his lips with her finger. "An Ian-made orgasm."

Ian's cock responded to the invitation. "You're very bad for taking out your vibrator. You disobeyed a direct order."

The elevator came to a stop on their floor. He turned her toward the open door and pushed slightly to get her to start walking.

She stumbled out. "You can spank me if you want. I'm not afraid."

He missed a step. Ever since she'd come back into his life, he'd felt off balance—as if walking on a wire, where one misstep could end things. But making it all the way across could be the start of a new venture in his life.

In their room, he walked to the couch, sat down, and patted the cushion next to him. "I don't ever want you to be afraid of me."

"That's good because you're not the least bit scary." She wiggled her eyebrows. "Is it time for my spanking?" She used a purring tone. Like someone looking forward to what they were proposing. Did being spanked turn her on? Well, hell, that was the point—to excite both of them.

She sat down with the grace of a newborn colt—all arms and legs going everywhere.

"Not just yet." He'd been hard for her all evening. Hell, probably since he laid eyes on her in the airport wearing that ridiculous pillow around her neck.

She waved a finger at him. "So then what?"

He grinned. Kinley Foster was more than just a little tipsy. He should put her to bed, but a person could find out a lot about another person when they were sloshed. And there was something he was dying to ask her. "If I ask you a question, will you promise to tell me the truth?"

She awkwardly laid her head on his lap, mouth facing his cock, and curled up.

He groaned silently and rubbed her hair.

"I never lie," she said.

"Me either."

She rolled over on her back and peered up at him. "Since when?"

He ran a finger across her brows, smoothing them out. "Since always." Should he ask her? Was that taking advantage of a boozed-up—

Kinley took his finger and kissed the tip and then bit down. "Tell me about you and my brother's fiancée."

He pulled his finger out of her grip, away from her teeth. "You're not sober enough to have *that* particular conversation."

She placed her palm on his chest. "You started this tête-à-tête, not me."

He smiled. With her speech slightly slurred, it sounded like she said tit-on-tit.

She had a point. He decided to give her a straight answer. Maybe because he was tired of keeping the truth to himself. Maybe because she finally asked. Maybe because he was beginning to think he wanted a relationship with Kinley, and the truth was necessary. Maybe his behavior in the bar was his roundabout way of telling the world, she was his. Maybe…

"Stacy wasn't good enough for your brother."

Kinley's roving hand stilled against his chest. "Who said you got to be the person to decide who was or wasn't good enough for my brother?"

Ian hoped she was too drunk to feel the rapid beat of his heart under her hand. "She did when she came to my apartment to tell me she was in love with me. That she never loved your brother."

Kinley's eyes narrowed. "I think you seduced her into coming to your apartment."

"You're wrong."

"I saw her in your apartment. Naked."

"Then you ran home and told your brother."

She sighed and raised her legs in the air and kicked off her shoes. "Don't you think he had a right to know?"

"He had a right to hear the story from me."

She unzipped her jeans then raised her hips and wriggled out of them. "You wouldn't have told him the truth," she said, tossing them on the floor. "Guys never tell the truth."

Ian swallowed hard. "We'll never know, because you didn't give me a chance." When she reached for her shirt to take it off, he placed a hand over hers and held it in place.

Kinley rolled her eyes like she was upset he wasn't going to let her get naked. "When he confronted you and Stacy, you didn't deny her story. She said you two had been sleeping together for quite some time."

"I wouldn't contradict her story." He couldn't believe they were having this discussion. After all these years. With her drunk and in her panties, lying on his lap. Her brother had simply taken his word for it when he told him there was more to the story, but he wasn't at liberty to tell all. That's what best friends do.

Would she remember a damn thing come tomorrow?

She pulled her hand out from under his. "You wouldn't

contradict her story because you don't lie, and what she said was true?" She slipped her hand inside her tiny red panties that matched the red bra she'd shown everyone in the bar.

He gulped. God, he couldn't think with her doing *that*. Was she distracting him on purpose? If so, the plot was working. "If I tell you the reason, do you promise not to tell anyone?" He tugged her hand out and laced his fingers with hers—like a girl wanting to hold hands. What was wrong with him?

"Absooooolutely you can trust me." She giggled, ruining the believability of her response.

He ran his free hand down the side of his face. How much and where should he start with the story? "Stacy came to my apartment about a week before their wedding and said she was in love with me. I sent her home. Told her she was having cold feet. Perfectly normal."

"I never did like her feet. She had the ugliest toes of anyone I've ever known." Kinley raised her foot and twitched her toes. "I like my toes. Do you like my toes?"

"You have lovely toes," Ian said, chuckling. "Then the day you came by, Stacy dropped by about twenty minutes earlier. Drunk and crying. I told her to go lie down and sleep off the alcohol. She went into my bedroom, and I thought that's what she was doing."

Kinley hiccuped. "Sorry. Continue."

"You knocked. When I opened the door, you threw yourself in my arms and kissed me, and offered me your virginity." She'd been wearing a raincoat. She'd opened it, showing him her school uniform. The skirt rolled up at the waistband. She'd been so adorably sexy and naive.

"Technically, I tripped and landed in your arms and then just decided to kiss you while I was there."

That would explain the velocity with which she came at him. "Unbeknownst to either of us, when you rang the doorbell, Stacy heard. She recorded our interaction."

"The bitch."

"When you left, she said I either had to back up her story, or she was going to post the video on Facebook."

"Why? What did I ever do to her?"

"Nothing. She wanted me, and I guess she thought I'd marry her to keep her quiet about you. You were underage at the time, and she probably thought that would be enough for me to yield to her demands."

Kinley pulled her hand out of his. "And then you slept with her?"

Their gazes locked. "I didn't sleep with her."

"Why didn't you just tell my brother the truth?"

He glanced away. "I couldn't let Stacy ruin your reputation. You were still in school."

Kinley sat up. "Shut up. That's too sweet to be true."

"I don't lie." There were a lot of things he did wrong, but he wasn't a liar.

Kinley's eyes took on a glassy appearance. Almost as if she were on the verge of tears, but more likely the result of alcohol. "How did you keep her quiet when she realized you weren't going to marry her?"

"I paid her off."

Her eyebrows furrowed. "So you just let half the town think you were the reason my brother and Stacy didn't get married?"

He popped his neck. "It's what you do for the people you love."

She bit her lip and glanced away.

He waited.

After what felt like a century, she glanced back at him and grinned. She gave him an I-know-what-you're-up-to nod. "Is this all an elaborate lie so I'll have sex with you? Because you should know, I'm going to have sex with you."

He exhaled. "I don't lie." He should record himself saying

that on a loop and send it to her so she could listen to it over and over when she was sober.

"Did you know I design T-shirts ranting about how we live in a society where trust is a stupid emotion?"

As a matter of fact he did. "Have you sold many?" He was the proud owner of one.

"Enough to pay for this trip."

He raised an eyebrow. "I've answered your personal question, may I ask you one?"

"Seeing as I'm lying here in my panties"—she did a Vanna White over the lower half of her body—"I'd say that's going to be a request I approve."

He laughed. He found himself laughing a lot around her.

His laughter died away, and he took a deep breath. The weight of what he was about to ask settled on his shoulders, and a decade's worth of doubts slammed like a linebacker into his chest. "When you lost your virginity, did you think about me?" It was the million-dollar question. The one he'd wanted to ask her for ten years. He stared into her eyes and waited for a response.

She blinked several times. Closed her eyes.

He waited. Not breathing.

Nothing. Had she passed out?

He exhaled. "Are you going to answer me?"

She opened her eyes. They were full of distress. "Do you care if we talk about this tomorrow…? I think I'm going to be sick?"

Chapter Twenty-Two

Kinley woke—unfortunately. Her head felt like a garage rock band was practicing in between her ears, and the poison thorns from a thousand cursed rose bushes were poking her in the eyes.

"Rise and shine, superstar," Ian said, drawing the curtains open.

She placed her hands over her eyes. What did he call her? "Don't." Her voice sounded like hell. A bottle-of-tequila hell. How many margaritas and shots did she consume? She forced one eye to open and peeked out between fingers.

Ian strolled toward her, an evil smile on his face, and yanked off the covers.

The sensation of cold air over bare skin told her she was naked except for her panties. What happened last night? Did he spank her? Did they have sex?

She couldn't remember beyond him carrying her to the bed—maybe because her head was full of remembering what they'd talked about before that point. It's like they'd had "the talk" and then everything else was a blur. "Did I pass out?" She moved her hands and cringed her way through the opening of her eyes.

"I'm afraid so. How is your bottom this morning?" He was fully dressed. Professional casual. Black slacks, long-sleeve, v-neck, gray sweater that fit his torso snugly, showing off his body.

She squirmed—once, twice—against the sheets. Her ass felt fine. But if she said that, he might be tempted… "Sore. Very sore." Were there do-overs if the spanking didn't hurt?

A smile lifted his sexy lips. "Did I spank you too hard?"

Her gut told her not to reply. To roll over and go back to sleep. "Of course you did. You're a beast." She had to whisper. Anything above that decibel made her want to cry.

"You're lying," he said quietly.

"How do you know how my bottom feels? Was yours spanked last night?"

"No, and neither was yours. Although you richly deserved one."

She stilled—not that she'd been very active to begin with. Even breathing hurt. "You can't blame me if my memories are foggy this morning." She gently sat up and pushed her hair out of her eyes. "Please tell me the things I do remember about last night aren't real."

He sat on the edge of the bed. "What do you remember?"

"Did I sing in front of people?" Her cheeks burned at the sketchy memory. He gave her a wide grin. "I'm afraid so."

Her breath quickened, and that hurt so much she lowered herself back into the soft mattress. "I can't go to sessions today. Everyone will be talking about me." How would she ever live through this humiliation?

"If they are talking about you, and I doubt that they are, it will be about the handsome guy who carried you off the stage. It's much more gossip worthy than your terrible singing."

She shivered. Not that she would tell him, but his carrying her off the stage had been the hottest thing that had ever happened to her. Worth getting up there and making a fool of herself.

She threw the pillow at him. "Why did you turn on the vibrator?" she whispered. She wanted to yell, but that wasn't happening anytime soon.

"Why did you tell some guy I was gay? And give him my number?"

She giggled. The guy had actually called him. "I didn't tell him you were. Just that there was a rumor you were. So that's why you turned on the vibrator? As revenge?"

"Yes. And I couldn't get the damn thing to turn off."

She rolled her eyes at him. "You are…an idiot."

He nodded. "If it makes you feel better, before I came into the Karaoke Lounge, I witnessed the piano player in the piano bar making out with a publishing editor last night."

"That doesn't make me feel better." A faint memory surfaced. "Aren't we supposed to meet with an editor this morning?" How had she lost track of that? Why didn't she quit drinking the minute she found out? There was no way she could function as an author this morning. Just lying still made her feel woozy. When she felt better, she was really going to hate herself for last night.

"I cancelled." He got up and walked out of the room.

She closed her eyes, relieved and disappointed and queasy.

He came back and set a tray with a coffee pot and a bottle of aspirin on the bed and then climbed onto the bed beside her. He leaned against the headboard, put the tray on his lap and poured them both a cup of coffee. "Coffee with too much sugar?"

"You remember?" She wanted to be mad at him. But anger took energy, and energy required her brain to work, and her brain was wearing a do-not disturb sign.

"I could lie and say yes. But, I watched you make yourself a cup the other morning. Although, I remember a lot of things about you." He poured the sugar into her cup and stirred, handing the china cup and saucer to her along with two aspirins.

She took a sip. A sigh of appreciation slipped past her lips. "Like what?" Other than she used to be: bucktooth and chubby.

"Like how pretty you are without any makeup. How your eyelashes are incredibly black and long. Like how smart you are. Like how uncoordinated you are on the dance floor."

"I am not uncoordinated on the dance floor. That was you."

"Are you kidding me? When you get your moves on it's like watching someone trying to pat their head and rub circles on their stomach at the same time."

She glared at him—and it wasn't easy to glare when your head wanted to die. But she did it anyway because how dare he make fun of her dancing. He was the one who wouldn't win if he was in a dance off between himself and a stuffed turtle. "Well, watching you dance is like watching a nerd with his hand in the air and the teacher won't call on him." They'd been paired up to take dance lessons before her brother's wedding, because they were to be a part of the wedding party dance. The lessons had been agony.

He gave her a somber expression. "If I forget to tell you before you leave to go home, I think you're beautiful. And funny. And the man who finally makes you forget to distrust—the man who finally wins your heart—is going to be one lucky bastard."

She took another drink of coffee to buy herself a moment to process what he'd said. "Why are you being so nice to me?"

"I don't have a reason to be mean to you."

"Well stop being nice. We're enemies with benefits for the next few days. That's all."

He set his cup back on the tray, then took her cup and did the same. He set it all aside then took both of her hands in his. "Kinley…I like you. I'm not going to lie about that. But, if it makes you feel better, I do owe you a couple of spankings."

Chapter Twenty-Three

Two hours later, it was time for Ian to stop mollycoddling Kinley and get down to the business of being a dominant. *Hell.* Did he just use the word mollycoddle in his thoughts? He needed to cutback how many Regencies he was representing.

He took the bottle of water from her and placed it on the coffee table. She'd taken such a long shower he'd been tempted to call in Search and Rescue. Once she'd finished, he'd ordered room service and fed her toast and a scrambled egg.

"Hey, I wasn't done with my water," she complained, showing all the signs of someone who was going to be grouchy for the rest of the day.

"You said you wanted to be in a relationship where you were spanked when you misbehaved. Correct?" They were sitting on the couch, at opposite ends. She'd put on a pair of jeans and an antitrust T-shirt. *Never waste your feelings on people you can't trust.*

"Because you said I suck at writing sex."

She looked like hell. Like a woman with a hangover. And

yet he was completely turned on by her. "And you agreed to the rules of the game we're playing. Correct? I'm the dominant. You're the submissive."

She curled her feet underneath her. "They were your rules, but I didn't argue with them."

"Which means I get to spank you when you break the rules."

She sat up straight and moved her feet to the floor. "Which I haven't done."

He maintained eye contact. "Lying about breaking the rules could count as breaking a rule."

She rubbed her forehead. "Okay. Maybe I broke one or two of your stupid rules."

Damn she was cute when she was grouchy. "Have you changed your mind about being in a D/s relationship with me?"

She nibbled on her bottom lip, turning her body so that they weren't looking at one another. "No."

He hid a smile, not wanting to provoke her into changing her mind. "Remember the scene in your book where your heroine is about to get spanked for the first time?"

She looked back at him with a haughty expression. "Of course I do. I wrote it."

He nodded and remained quiet for a moment, choosing his next words carefully. "It's a great scene, but you left out the emotions of your POV character. The reader has no idea what she's feeling. If she's excited. If she's frightened. If she's both."

He listened to the laughter of hotel guests walking down the hallway and waited for her response. Would she take the criticism as constructive or would she get mad?

She slowly turned back toward him and gave him a quizzical look. "She resists. Doesn't that say what she's feeling?"

"Not all of it. Why is she resisting? Is she trying to figure out what it is about being spanked by a dominant that turns her on? Or is there another reason for resisting? Like she's changed her mind? She doesn't like the act as much as she thought she would?"

She wrinkled her nose. "I thought adding too many thoughts would be boring."

"Too many would be. But you need some."

"Oh." She nodded her head. Like what he'd said made sense.

He shifted so that he was sitting in the middle of the couch. Enough with the verbal mentoring on how to be a better writer. Time for some physical mentoring. He patted his lap. "Take your jeans off and lay across my legs."

She jumped up. Hurried to the table. Grabbed the top of a chair and stood behind it as if it could protect her. "Now? You want to spank me now? Why?"

He knew exactly why he wanted to spank her. He wanted to see her ass rosy from his hand again. But why he wanted to and why he was going to were two different things. He was going to spank her because of their agreement. "If I'm going to do my job as a mentor to you this week, then it's necessary for me to keep my word and spank you when you've broken the rules."

"And then what?"

"Then you go downstairs and attend the sessions like you planned."

She moved from one chair to the next, keeping as much distance between them as possible. "I don't want to go downstairs. People will whisper."

Ian wanted to pull Kinley in his arms and assure her no one would make fun of her on his watch.

But right now, he was playing the part of a dominant.

A part he'd been thinking a lot about making a permanent

part of his lifestyle. He wouldn't chase her. She would come to him. "What is your safe phrase?"

Kinley blinked. "Excuse me?"

"The first time I spanked you, it wasn't planned. This time is different."

She nibbled her lip. "Why is this time different?"

"Because I'm in control of what I'm doing."

A look of doubt clouded her eyes. "Why a phrase and not a word?"

"Because a phrase takes longer for the submissive to say. Not as likely to be a knee-jerk reaction because your bottom is stinging."

She chewed on her lip. "What happens when I use the safe phrase?"

"I quit spanking."

"What if I said I love you?" she said in a matter of fact tone.

The panic he would expect to feel at the declaration didn't occur. Confusion, yes—but not panic. "What?"

"What what?" She placed her hands on her hips and cocked her head like a diva.

"What do you mean?"

She laughed. "Don't look so hopeful, I'm not telling you I love you."

He frowned. What sort of game was she playing? "You know damn well I didn't give you a hopeful look. But if you don't mean it, why did you say it?" Since when had his face become so easy to read?

She gave him a smile so dazzling it could light up the Strip. "That's my safe phrase."

He swallowed. Since when had she become so good at messing with his brain? "That's your safe phrase." He refused to analyze the emotions surfing inside of him. Refused to think about the taste of disappointment in his mouth.

"Yes," she said in a saucy voice.

"Why?"

Her mega-watt smile faded like the setting sun—not fast, but slow, like each thought going through her brain pushed it down a little further in the sky until suddenly it was gone. "Because it would take a lot to ever say that to a man, let alone to you."

He winced. "I get the part about not wanting to say it to me. But why not to any man?" Was that his fault?

Her eyebrows pulled together. "Do you believe in love?"

"I can't wait to fall in love and have a soulmate." Why did an image of her and him sitting in rocking chairs on a huge front porch overlooking a picket-fenced yard pop into his brain? And why were there little girls playing in the yard? *Hell.* Who was he kidding? He knew why. He'd been keeping up with her every way he knew how over the years. Waiting for his chance to come back into her life. Waiting to see if grown-up Kinley played havoc with his emotions the way young Kinley did.

God. She was the reason he decided to represent romance writers. He'd been perfectly happy leaving that genre to other agents until her brother mentioned that she had a dream of someday being a romance writer.

"Do you believe in love at first sight?" she asked him.

She wasn't the first female to ask him that question. Normally all of his defenses would fly up, and he'd be itching to escape the woman asking the question.

But not this time.

This time he found himself actually considering the question. Actually responding to it. "I think love at first sight is overrated. I get much more excited at the idea of falling in love with..." He stopped and clamped his mouth shut. *Hell.* He'd been about to say his best friend's little sister. Where had *that* answer come from?

"With?" she prompted.

He shook the image and thoughts away. "With a rare steak and a double bourbon." He glanced at his watch. "We're out of time. There will be a spanking this evening. Right now, we have sessions to attend."

Chapter Twenty-Four

The day took forever to end.

Ian sat through fifteen pitches and attended a few sessions. He had lunch with an editor from Hachette. Kept an eye out for Kinley the whole day and never saw her. He'd thought about calling her or texting her, but that felt too much like a real relationship.

Finally, they were alone in his suite. And the time had come for the spanking.

He leaned against the bar. "Take your jeans off," he said, aware his voice was low and rough. Not the calm tone he'd been attempting.

She lifted her chin. Her eyes flashed with mutiny, but she reached for her waistband. She unsnapped her jeans and slipped them off.

An ache to possess Kinley rocketed through his body. He took a deep breath and exhaled. Reminded himself of the role of the dominant. To be her protector, her strength, and her biggest fan. But mostly, to be in control.

He'd figured it was a long shot that she would actually let

him spank her when the time came. His heart drummed in his chest as he waited for her to comply. He needed to spank her, for himself as well as for her. This was the first step in her admitting he was a man she could trust—something he needed from her.

She reached for her panties.

Heat coiled in his stomach. "Leave them on."

Her long, toned legs were amazing. The scrap of silk panty was tantalizingly small. He pointed to the couch. "Lay down. With your head on your forearms and your ass in the air." He folded his arms and waited.

She set her lips in a stubborn line. Her breasts rose and fell with each breath under her T-shirt. She walked to the couch. Her movements were graceful, haughty, confident. So unlike the sixteen-year-old who'd literally fallen into his arms and asked him to take her virginity, back when she trusted him.

She stretched herself across the couch, her bottom in the air, facing him.

He ached to touch her. To explore her body. To give her the man-made orgasm she'd asked for the night before. But to do so would threaten his ability to finish the punishment. There would be time later for caresses.

He crossed the room and reached for her panties and slid them half-way down her thighs.

Her skin was creamy, unflawed. Her hips womanly, her ass voluptuous, perfect.

She spread her legs slightly, and his blood heated.

He could see her engorged, glistening sex. This aroused her. The realization caused his cock to harden. His muscles tensed. He imagined exploring between the plump folds of her sex. Anticipation pushed him to hurry, so they could get to the part that happened after punishment.

"Before I spank you, I'm going to take a picture of you in the submissive position. When I'm finished, I'm going to take another picture of your bottom, branded from my hand."

"Why?"

"Because being photographed is another angle of—what did you call it? Oh yeah, non-vanilla sex."

"Does it turn you on to snap shots of me in this submissive position?" Her voice sounded breathless.

He stood over her and shook his head in wonder of her breathtaking sexiness. "If I told you the things I want to do to you right now, bent over with your panties pulled down, you would faint from the shock."

...

Kinley thought about telling him no, he couldn't take pictures, but what he said made her more than just a little aroused. She'd never thought about being photographed. But now that it was about to happen, a barrage of ideas and other scenarios in which he could photograph her poured through her brain. Damn. She might come the minute he spanked her. "When this week is over, you have to promise to delete them."

She had spent the day writing. An idea for a novella, based on what she and Ian were doing, came to her during her shower. She'd skipped the sessions and found a quiet place to type. The story flowed from her fingers to the keyboard at an unbelievable rate...until she reached the ending. She was going to have to go back in and add a photo-shoot scene.

He laid his hand on her bottom and rubbed.

She jumped. Man, his hand was big. Did that mean the spanking would hurt more?

"If I say yes, do you trust me to keep the promise?" he asked.

She started to say no but realized she did trust him to delete the embarrassing photos. The realization caused something hot to rush up her throat. She didn't do trust. Yet here she was…trusting. Him.

A dynamic had changed between them.

They were bonding. When did that happen?

"I didn't hear your answer."

"Yes." How could one word be so full of meaning? She wasn't sure how she felt about bonding with Ian. It was one thing to have incredible sexual experiences with him. But trust?

He removed his hand.

She turned her head to see him.

He took his phone out of his pocket and took a picture of her looking up at him with her head on her arms, her ass in the air, and her panties pulled down.

Then he stepped behind her and took a picture from that angle.

"Spread your knees a little."

She did, and her heart thumped against her chest like a woodpecker trying to peck its way out of a cage to get to its mate. Could he tell she was aroused?

She noticed the bulge in his jeans. He was as aroused as she was.

He took another picture. Then he walked back to her side and placed the phone—with the picture showing—on the couch beside her arms so she could see herself. He laid a hand on her behind. Rubbed.

The soft stroking relaxed her. "You'll stop if I use my safe phrase?"

"Of course. Tell me why I'm spanking you."

"Because I broke the rules." What would her heroine say? *Because you're an ass who told me I can't write sex?*

"Correct. I'm spanking you to remind you of who is in charge in this relationship. Not to bully you."

She swayed her hips, wanting him to slide his fingers between her legs. To feel her wetness. "And to teach me about kinky sex." This was kinky for her. Would they get around to exploring the other avenues of kink she'd mentioned? Their time was running out.

"When engaging in the kind of sex you want to write about, someone's the dominant partner. For us, that's me." He spread his fingers and squeezed her glutes. He leaned closer to her. "I'll never lie to you. Do you believe me?"

She glanced into his eyes. His expression gentle and loving. She tried not to shiver. Didn't succeed. "I'm trying." Was he telling the truth about Stacy? Had she hated him all these years unjustly? He'd asked her if she remembered their conversation the night before about Stacy. She'd lied—told him she didn't. But she did.

His jaw clenched. He placed one hand under her hips to hold her in place and then administered the first slap.

The contact stung, and she jumped. "Damn it. That hurt." A good kind of hurt. Here was a man bold enough to be in charge. Strong enough to take over when she wanted to relax her guard.

"This is for calling me a liar." Three swift smacks landed on her bottom in the same place.

Tears sprung to her eyes. *I will not cry.* She may be playing the part of a submissive, but she was going to play the part of a strong submissive. One with a mouth that would drive her dominant crazy.

He stopped and rubbed. "Are you okay?"

She nodded.

"I can't hear a nod."

She bit back a smile. "I'm just peachy."

"Good." Three more, quick, hard thwacks scorched her bottom just above the crease where her bum and legs joined. "Those were for taking out your vibrator when I told you to leave it in."

She tried to roll away from him. To see how dominant he

was going to play his role.

He held her in place. "Do you have anything to say for yourself?"

Dear Lord, he played the alpha beautifully. "I'm sorry. You had me so horny I couldn't think straight."

"Who were you thinking about when you were singing?"

She shook her head—didn't answer.

He landed another swat on her cheeks. "When I ask you a question, you must answer me."

She groaned. "Being satisfied by you." She glanced up at him and gave him a sultry look. She wanted to distract him, so he'd be done with the spanking and get on with the pleasuring.

He stroked her bottom. "Do you have a desire to have sex in a public place some day? Where others can watch?"

She moistened her lips with the tip of her tongue. "Absolutely." *Maybe.*

His hand came down hard.

She cried out in surprise. That one felt more real. "You're hurting me."

"That was for tattling to your brother about Stacy, before I could speak to him."

She flushed. "You can't spank me for something that happened in the past." She collapsed on the couch and rolled over on her back before he could react. She kicked her panties off and tried to get up.

"Where do you think you're going?" He held her down with an arm against her stomach, his expression fierce and determined. "I didn't hear the safe phrase."

She clenched her jaw. "Because I didn't say it."

He made a noise that sounded ominous. "Then this session isn't over."

She felt her stomach free fall as if jumping out of a plane's window. This felt real. Like they weren't playing a game. Like they were really in a relationship in which he ruled. "You can't punish me for something that didn't occur this week."

"Roll over." The two-word demand left little room for argument.

She clenched her fists. "I don't have to. I can use my safe phrase." She refused to make it easy for him to be the dominant one. He was going to have to earn the title.

Their gazes locked.

Neither of them blinked.

"Kinley, who's in charge?" his voice was steady, soothing. Nothing like her angry one.

A knot formed in her throat. Damn him for being sensible. She couldn't argue with sensible. "You are."

"Roll over," he said softly.

She hissed out a breath. She flopped over and stuck her ass in the air. She gritted her teeth and waited for the contact of his hand on her derrière.

He spanked her several more times. She didn't make a sound. She refused to give him the satisfaction.

Then he stopped.

She waited to see if it was a trick. When nothing else happened, she glanced back at him.

Beads of perspiration dampened his temples. His nostrils flared.

He picked up the phone and took a picture of her bare ass—no doubt bright red from his hand. Then he tossed the phone on the coffee table and stood. He held out a hand to her. "Come."

She sat up on her knees. "Where?"

His face softened. "We need to take care of your bottom."

She lifted her brows. "You mean my ass?" She wasn't sure how she felt about that. He'd just gone all real-dominant on her ass. And…and…it turned her on. But he was the enemy.

No—not the enemy.

A man who would always have her back if she gave him

her backside. Or that's how it would work if they were in a real relationship between a dominant and a submissive. This was just for research.

He gave her a lopsided smile. A smile that shouted "I'm a man who can be playful." A smile that melted her defenses. "And a fine one it is," he said. "Then I'm going to fuck you senseless."

Her girly parts applauded. He knew exactly what to say to make her pant, to make her forget her misgivings. To remind her how much she wanted him to give her an orgasm that had nothing to do with a vibrator. But she wasn't ready to make it easy for him. "Let's get one thing straight." She walked toward the bedroom.

"And what would that be?"

"Now, that my punishment is over—I'm the one in control."

He chuckled: a rich, warm sound. "That you are, love… that you are."

Chapter Twenty-Five

Kinley unzipped Ian's slacks and lowered them down his muscular legs. His erection sprung to life. "Commando?" She didn't take him for the sort. She had him pegged as a Versace boxer boy.

"I like the freedom." He stepped out of his pants and kicked them away.

Kinley licked her lips. Her eyes fixed on him. On an aroused cock that intimidated and thrilled her at the same time. "Did spanking me do that to you?"

He didn't reply immediately.

She peeked up at him with heavy eyes—desire making it hard to keep them open.

"I couldn't help but notice being spanked turned you on," he said, standing at ease. Broad shoulders. Lean hips. Legs wide apart. Completely comfortable being stared at by her. "Do you forgive me for hurting you?"

"I wanted you to slide your fingers in me between spankings."

His jaw clenched. "We can't mix punishment with

pleasure."

She gulped. "What if, next time, I pleasure myself while you're spanking me?"

His nostrils flared. "Does that mean you're going to let me spank you again?"

They only had two days left. She didn't plan on giving him any reason to spank her between now and then. Which meant this part of their experiment was over. She couldn't help but feel some sadness at the realization. She shook off the melancholy. "Not likely," she said with a cocky smirk.

She walked to the bed and crawled to the middle of the king-size mattress. She rested her forearms on the bed and raised her ass in the air before glancing back at him. "Do you know anything else to do with a woman's ass besides spanking it?"

"Oh, I think I can come up with a couple of things you might enjoy." He walked to the bed, bent down, and kissed her ass. "Watching you sing on stage last night was the most erotic thing I've ever witnessed." He dotted kisses everywhere.

She stilled. Had her singing been okay? "So I wasn't awful at karaoke?"

"I didn't say that. But you had a slow burn in your eyes. The same burn you get when you're coming. And I knew, when the night was over, your cute ass would be tumbling into my bed. Grasping my sheets. Crying out my name. Not the name of those idiots in skirts you were flirting with."

Kinley didn't want to dwell on last night's fiasco. "Did you know they go commando under their skirts?"

He bit her bottom. "I'm not happy that you know."

She jerked. "Don't even think about spanking me for something that's said during foreplay."

He laughed. "I bet they jacked-off thinking about you last night."

She scooted away and lay down on her back. Spreading

her legs, she ran a finger over her center, causing her hips to lift off the bed. She touched herself again, and a low moan escaped her lips. "Did you?"

"Did I jack-off thinking about you?"

She nodded.

He smiled—a smile that had power shining through. "What do you think?" He went between her legs and spread them wider. Opened her folds with his hands and then flicked her pink bud with his tongue.

Her back arched off the bed. "Oh God."

"You like that, do you?" He flicked it again and again and again. Then he licked her center.

"It's beginning to give me some satisfaction." Her voice was breathless. She lifted her legs in the air.

He bent them until her knees were flush with her chest.

She squirmed, liking the feel of the sheets against her bruised ass.

He held her firm. "You're clitoris is so engorged." He pinched it.

She gasped. No one had ever done that. It wasn't proper. Nice guys didn't do that.

He pinched it again.

She squirmed. The pain made her hot. Hot for him. "Don't make me wait."

"Are you sure you're ready?" He placed his cock at the apex of her warmth and teased by sinking the thick tip in. "Or do you need more preparation?"

"Don't be an ass."

He ran his finger around her anus. "Did you say go in your ass?"

She stilled. "No." There was not proper and then there was NOT PROPER.

"No what?" He sounded so caught up in the moment, almost as if his control was about to snap.

"Not there." She couldn't cross that bridge with him. A lady could only take so many new experiences in one week.

He pinched her clitoris again, and she groaned.

"Someday—I'm going to go there," he said.

She shook her head.

"But not until you're ready."

"Okay." The word of permission slid out easily. They both knew someday wouldn't—

He moved back, leaned down and licked her hard. He didn't let up on the pressure until her breathing sounded like the steam coming from a freight train.

"Don't," she gasped out. She didn't want to come yet.

He gave one more long, rough lick. "I want to hear the soft mewling noise you make when you come."

She dove her fingers into his hair. "Then satisfy me like you promised everyone in the club you were going to do."

He dropped her legs and raised above her. Grabbed the condom off the nightstand and put it on.

She watched, her body pulsing with desire. "I need you inside of me." She wriggled and felt the soft scrape of satin across her ass… Her ass that no doubt held the imprint of his hand. She moved again enjoying the sensation. Enjoying the memory of his dominance.

He shifted his hips above her. "Say please."

She'd never begged a man for anything. "Please."

"Happily." He lowered himself and thrust in. Not slow. Quickly, as if his control broke.

She arched hard. Her mewling turned to a growl. God. They'd just started, and her orgasm was about to happen. Was that what spanking did to her?

An assault of energy vibrated through her, wiping away her ability to think, leaving unfettered throbs in its wake. She rode the derailment of sensations that seized and swirled, bucking against him until the storm of pleasure quieted.

"I take it you liked that?" he said.

Somehow, she managed to open her eyes.

Ian stared intently at her, his blues dark and heated.

"Oh God, that was beyond like." Every inch of her skin tingled as her muscles continued to softly contract around him.

His lips tilted up. "You're so beautiful." His hair was damp from sweat. A sex-tousled mess. And she'd never seen him look so gorgeous.

She dug her nails into his shoulders. "Your turn. I want you to feel what I just felt."

He kissed her forehead. "Not yet." He reached between them. His thumb did magical things.

"Ooooh." Another surge of heat enveloped her with ripples of ecstasy. "I think I want you to spank me every night." She leaned up and bit his ear and then fell back on the bed.

His eyes glazed over. "I'd be happy to." He pumped fiercely.

She watched his face as she met his thrusts with her own, fascinated by the flush that darkened his cheeks. When he stilled and closed his eyes, she wrapped her legs around his waist and squeezed. At the same time, she grabbed his ass and dug her nails in.

A sound that was all satisfied male came out of his throat.

She laughed.

Pure, powerful, female, happiness.

Chapter Twenty-Six

The next morning, after several more kissing sessions once Kinley pointed out he'd failed to kiss her the night before, and fucking sessions, which cracked and corroded the wall of protection Ian normally wore around his heart, he was lying on the bed. Happy. A little too happy.

Sex with her was extraordinary. Wanton. Mind-killing.

Thus his happy-ass state of mind.

He wasn't against feeling happy, but Kinley wasn't the right girl to feel this way about. She was his best friend's little sister. And she deserved a man who could give her more than a few nights of himself.

And even if he was a man who could give her a long-term relationship, he still wasn't the right man for her.

As much as he and her brother had mended their fences, Jack still wouldn't want a constant reminder around the family of the wedding that never happened.

Besides, Ian wasn't ready to settle down into a long-term relationship. He liked his life the way it was. No complications. Then again…

He rubbed his temples. He didn't want to think very hard along those *then again* lines.

He needed to get his head out of his ass and refocus on what he'd promised Kinley—a no-strings-attached introduction to non-vanilla sex. Any feelings his heart was nursing needed to be killed.

He picked up some conference notes and straightened them with more force than finesse, only to become distracted by Kinley when she walked out of the bathroom wearing a white fuzzy robe.

Still holding the notes, he turned to get a better look at her, and a card slipped to the floor.

She bent down to pick it up. "What's this?" She read the information on the card and then gave him a beaming smile. "A REAL sex club?" she squealed. "Oh my God. I can't believe you have an invitation to one. They were all the rave when I started reading erotica."

Shit. He'd meant to toss that in the nearest trash can after the lady in the elevator dropped it. How did the card get mixed up with his pitch notes? "It's nothing. Just something I found." He didn't correct her and tell her the invitation was for a private sex party, not a sex club. That there was a difference in the type of individuals you'd come across in each. That bit of information was beside the point.

As if clueing in to his lack of excitement, she gave him a beguiling look of female begging. "Can we go?"

His throat tightened. "Absolutely not."

"Why? Isn't your job this week to teach me about things I want to write about?"

He pinched the bridge of his nose. "It's also my job to keep you safe. I can't take you to a party where I don't know the host."

She rolled her eyes. "Stop being such a worrywart. If I can walk on the wild side this week, surely you can as well.

Where's your sense of adventure?"

He fingered a curl of her hair, still wet from her shower. "I left it in New York. One of us has to be sensible." Actually, back in NY, when he'd been doing his BDSM research, he'd ventured into a couple of "dungeons" and, no, they weren't the dark, dangerous places that one might think. Most had rather ordinary-looking people entertaining extraordinary fetishes. Few had people actually having sex—that was more common on the international scene. Here in the US of A, actual "sex" was illegal in most states.

She collapsed back on the bed, causing her robe to gap open, showing him enough skin to rattle his brain. "We're in Vegas, baby. The city that frowns at sensible people."

Chapter Twenty-Seven

"How much do you know about story structure?" Ian asked Kinley. She was wearing a white turtleneck and black slacks. Her hair was up in a bun, and her glasses were perched on her nose. A very prim and proper look for a vixen he'd seen naked only hours earlier.

They were having lunch in the same café they'd dined in on the first day at the conference.

She took a bite of her omelet. Swallowed. "I think I know more than the average writer."

"Good. Pretend we are a love story. What would the inciting incident be?" He hadn't meant to ask her to use them as an example in the teaching of story structure. So why did he?

Her cheeks flushed a pretty shade of girly pink. "Actually, I started writing a novella yesterday, and I'm loosely using our setup as the backbone of the story."

He sat back in his chair and steepled his fingers. "Interesting. So, what's the inciting incident?"

She took a sip of her orange juice. "My heroine's inciting

incident is when she boarded a plane full of ladies who sell sex toys."

He nodded "That explains your vibrators."

"That's where my heroine's sex toys came from. And the lady sitting beside her in the plane becomes her mentor in the seduction of the story's hero." She dipped her hash browns in the glob of ketchup she'd poured on her plate and took a bite.

He grimaced. He didn't like ketchup. It reminded him of the blood that had gushed from her head during their unfortunate sledding accident that had left her scarred for life. "You've had some help in your game plan to seduce me?"

She patted the corners of her lips with her napkin. "In my novella, my heroine has had some outside help."

He took a bite of his bacon. "And in your novella, did the mentor tell the heroine to masturbate in front of the hero?" he asked, feeling wicked talking to Kinley about masturbation in the middle of the day in the middle of a busy restaurant.

She dropped her fork on her plate and it clanged loudly causing some to glance their way. "She told her to leave the bar without the hero," she whispered.

He leaned closer to her and whispered back. "Nice. What's the hero's inciting incident?"

She pushed her plate away and folded her hands prissily on the table. "His is a little more complicated. An unlikely friend calls and asks him for a favor."

He reached out and stroked the top of her hand. "You really don't remember anything we talked about the night you sang on stage?" He found himself wishing she did. Wishing they didn't have that black cloud hanging over their experience this week.

She dropped her gaze and laced her fingers with his. "I thought we were talking about story structure, not the most humiliating night of my life."

He released her hand and sat back, shifting in his seat.

"What is the first turning point of…your hero and heroine's love story?" The restaurant was filling up.

"For my heroine, it's when the hero bets her she can't seduce him. She takes him up on the bet. And for the hero, it's when he realizes she did seduce him, and he so arrogantly assumed she never could."

He glanced back at Kinley. Her comment surprised him. "Arrogant?" Is that how she saw him?

"Absolutely. It's my story. I have an arrogant hero who needs to be taken down a notch or two before he makes a great hero."

He never meant to come across as arrogant. Mostly, he said and did what he said to protect against poor choices. "What do you have planned as the climax in your story?"

She chewed on her bottom lip. "That's where everything goes to hell between the hero and heroine—right?"

His groin tightened. He felt a pull of temptation to reach across the table and kiss her bottom lip. "Sometimes. But sometimes it goes great."

"The hero falls madly in love with the heroine and tells her so in a very public setting." Her voice held a wistful quality.

Was she secretly hoping he'd fall in love with her? "And how does the heroine respond?" Was he secretly hoping she'd fall in love with him? *How public is his declaration of love?*

"I haven't gotten that far in my planning. But I'm thinking, she's going to shoot him down. Wipe the arrogance out of him in a big way."

He tugged on his ear. "You've got a mean streak."

She shrugged one shoulder. "I prefer to call it an ornery streak."

His gut tightened. "You're writing a romance, so there has to be a happily ever after resolution."

She shrugged. "I'm thinking about giving it the Nicholas-Spark's-Ending Treatment. The hero's heart gets broken, and the heroine regains her independence and dignity. And revenge for her brother."

"Your brother doesn't hate me. He trusts me."

"This story isn't about my brother. It's about my heroine's brother."

He frowned. "I don't think I can sell that." Nor would he want to.

"You're not going to be my agent, so that's not a problem."

His palm itched to make contact with her ass. "If your heroine is so fabulous, why doesn't she have a boyfriend? Why is she single?" He held his breath, waiting for her answer. Would she tell him?

She gave him her sassy look. "She's between boyfriends."

He exhaled. "What happened to her last boyfriend?"

Her eyes narrowed, and she glanced away. "He reminded her too much of her first love…but she didn't realize this until he declared his love."

"And?"

She took her glasses off and wiped them with her napkin. "Have you thought anymore about taking me to the fantasy bash?"

Ian frowned. She wasn't going to kiss and tell. "What if I said yes? Are you saying you'd be okay watching me have sex with another woman?"

She propped her elbows on the table and cupped her chin with her hands. "Could you watch me with another man?" she asked, a wicked grin on her face.

Was she purposefully pushing his buttons to see how much he cared? "Honestly?"

Her smile didn't waver, but the gleam in her eyes turned a darker shade. "Of course."

He'd promised her a lot of things this week. One of them being honesty. "I don't think there's a chance in hell I'd ever be able to share you with another man. The thought causes me to want to punch something."

"We're not a real couple. Just a short-week couple."

"I know."

She leaned back and picked a piece of lint off her sleeve. "And we're not in love."

He waited for her to look up at him. "I know."

"Then take me to the sex party."

He ran his hand through his hair. "I don't understand why it's so important to you to go to one. You don't have any sex-party scenes in your manuscript. Everything you have is between one man and one woman."

"This may be my only chance to experience all of these different sexual avenues with someone…like you."

"Like me?" He didn't want to do this. He couldn't do this. He wouldn't do this.

"You know. Safe. Non-judgmental. Someone who lost a bet and who has to keep his end of the lost-bet bargain."

Ian's stomach dropped. The friggin' bet. Neither of them had mentioned the bet. Who was a better teacher or mentor? That was the question, wasn't it? And then, she'd gone and seduced him, and he had to concede she had in fact won that round. But, damn it, they'd come farther than that. Hadn't they?

She stared at him as if daring him to argue. "I did lose the bet, didn't I?" Damn this arrangement. Surely she was feeling some of the same doubts he was feeling about their ability to keep their relationship purely a mentor/mentee bargain.

"You did indeed *lose* the bet?" She did air quotes around the word lose. "Which by default means you have to teach me everything you can about sex and sexual tension."

He stamped down the desire gnawing at his throat to once again say this was a bad idea. "Please remind me to never take you up on a bet ever again."

"Does that mean you're going to uphold your end of the

one we have in place?"

"I'll make you a deal, if I can find out more about the people hosting the party, and they are legitimate, then we'll go. Not because I want to, but because I'll keep my promise to teach you about sex this week."

She cheered and clapped her hands. "You're the best. How will you do that?"

He shook his head. He was a friggin' idiot. "I'll do what any endowment brat would do. I'll hire a private detective."

She plopped her elbows back up on the table and rested her chin in her hands. "Speaking of endowments. I should say, yours did not disappoint."

He chuckled. "I aim to please."

The waitress came and cleared their table.

"Oh that you did," Kinley said, giving him an exaggerated wink. "In fact, let it never be said I'm not anything if not a gracious bet winner. That being said, I owe you big time for agreeing to take me to a sex party."

He crossed his arms and sat back. Was there a silver lining in this fiasco? "Big enough to answer a question for me?"

She pulled her glasses down to the tip of her nose and glanced at him over the top of them. "I was thinking a blowjob would be a great thank you. But sure, if you want the answer to a question, I guess I could grant you that instead."

"Tell me why you and your last boyfriend broke up."

Chapter Twenty-Eight

Ian and Kinley slid their masks into place before he raised his hand to knock at the front door of the Robinson House, a pre-Civil War reproduction of Tara from *Gone with the Wind*. Before he could knock, an intimidating black man dressed in a red tuxedo, wearing a black half-mask, opened the door.

Kinley stiffened next to Ian.

Was she afraid? He drew her to his side. Or was she having second thoughts about what they were doing? He kissed her temple. It had been twenty-four hours, but he was still reeling from the knowledge she'd cried out his name during an orgasm given to her by another man. Of course she'd gone on to say that it was a fluke, a mind-meltdown on her behalf because her brother had mentioned Ian's name earlier that day in a conversation, but Ian had latched onto that tidbit of information like a pit bull to a steak. Because, come on, it'd been *ten years*. If he was still on her mind—and while in the throes of passion, no-less—then Kinley hadn't been nearly as indifferent to him as she'd claimed.

He cursed this wretched deal they'd struck yet again.

They should be back in their hotel room, in bed, where he'd devote the next twelve hours to making her scream his name, over and over again. So he could etch himself into her mind for another ten years.

But no. A promise was a promise. That promised stemmed from a bullshit bet. And here they were. At a friggin' fantasy bash.

One of these days, he really needed to learn to tell this woman no.

The man who answered the door didn't smile. "Names?" He had a no-nonsense voice.

"Brad and Angelina." Ian gave him their stage names. Names they were assigned after being selected to attend the party. The invitation he'd found in the elevator had only been the beginning of the process.

Once he called and RSVP'd, he'd been required to send photographs of himself and Kinley. From there, he had to wait to hear back from the hostess to see if they'd been chosen by a committee to be allowed to come to the party.

Then he had to give permission for them to do a background check on them.

His detective reported that Fantasy Bashes threw friendly parties all over the country for young couples and single women. They were regularly attended by beautiful partygoers from all over the world.

They were known for their intimate sensual ambiance and welcomed newcomers and first-timers.

"Very good." He stepped back. "My name is Dan."

A woman stepped out from behind Dan. She had on a dark green nightgown that squeezed her boobs into a gravity-defying display of cleavage.

Dan placed his hand on her shoulder. "This is my wife, Charlie."

"Nice to meet you," Ian said. "I'm Brad and this is

Angelina."

Kinley stepped forward and held out her hand. "It's nice…to meet you." Her voice sounded different to him. Hesitant. He placed his hand in the small of her back. If she was having second thoughts, they would go.

"It's very nice to meet the two of you," Dan said, shaking Ian's hand and kissing Kinley's. "Have you done this before?"

Was the tension in the air his imagination or real? "This is our first." Ian glanced past the host. He saw a wide hallway painted a rich red with a lot of doors. No people spilling out. No shindig underway. No sound, barring faint jazz music.

"Then my wife will explain the rules. Rules you must follow."

Charlie smiled. Her eyelashes fluttering through her white mask. She stepped away from the door. "Please follow me." Her voice was low, soft, and perfectly southern. Charming.

Dan stood back and allowed them to enter.

Ian took Kinley's hand and followed. "Do you live here?" he asked Charlie. His detective said the house belonged to a couple, not Fantasy Bashes.

The house sat in the middle of a secluded lot. A wall of trees surrounded the perimeter—a throw-back of a large plantation home. From what he could tell in the dark, while the car-service drove down the winding driveway, the groomed grounds were top notch. Obviously an expert cared for them. They were a long way away from the Strip.

"No one lives here." Charlie stopped next to a door and opened it. She motioned for them to enter first.

A large red divan was situated in the middle of the room. A fire burned low in the belly of a fireplace whose chimney extended to the top of eighteen-foot ceilings. On the wall above the mantle hung a huge flat screen television.

"There is a remote on the divan's arm. Please turn the television on and watch the video. When you are ready, knock on the door, and you will be escorted to the party. Or, if you desire, you may go home." With those simple instructions, she turned and left them alone in the room.

"Are you okay?" he asked Kinley, who'd been unusually quiet. Since when did she become the silent type? "We can go home at any time."

She lifted her chin and glanced at him. "Do you know Dan and Charlie?"

The question surprised him. "Not exactly. I think I met her in an elevator at the conference. But with the mask, it's hard to say for sure." He took her hand and kissed her palm.

She gave him a smile and then tugged her hand away. "That tickles."

"You look so beautiful." It was all he could do to keep his hands off of her. He'd thought of a few other ways he wanted to make love to her. "Perhaps, we should leave and go back to the hotel. Do what we do so well."

"You're looking mighty fine yourself in your tuxedo, Mr. Thompson. But I do declare, it sounds like you may be getting cold feet."

He wrapped his hand around the back of her neck and pulled her close. He leaned down and captured her lips in a short kiss. "Or maybe a case of possessiveness."

She touched her fingers to her lips. "You're very good at confusing me. You're the one who said I needed real experience in order to be able to write erotic romance well."

"I did, didn't I? Shall we watch the tape and see what we're getting ourselves into?"

She nodded and walked to the divan. For a moment, he just stared. Dressed in a long red dress that hugged all her curves, and displayed her ass like an hourglass, he'd been entranced all evening. Her hair was pulled back away from her face and hung down and around her shoulders in a cascade of curls. A zipper held the dress up. Easy to unzip. Easy to step out of. Easy to have sex in.

He sat down beside her and turned on the television. The first scene on the screen was of a bedroom. A bed—the size of three king beds pushed together—crowded the room. On the bed were a group of men and women engaged in sexual acts.

"Oh, wowza," Kinley said, her hand coming to her mouth. "I wasn't expecting that right off the bat."

Ian chuckled.

To the side were cafe style tables. Men and women sat at the tables. Some were watching those on the bed and openly masturbating, others were drinking and talking as if alone in the world.

As quickly as the show appeared, the screen went dark.

"Shall we go home?" Ian asked, willing her to say yes.

Kinley glanced at him. Glanced at the door. "Did you notice they were all wearing bracelets?"

He frowned. She didn't sound like a woman ready to go home. "Really?" He tried to hide the disappointment in his voice.

She smoothed the skirt of her dress. "Men don't wear bracelets. How could you not notice they had them on?"

He crossed his leg, resting his foot atop his knee, and reminded himself of his promise to her. "What kind of bracelets?"

She shrugged. "Some type of charm bracelets."

The movie came back on. Charlie and Dan were sitting on a couch. They were dressed in sleepwear. Charlie spoke. "Anything legal or within reason is allowable at one of our bashes. Everyone here is an adult and consenting."

Kinley shivered. She reached out and touched Ian's hand, lacing her fingers with his.

He kissed the top of her head. "You okay?"

"Perfect. Just a little nervous," she responded.

"In the baskets, sitting on the table under the window, are

charms," Charlie said.

Ian fetched the basket and placed it on the couch between them.

"Choose the charms that represent the things you are willing to experience. The ping-pong paddle represents your willingness to allow another couple to spank you. If you wear a paddle with a pair of eyeglasses, it represents that you are willing to allow another couple to watch you being spanked," Dan said.

"If you wear the number two on your bracelet, this symbolizes you are willing to swap partners," Charlie said.

Kinley picked up a charm of the number two. She held it up to the light and stared at it before placing it back in the basket.

Ian sighed in relief.

"A three or higher represents your willingness to participate in group sex similar to what you just watched," Charlie said.

Kinley explored the charms in the basket but didn't pick any up.

"The handcuffs tell other couples you are into bondage and are willing to participate in light BDSM. We do not allow anything beyond light BDSM," Dan said.

Kinley glanced up at Ian. "Let's not do that."

"Okay," he said, smiling. "You don't have to do anything you're not comfortable with doing." He cupped her cheeks and kissed her forehead, glad she'd said no to that experience. He'd never be able to allow another person to harm her in any way.

On the screen, Dan spoke. "If you wear a bracelet with no charms, you are telling other party participants you are new, and you want to watch and learn. We recommend this for all first-timers."

The television went black.

Kinley and Ian stared at one another.

"I'm good with just watching," he said.

She licked her lips. Shook her head. "Nope. I'm doing this. We're here. There's no going back now."

He swallowed the bitter tasting lump in his throat.

She squared her shoulders. "I say we wear the number two on our bracelets."

He hissed out a breath. The words were like a gunshot to the heart—the pain intense. "You're killing me, Foster." He said the words in a joking tone, but he wasn't joking. At all. What was wrong with him? Why had he brought her here? He wanted more than a few nights with her. A lot more. Why was he just now letting that truth into his brain?

The fact was, he didn't want any of this. He didn't need a threesome to be happy. He needed Kinley. And if she wanted non-vanilla sex, he could give her that. Without adding additional people to the mix.

But he'd made a promise. To go back on the promise would be to break his word. He wasn't a liar.

She smiled like he'd made her extremely happy. Like she was completely unaware of the storm raging inside of him. "Somebody should have done that a long time ago."

She'd have her week of kink. "And somebody needs a spanking."

Her brows furrowed.

Ian figured the best way to handle tonight was to approach it like the pulling off of a band-aid—just get it done. He grabbed a bracelet, slipped the number two on the silver band, and placed the bracelet on her wrist.

She created a matching bracelet for him and then insisted on being the one to take the basket of bracelets and parts back to the window desk when he made a move to do it himself.

He walked to the door and knocked as they'd been instructed.

The door opened.

Charlie and Dan came in. "Ian, you will go with Dan. Kinley, you will come with me. You will meet at the party. If you want to come together as a couple you may. If you want to circulate as singles you may."

"I prefer walking into the party with Kinley on my arm," Ian said. He needed to claim her as his.

Kinley laughed. "Nonsense. If we're going to do this, let's go all the way. Let's be mysterious and seductive."

He frowned but allowed himself to be led out of the room.

• • •

As soon as the door closed, Kinley turned on Charlie. "What in the hell are you up to? Why are we here? Why are you here?"

Charlie laughed loudly. "Hosting a party."

"Is this a Passion Party?" Kinley felt like the universe was spinning out of control, and she didn't have a tight grip on reality. And why in the hell did she insist on wearing numbers on her bracelet?

She thought for sure Ian would put his foot down and demand they only watch tonight. What in the hell was he doing letting her have her way in all of this? Did keeping a promise mean that much to him? She'd been ready to shove that number two charm up his nose—gah, that stubborn man!

"This is our first business. Selling Passion Party products is a natural extension of what we do as sex party hosts," Charlie said.

Kinley took her glasses out of her purse and slid them on. "How does one become sex party hosts?"

"The journey is really quite simple. My grandparents owned the business. I inherited their Bash Homes, and thus the tradition, when they died." Charlie handed Kinley a black mask with beautiful beading attached to the front and a different bracelet. "Put these on."

Kinley removed hers and did as she was told. "Why have you been acting like we don't know one another? And why do you want me to wear this mask? Are you the one who gave Ian the invitation?"

"Because this gives you the upper hand in what happens tonight. And yes, I may have interfered a tiny bit and made sure Ian found out about tonight's event. And then placed the seed of the thought in your head by casually mentioning swinger parties in a comment."

Charlie had masterfully manipulated them both. Wow, she was good. "Why do I need the upper hand?" She glanced at her bracelet, the three jingled from the gold band.

"You're scheduled to go home tomorrow—correct?"

"So?" What was it the three represented?

"Honey, I've seen a lot of couples in my life. I have a sense when it comes to who will fall in love and who won't. You and Ian are destined."

Kinley dropped her arm to her side and made a noise that defied description other than a donkey's laugh. "Not in this lifetime. I don't trust him…he's an ass." Even to her own ears, she sounded like she was protesting too much.

Charlie raised Kinley's chin with her finger, her bracelets clacking noisily in the room. Charlie had a gazillion trinkets on her bracelet. "He's a keeper."

Kinley stepped away from the touch. "And you know this how?" She didn't disagree with Charlie. Especially now that she knew the truth about the Stacy incident. But falling in love with Ian was a wasted cause. He'd never feel that way about her in return.

"Like I said. I have a knack for reading people."

"Whatever."

"Tell me. Do you love him?"

"Of course not. Maybe. I don't know."

"But he's your dom—right?"

Kinley flushed and tingled and wanted the floor to swallow her. "Well, yes. But only for the duration of the conference. And it's all in the name of research…" She licked her lips. Was Charlie a freaking psychic?

"That may be true—but you're not the type to let a man be in charge of you if you don't trust him. And, you have a personality that finds it very hard to trust. In fact, the only men you are ever going to trust are those you love."

"You're talking in circles," she argued.

"Do you want to know how to find out if he loves you?"

"Of course…not…maybe." That was her new favorite response. There was so much conviction in it. She was a woman who knew her mind.

"There's a couple at the party. Do you remember the sale's lady from the boutique?"

"Sure."

"She's the female. The male is her current lover. They'll know you by your mask. They are going to approach you. Her lover is going to whisk you away. You're going to go willingly."

Kinley placed her hand over her chest. "I don't want to have sex with her lover! I just told Ian I did so he'll stop saying I don't have what it takes to write sexy fiction." Could a woman have a heart attack from sexual shock?

Charlie's smile faded, and she folded her arms across her chest. "Why don't you want to have sex with another man? He's quite delicious to gaze upon."

Kinley walked across the room to glance at a picture of a threesome in progress. "Because… Just because."

Charlie walked up beside her and placed a hand on her shoulder. "Because you're in love with Ian. There's nothing wrong with that."

"Absolutely not," Kinley said, stepping away from the

touch.

Charlie laughed. "You protest too loudly. If Ian allows you to go, that means he hasn't realized his own love for you. Your act of leaving will push him to realize how deep his emotions go for you. Don't stop leaving until he declares his love."

"That's a ridiculous plan." *Was* she protesting too much?

"When you left him in the bar, he chased after you, didn't he?"

"Yes."

"That's because by leaving, he realized he wanted you more than he wanted his pride to win."

"What?" Kinley asked, intrigued.

"Men don't know what they want until what they want leaves, and they have to chase to get what they want back."

"Are you sure about this?"

"Of course. And once a woman realizes this, they have the upper hand. You just keep leaving until your man stops letting you leave. Then you let him catch you."

Kinley went to the couch and sat down. She forced herself to think logically. "Your theory is all fine and dandy if this week had been spent with us falling in love with one another."

"And isn't that what you've been doing?" Charlie came and sat down beside her.

"The sex is spectacular. But part of the reason it's so great is because at the stroke of midnight, I leave for the airport and we go back to being childhood acquaintances. We promised each other a no-strings-attached week in which I get to learn about kink."

Charlie took Kinley's hands in her own large ones and squeezed. "Do you think you are the only couple faced with complications to falling in love? History is full of fabulous couples like you. The best love stories are complicated. You should know that as a writer."

"Of course they can be complicated. But we're not a love

story."

"Trust me—you are. And the universe has placed me in the middle of your business to help you remove the complications to your happily ever after."

"How do you know that's what the universe wants you to do?"

"I saw it in the cards, of course."

Kinley didn't know how to respond to that type of logic. Charlie was—what? A tarot-reading, sex toy selling, blackjack playing, sex club owner?

"You're not going to let this go, are you?"

"Bless your heart, you know I'm not."

"What are you? Like my sex-fairy godmother?"

Chapter Twenty-Nine

Ian glanced at a couple humping on the dance floor and frowned and wasn't sure why he wanted to cover Kinley's eyes and wasn't sure why he was regretting RSVP'ing for this party. His reaction didn't make sense. They were at a party that was all about sex. The couple wasn't acting inappropriately.

And he didn't consider himself old-fashioned.

Old-fashioned described his parents, who'd married at the age of eighteen and never regretted the decision.

Old-fashioned described his grandparents, who were married sixty-two years before separated by death.

Old-fashioned described those who followed society's rules.

Rules he'd never especially cared for, because they were too old-fashioned.

So why did he feel the need to grab Kinley and protect her from the debauchery rampant in the massive ballroom decorated with pictures and statues of scantily clad individuals engaged in every sex act one could imagine, and some he'd never thought to?

"Have you ever seen so many beautiful people in one room?" Kinley asked next to him, her voice a little high-pitched. As if overly excited, or overly nervous, or both.

One couple waved at them from across the room.

Kinley raised her arm and waved back.

He pulled her arm down. "Don't encourage them." They shouldn't have put charms on their bracelets. They should have committed to just observing. Why hadn't he insisted? Why had he agreed to this party to begin with? When in the hell had he become such a moron?

She pulled her brows together. "Why not? How are we going to meet a compatible couple if we don't mingle?"

He ran a hand through his hair. His gut was tight. He reminded himself he'd promised her a week of learning kink. "I don't know why you don't just agree to write Amish romance."

Her jaw dropped, and she punched him in the shoulder. "You're not having second thoughts, are you?"

Fuck. He was way past second thoughts. He wouldn't lie to her and say no. But he wasn't ready to analyze his feelings too closely. "I want you to be happy." That much was true.

"Being the best possible writer I can be will make me happy. If experiencing the act of swinging helps my writing, then I say let's go find us a good looking couple and make us a swap."

He glanced away. She sounded positively eager. Like a writer in a bookstore with a no-limit credit card.

She obviously had no problem trading him in for a different model. Why wasn't he feeling the same? "Why don't we have a seat and observe for a moment? Take this slower rather than quicker."

She shrugged her shoulders, and he was pretty sure she rolled her eyes at him. But the mask made it difficult to know for sure. Was she wearing a different mask?

He took her hand and tugged her to a set of chairs that were in a corner by themselves. "This is better. We can enjoy a drink, listen to the music, and people-watch."

"Wow. He's hot." A guy wearing a cowboy hat, a snug white T-shirt, jeans, and boots walked by. "So rugged." Kinley fanned herself, drawing his attention.

A bolt of jealousy stabbed Ian. She didn't like country music. And she'd never used to like cowboys. Why did she like cowboys now? He had a cowboy hat and boots in his closet in New York. If that's what turned her on, he could give her that. "She's not bad herself," he forced himself to say.

She glanced at the woman and frowned. "What time does your plane leave tomorrow?"

"It doesn't. I leave the following day. How about you?"

"Mine takes off at four a.m. It was the only one I could get at a rate I could afford. I'll probably leave this party tonight, go back to our suite and pack, and then leave for the airport." Her words were running together like two colors of paint when the tape is removed before they dry. "Unless I'm with someone else, then maybe I'll just have you pack my stuff and send it to me. That is if I'm running late and have to make a mad dash for the airport."

Hell. Why was he just learning of this? "We should leave early. This isn't a good night for us to do this. You'll need some sleep. And you don't really want me to pack your toys—do you?" And they needed one more night of passion.

The woman he'd mentioned earlier walked back into their line of view and gave Ian a thorough look.

Kinley exhaled loudly. "Oh, I plan to stay here as late as I possibly can." She gave him a wicked smirk. "And you've already seen my toys, I don't care if you pack them."

Before he could respond, the couple came to a stop in front of them. "Hello," the male said.

Kinley hopped up. "Hi." She held out her hand, but

instead of shaking it, he kissed the back. She giggled.

Reluctantly, Ian stood and said hi to the female. "You're a breathtaking sight in the midst of a breathtaking scenery," he said stiffly, using a line he'd used often on the dating scene.

She smiled tranquilly and ran her hand down his arm. "And you are fresh blood. We haven't seen either of you at one of these parties before."

"This is our first time," Kinley said.

"You're beautiful," the female purred to Kinley, taking both of her hands in her own, lifting their hands in the air, and then spreading them out. She glanced up and down Kinley's body and turned to her partner. "I'd say she is definitely someone we'd like to get to know."

Ian took a step back. This couple wasn't interested in him. They were interested in finding another female for a threesome. He glanced at the couple's bracelets. A number three dangled from them.

He glanced at the two on his and then glanced at Kinley's. He frowned. When did she add the three to go with her two?

"I'm Donnie, this is Marie," the male said. "Perhaps we can talk later." He spoke directly to Kinley.

She blushed. "Perhaps."

The couple disappeared as quickly as they'd appeared.

"Take that three off of your bracelet," Ian hissed.

They both sat down.

"Why? I'm not opposed to trying a threesome. And, gawd, he was a male specimen of perfection. I wonder how big he is beneath that buckle?"

"Really? You'd be willing to go into one of the bedrooms around here and have a threesome with those two?" He sounded like a spinster judging.

Her lips parted. Her eyes flashed daggers. "I'd consider the possibility. For my writing. Are you jealous? Or is your male pride hurt, because they wanted me and not you?"

He shook his head and sighed. "This was a fucking stupid idea. Your brother trusts me to keep you safe."

She lifted her mask then reached over and lifted his. "You're so cute. You think because we've had sex this week that I belong to you? And/or that my brother and you can still rule my life?"

He pulled his mask back into place. "I didn't say that. You're your own person. The only person you belong to is the person you decide to belong to."

"Would you like to dance?"

Kinley and Ian both jerked in surprise at the sound of a female voice. They looked up. A couple was standing in front of them.

Hell. Had they sat down in a spot that said, "we're new, come to us?"

"I'd love to dance with you," Kinley said pulling her mask down. She took the man's outstretched hand, and sashayed away.

"How about you? Would you like to dance?" The woman had a short pixie haircut and huge blue eyes. Built like a petite Dolly Pardon.

He stood. "Why not."

He glanced around the room for Kinley and didn't see her. He wanted to leave. He wanted to get her alone. Enjoy together what little time they had left this week. He was going to insist they leave.

Where had she gone?

He spied her in the corner dancing like he remembered her dancing. Fantastically poor. He chuckled. Her suitor would leave her soon enough.

He led his dance partner to the same corner and danced just as poorly. Because that's all he knew how to do. He and Kinley smiled at one another. Their arms flailing. Their legs twitching. Sure, he could make a better effort if he'd tried, but their own brand—dare he even call it dancing—was more fun.

Amidst a twisting turn on Kinley's part, he grabbed her arm and led her off the floor—to a door. Without giving her time to speak, he opened the door, pushed her in, and shut it behind them.

"What the hell are you doing?" she demanded, yanking out of his grip and taking a step away.

"I could ask you the same thing." He turned on the light and glanced around the room. A playroom. A lady's boudoir.

"I'm conducting research for my writing. Something you're supposed to be helping me with—not hindering my progress in."

"I am helping you. I'm giving you a lesson in what it means to be a submissive."

She jammed her hands on her hips. "Don't even think about spanking me."

He hadn't been. But now that she brought it up… He ran his hand through his hair. Frustrated with himself. Frustrated with her. "Why shouldn't I?"

"Because…because…" Her voice was husky. Aroused. Defiant.

He took a steadying breath, walked to a wall of scarves, and grabbed one. Then he walked to the dressing table and picked up a flat head brush. "These should work." It was time for him to reclaim his control of their experiment.

She raised her mask and backed toward the door. Her over-sized brown eyes were flashing fire. She sucked at being a submissive. Which suited him just fine. He liked her spunk.

He reached out—grabbed her arm. "Because isn't an answer." He removed his mask, and their gazes locked. He glanced away from her far too spellbinding eyes…eyes that could make a man forget his mission.

"Because is as good as any," she said in a voice that charred his brain with its heat. There was some new nuance to her voice. Something he couldn't quite put his finger on. Whatever it was, he liked it.

"Is it because," he said the word because very softly, "you'd prefer I kiss you right now? And then whisk you away from this circus?" He lifted his gaze from her lips to her eyes.

She shook her head and tried to yank her arm free. "Who's to say I didn't want to kiss the guy I was dancing with instead of being pulled in here and manhandled by you?"

He pushed her against the wall. Trapped her there with his hands on either side of her face. Felt her heart pounding against him. "Did you?" He leaned in close. Close enough to smell her mint toothpaste. To feel the heat coming off her body. To see the dilation of her pupils.

...

"When in Rome…" Kinley quipped. She wasn't sure her heart had ever pounded so hard and fast in her life. She noticed the freckle next to the scar on his forehead, adding a sweetness to the physical reminder of his kindness when they were young.

That was the day she fell in hero-worship of Ian Thompson.

His lips parted. She inhaled the scent of a fine scotch on his breath.

Was Charlie right? Did he love her? Was tonight going to be the night he declared his love? Would he do it here in this room?

He leaned in closer. "We're not in Rome." He placed the scarf over her eyes and tied it gently behind her head.

"You know what I mean," she whispered.

"God, you're beautiful," he whispered back. And then his lips were on hers. Soft at first. Caressing.

She placed her hands on his shoulders to remain standing. Her legs wanted to fold underneath her. She couldn't believe this moment was happening. Couldn't seem to focus on anything beyond the rapid rhythm of her heart pounding in her chest and how much she hadn't even known she wanted this moment to happen.

Someone knocked on the door.

"Occupied," he growled.

Why didn't he just say I love you and whisk her away? Take her someplace where they wouldn't be interrupted? Someplace worthy of a declaration of love?

Did he have any idea how much courage it took her to come to this party? Not knowing if she was going to find herself researching acts of sex up close and in person with someone other than Ian? Just to prove to him—to herself—that she could write steamy romance?

When she thought about it, wasn't that a tad ridiculous? Okay, it was *entirely* ridiculous. But seeing how she'd been in denial about this man for over a decade, what was four more days of delusional thinking?

She had nothing to prove and only herself to make happy. She knew that now.

And Ian made her happy.

He pressed closer to her. Close enough she could feel his arousal. Not being able to see heightened her other senses. Heightened her emotions.

She opened her mouth against his and demanded more than sweetness. She wanted rawness. Being so near him made her feel safe. Safe in a place that scared the crap out of her. Not that she would ever admit that to him.

He groaned. Picked her up, carried her across the room, and sat her on a hard surface.

His hand found the zipper of her dress.

She whimpered. The heat was building in her body at a rate so fast she found it hard to breathe. She searched blindly for the buttons on his shirt.

He laughed. Like a man who was very pleased with

himself. "I knew you weren't cut out for kink. You're a one—"

She stilled. Her mind cleared. "What?" How could she be so wrong about what was going on between them? *Gawd.* He wasn't thinking about declarations of love. He was thinking about the fact he was right, and she was wrong. *I'm such an idiot for romanticizing what we've been doing.*

She slid down the scarf and stared silently at him, biting her tongue so she wouldn't blurt out something without thinking it through.

He stared back, his eyes heavy with desire. "Why did we stop?"

She forced herself to shrug. Her heart tried to convince her she was overreacting, but her brain argued a good case. If he'd been thinking about them as a couple, about loving her and wanting to know if she loved him back, those are not the words he would have breathed into existence. He would have been pulling out all of his romantic moves. Declaring your victory over a bet wasn't even a little romantic. It was time for her to react according to what was truly going on between them and not her Romance-writer delusions of happiness. "Although kissing you is fun, we didn't come here to make-out with *each* other." She wanted to feel mad, because mad was an emotion she knew how to handle. Instead, a raw sadness that she'd been holding at bay for ten years, thundered to life, screaming in her ear, *he didn't love you then, he doesn't love you now.*

But she couldn't tell him *that*. The truth would make him feel guilty about something that wasn't his fault. It was really her fault. After all, he'd more or less kept his end of their crazy bets and promises. So she would too. This was a one-week experiment, and she needed to move on with said experiment.

He blanched. "That doesn't mean we can't."

Her girly parts woke up to his suggestion. *Say yes. Say*

yes. Say yes. "Where's the fun in that?" she replied, ignoring her baser needs, intent only on guarding her heart. She fought back the tears threatening to fall. "Besides, I think it's time for this student to graduate."

He pinched the bridge of his nose. "Kin—" He reached a hand toward her face and she leaned away.

Her throat was so thick she found it hard to speak. "Don't." His touch would unleash a flood of emotions. She gave him a false smile and jumped down from the table. He barely backed up, forcing her to crane her neck to see his eyes. Why did she believe Charlie that they were meant to be a couple? They weren't meant to be. They were old friends who'd finally hooked up. Nothing else.

A pulse pounded near his temple.

She stepped sideways and moved out of his space. Of course there'd be no declarations of love. This week was all about fantasy. Not reality. She'd momentarily forgotten that. But not any longer.

She reached behind and re-zipped her dress, hoping he didn't notice that her hand was shaking.

He pounded the table she'd been sitting on with his fist, causing her to jump.

Since when did he have a temper? That was her shtick. She leaned down, recovered her mask that had somehow ended up on the floor, and slipped it on.

"What did I really do?" he asked.

She opened her mouth to reply, and he held up a hand.

"I want the truth. Don't give me a line of crap," he said in a rough voice.

She untied the scarf that was still hooked around her neck and ran the length of it through her hands, stalling. He didn't want the truth. Not really. "Don't get your boxers in a bunch. Your mention of our original dilemma, my not being able to write sexy and all, caused me to suddenly realize I've lost my focus on what my mission is this week."

"Gather experience so you can write sexy?" he asked in a tone that was part-question, part-statement, and a whole lot of accusation.

"Yes."

"And isn't that what we were doing before you froze up on me?"

"I need to be out *there*," she pointed toward the door, "pushing the boundaries of my comfort zone, instead of in here where things are comfortable."

He scowled. "Damn it, Kinley. You can't really mean that. What we have isn't comfortable. It's hot, and incredible, and our time together is running out."

His words left her romantic heart no room to hide. How much clearer could he say what they had was temporary? All he wanted was to get laid one more time. "Our time together," she resisted the urge to put air quotes around *our time*, "ran out the moment you brought me to this party." She dropped the brush and walked to the door. If she didn't force herself to leave, she wouldn't leave. She'd stand here and let him talk her into one more night. "You've taught me a lot this week. In fact, everything you can teach me. But, as fabulous as you are, you haven't taught me everything I need to know." With those words hanging in the air between them, she opened the door and left.

She was pretty sure she left her heart in the room with him.

No. She wouldn't leave him her heart. It might be missing a big chunk, but the rest was still hers. She was too strong not to take back what he didn't want. *Wasn't she?*

Chapter Thirty

When Ian emerged from the playroom, his previous dance partner was standing there. Waiting on him. She grabbed his arm and pulled him onto the dance floor, where she proceeded to gyrate and bend and spin.

"I really didn't know the human body could bend like that," he said absently.

He saw Kinley talking with the same man as earlier. The prick's hand was rubbing up and down her arm. He wasn't surprised by his desire to kill the guy—Kin was his if only for the week—but he was surprised at how the sight made his heart ache. As if it didn't get the notice that they weren't a real couple with happily ever afters in their future.

"Don't worry about them," his *partner* said, pulling him out of his self-reflection, but not before he saw the guy grab Kinley's hand and lead her away.

"Where are they going?" Ian asked his dance partner. He wasn't sure what to do that wouldn't make the situation worse between him and Kinley. Was she right? Did he teach her everything he could teach her, and now she needed to experience seduction with other men?

It was his fault. He was the one who set her down the path to prove she wasn't a good girl. That she could indeed write erotic sex. That's why they were at a sex party. And she obviously wanted to be with that idiot she'd been talking to. She'd left Ian to go to him after Ian specifically asked her for one more night. She couldn't make her desires much clearer than that.

"They're just going to talk. See if they are compatible. See if there are any sparks."

His insides twisted into a tornado. "Sparks? They're not electrical wires."

"Sexual sparks. We should be doing the same." She grabbed his shoulders and danced into him. Her hands slid down, and she grabbed his ass, squeezing and pulling him against her.

He stumbled and stepped on her toe.

She yelped and took a step back. "How about we find a dark corner?"

He glanced around, looking for Kinley. "I think all of the dark corners are claimed," he said in a distracted tone.

"Why don't we slip into one of the playrooms?"

He spied Kinley, her back against a wall. The ass was dancing for her. Stripping while she watched. Hell, were those dollar bills in her hands? Where in the hell did she get those?

His abductor tugged him along by the tie. She stopped without warning, and he glanced at her questionably.

"I get the feeling you're very upset." She slid a finger in her mouth and slowly sucked on the tip and then the whole finger. And then she slowly licked her finger from bottom to top like it was a lollipop.

"Not with you," he said. How many other men had she performed this routine on?

"I like to be spanked. Do you want to spank me? Would

that make you feel better?"

"No spanking," he said gruffly. What was her name? Did he know it? Had she told him? The only woman he wanted to spank was Kinley.

Tears welled in the woman's eyes. "Are you sure? I've been a very bad girl. Very bad."

"What have you done that's so bad?" The question was asked without thought. Were those real tears or fake tears that women could produce when in the mood to manipulate?

She smiled. "I've been thinking about giving you a blowjob."

He sighed, wanting to get away from her without hurting her feelings. None of this was her fault. "I see."

"Don't you agree that makes me very, very bad?" She turned around so that her bottom was to him. She bent over and placed her palms flat on the ground.

He glanced around for Kinley. God. What was wrong with him? Was he seriously considering running after a woman? It wasn't like she was at risk. He'd done his research, and this party was probably safer than church on a Sunday morning. If she was ever going to indulge in her fantasies, this was probably the best place for her to do it.

"Baby—my ass is this direction. Not behind you." The sweet little school-girl voice transformed into a pissed-off female voice.

He glanced back at her. "I'm sorry. It's not you. It's me. Under normal circumstances, you and I…well, we'd be getting along okay." So why weren't these normal circumstances? He had the green light to screw anyone he wanted. Kinley said she didn't care. And this woman wanted to be spanked. And he fucking loved spanking Kinley, so why not the woman bent over in front of him?

She stood. "Whatever. You should have thought this through before you came. Asshole. I thought they vetted everyone who was invited."

Ian didn't respond. Instead, he turned and weaved his way through the crowd, a migraine was forming—something he had happen a lot right after the falling out with Kinley. He ignored the pain and searched for her. Where in the hell did she go? He opened and slammed doors. Playrooms. None of the couples consisted of her. He was going to break his promise to her. He wasn't going to give her full access to learning how to write kink. If she couldn't learn it with him, she didn't need to know it. If she was dead-set on having a one-night stand with a stranger from a sex party, she was going to have to do it on someone else's watch. Until her plane took off in the morning, he was in charge of keeping her safe.

He found their hosts. "Have you seen the woman I came with?"

The massive black man didn't smile. "The beauty in the red gown?"

"Yes," he snapped.

"She left with a regular."

Ian blinked. His heart rate exploded. "Left?" He hadn't really thought she'd leave with a different man. Try to go into a playroom and play, maybe, but not leave. *Hell.*

Dan gave him a bland smile. "That's my understanding. She said you were hooking up with the guy's wife, and they were going to go find a place more private."

"What made her think I planned to hookup with his wife?"

He shrugged. "I told her the last time I saw you, you were adjusting your Johnson and watching his wife sway her bare ass in your face."

"Why in the hell...never mind." Ian headed toward the front door.

"Where are you going?" Dan asked, his smile anything but innocent.

"After her."

"I wouldn't do that—"

"Why the hell not?" He stopped and stared hard at Dan. What was this guy up to? And why was his wife giving him a look of concern?

"—unless you're in love with her."

Ian frowned. "What's love got to do with any of this mess?" He rubbed his temples.

"Unless you're in love with her, and she's in love with you, you need to allow her to have this experience."

Ian inhaled sharply, the oxygen slicing his throat with a rusty razor. "Why?"

"Because now that she's gone down the path of sexual discovery, she's always going to wonder what it would have been like if she doesn't complete the task."

He exhaled a bloody breath. "And if we're in love?"

"I don't have the answer to that one. I don't know what your love can handle. For some, this brings them freedom to love each other unconditionally. For others, this brings them heartache."

Chapter Thirty-One

Ian ran out the door in time to see a yellow cab pulling away from the curb. He sprinted, got in front of the vehicle, and slapped his palms on the hood, shuffling back until the car came to a stop.

Kinley jumped out. She shoved her mask up so that he had a clear shot of her glare in the light of the full moon. "What in the hell are you doing?"

His heart shifted, like a poorly hung shelf with too much weight on one end. "Where are you going?" he asked, feeling stupid for not having a better answer. He hadn't planned what to say—just to catch her and keep her by his side.

"I don't know. A hotel room, I guess." Her heavy breathing sounded loud in the still night. Her breasts were rising and falling rapidly. Was she aroused? Had she been kissing the guy in the backseat?

"You guess?" He couldn't keep the disbelief from his voice. Did she really leave with a man and not know where they were going? What the fuck was wrong with her? That wasn't safe. Was there a small rip in her dress? Who did that to her dress? "Why?"

"Maybe I'm doing it to win the ultimate round between us," she snapped.

He rubbed his temples. "Is that why you're doing this?"

She sighed. "Does it matter?"

He shoved his hands in his pockets. "No. Because you're not going with him."

Her eyes widened. "Says who?" He could almost imagine her donning a pair of boxing gloves, ready to have a go at his face if he didn't answer correctly.

What was the correct answer? The words, *Me, because I love you* tickled the back of his throat. But there was no way that was the right answer. Obviously, he'd been reading too many love story manuscripts lately to have it even surface as a possibility.

He wasn't in love…was he? *No.* Being in love was different from wanting to have a relationship beyond a week. "Says me. I promised your brother I'd keep you safe." He couldn't promise her love. What if he was wrong? What if what he thought was love wasn't love? What if it was?

She laughed. A cynical noise with no pleasing qualities. "And you promised me a week of kink. Which one of us are you going to keep your promise to?"

He narrowed his eyes and thought about her question.

The guy got out. "Umm, the meter's running."

Ian stood like a stone statue and resisted the urge to deck the guy.

"Just give us a moment." She walked over to Ian, who'd stepped away from the front of the car. She didn't stop walking until the toes of her shoes where touching the toes of his shoes. "You and my brother are not my keepers," she whispered.

"I know that," he whispered back. "What if I said I'm in love with you?" There. He'd said it. He'd placed his heart on the line — a line he didn't even know existed until this moment.

Her eyes darkened to a burnt-chocolate brown. "I don't know? Try and see."

He combed his fingers through his hair. What was she talking about? Try what? Didn't he just say I love you?

Hell, was she deliberately misunderstanding because she didn't want to hear the words? That's what he would do.

He'd probably pulled that stunt in the past to keep from hurting a woman's feelings. "Let's go back to our hotel suite. Call tonight a failed experiment." Of course she didn't want to hear his confession of love. A week ago, she still hated him.

She glanced up at the sky and then at him. Her expression was indecipherable. Long seconds ticked by with just the whistle of the wind to be heard over the beat of his own heart. "Okay," she finally said in a no-nonsense tone.

He raked a hand down his face. "Okay you'll come back to the hotel with me? Or okay you agree tonight was a failed experiment?"

She turned to the guy who was still standing by the cab. "I've decided not to share a cab with you after all. Thanks for the offer of a lift."

Ian relaxed his hands. Were they really just going to share a cab? He snorted to himself. Maybe that's what she thought they were going to do, but there's no way a single man leaving a sex party with a single woman wasn't thinking about getting her dress over her head and her panties down around her ankles. He was smart enough not to mention his theory to Kin. "Does this mean you and I are okay?"

She nodded slowly. "We're okay."

She might've said so, but Ian wasn't foolish enough to believe it.

Chapter Thirty-Two

Ian wasn't speaking. He was staring moodily out the window.

Should she tell him the truth about the couple at the club? It wasn't like she was really leaving the club with a stranger. Charlie knew him. Too bad she couldn't call Charlie and ask her how to play this one out.

No. She didn't need Charlie to tell her how to handle this. Ian was great as a sex partner, but he wasn't life-partner material. And this arrangement had *always* been temporary. She might have been too weak to resist his final invitation to come back to the hotel with him, but that didn't mean she couldn't leave him feeling a little bit unsure of her. Unsure of what she may or may not have been about to do. It would do his ego good to be knocked down a few notches.

"Ian?"

"Yes?"

"You've been a great mentor. Heck, at the beginning of the week, I would have never considered leaving with a single guy from a sex party. I have you to thank for that type of confidence."

His response was a grunt.

She hid a smile.

Their cab pulled up to the hotel.

When they walked into the hotel, Ian said, "Go on up to the room. I'll be there in a minute," in a drill sergeant tone. Like he was in complete dom mode.

"But—"

"Don't argue."

Maybe she was wrong. Maybe he wasn't playing the part of a dom right now. Maybe he was just really pissed at her.

She might have been inclined to tell him the truth about the guy at the party if he hadn't backtracked quicker than a politician after election day on the whole "what if I say I love you" comment when she'd asked him to expand on what he meant by it. Sweet Jesus, for a few seconds, while standing there in the light of the moon with Ian, hope had sprung flowers inside of her dismembered heart, filling in the cracks and holes with lilacs and daisies. And then they'd wilted.

Frustrated with the whole situation, she tossed her hair over her shoulder and trounced off to their suite. She should have stayed with her stripper. At least he liked to laugh. Damn Charlie and her whole leave-until-they-stop-chasing-you advice. All it had done for her was totally piss Ian off. And a pissed off dom wasn't that much fun.

Inside the suite, she glanced around. Everything was a pristine white with black accents. Very modern. Very large. The kind of room a rich man reserves for a week at a conference. The kind of room a rich man can spend a week playing kinky games with a woman in and then walk away with no regrets. The kind of room she would have never seen the inside of if it hadn't been for him.

Not that you would know he was rich by talking to him. He never mentioned money.

She poured herself a glass of wine. She thought again

about Ian's words as they stood outside in the lights of the cab.

"What if I said I'm in love with you?"

Was that his idea of a true declaration of love? She sighed. Of course it wasn't.

He'd simply said what he thought he needed to say to get her to go home with him. If he'd meant it, he would have repeated it. Made sure she knew he was serious.

So what would happen if she told him she loved him? No. She couldn't do that. They'd entered into a deal. He shouldn't have to listen to her declare her love and then feel like a jerk for not loving her back. Besides, all she had left was her pride. She wasn't giving that up on a whim.

No, if he loved her, he was going to have to make it very clear to her.

She didn't have to wonder or worry for long what Ian's plans were for the evening.

Within minutes, he came in carrying a bag from a gift shop in the hotel. He held the gold colored bag out to her. "Go take a shower and put this on. No makeup. If it's not in the bag, don't wear it."

Her chin came up. "What if it doesn't fit?"

"Wear it anyway."

She swallowed her retort, grabbed the sack out of his hand, and stomped her way to the bathroom. She wasn't sure who she was mad at—him, or herself. Or her dumb pride.

She opened the bag, and her heartbeat ratcheted up. Ian's version of a schoolgirl uniform. Similar to the one she'd worn in high school.

Similar to the one she'd been wearing the day she asked him to take her virginity. She pulled the pieces out and laid them on the counter.

Well…maybe not *that* similar.

At her school, the black skirts were required to hit mid-knee. This skirt would hit her upper thighs. At her school they wore pristine, white, loose-fitting blouses. This form-fitting blouse had tiny buttons stretching from the high-collar to the hem—a size small. A pair of white, thigh-high stockings were included.

No shoes. No bra. A tiny pair of panties.

Her heart ached at the realization that they were going to end their week on a nostalgic note. Recreating the event that brought them to this point in their life.

Was this his idea of bringing closure to their relationship? Had this week just been about them getting each other out of their systems? Would it work? Would she be able to walk away a whole person?

Chapter Thirty-Three

Ian had a drink in his hand when Kinley walked out of the bathroom. His heart fell to his toes and landed with a noisy splat. He set the glass on the counter and walked closer.

She had her hair pulled up in a ponytail. Her red-framed glasses perched on her cute nose.

Her breasts were straining to escape through the buttonholes of a white blouse that was buttoned up to her chin.

The skirt skimmed her thighs. A quarter of an inch shorter and he could see her bare pussy.

"So our last night is going to be about roleplaying?" She gave him a smile that wasn't quite happy but not quite fake. Sort of sad.

"No. It's going to be about you and me. About something that's been ten years in the making."

She tugged at her bottom lip with her teeth. "That sounds nice."

"Turn around slowly," he ordered.

White stockings encased the length of her legs, stopping at the hem of the skirt.

Her legs were shoulder-width apart.

He remembered the beauty of her ass after he'd spanked it the last time. Rosy and begging for attention. He wanted to see it that way again. But not tonight. Tonight was for other things.

"Go out in the hall; knock on the door. When I answer, I want you to ask me to take your virginity."

She turned around slowly, her lips slightly parted. Her breasts were rising and falling rapidly with her breathing. She nodded. Walked out in the hallway.

He waited for a knock. He didn't answer.

A second knock. He didn't answer.

A third knock. Loud.

He opened the door just as she raised her hand to knock the fourth time.

She lost her balance and fell into him. He placed his hands on her shoulders, pushed her back slightly, and steadied her. "Kinley, what a surprise. What are you doing here?"

She glanced up at him with large brown eyes. Innocent eyes saturated with lust. She raised her hands and wrapped them around his neck and kissed him.

It was an awful kiss. All closed mouth and inexperienced. Exactly the way she'd kissed him ten years ago.

Her body collapsed against him.

His hands went around her, trying to steady them both, and they landed on her ass. She jumped. Pulled back. Out of his arms. "I want you to take my virginity," she said in a breathless voice. The same breathless voice she'd used ten years ago.

Only this time she was all woman. His for the taking.

He shut the door and pulled her into the hotel room. Past the living area and into the bedroom. He left her standing at the bedroom door, and he sat down on the bed. "I can't take your virginity. You're a good girl."

A small smile tugged the corners of her lips. "You're

wrong. I'm not a good girl. I'm a very bad girl." She walked halfway in and stopped.

He spread his feet. His cock was hard. He adjusted himself while she watched. "I don't believe you're bad. I would never forgive myself if I took what you're offering."

Her eyes grew stormy. "But I want you to. I've dreamt of this for years."

"I'm too old for you. You need someone your own age."

She raised her hands to the buttons on her blouse. "What if I change your mind? Then will you take my virginity?"

He swallowed the desire to get up and strip her naked. "If you can change my mind. But you won't." God, it was their arrangement, all over again. Only this time, the stakes were so much higher. This game meant so much more. At least to him, it did. He wasn't sure about her.

She unbuttoned her shirt—one tiny button at a time. Her nipples were so erect he could easily see their rosy color through the thin material. She stopped about midway, pulled the shirt apart, and let her tits pop out.

The breath swooshed out of him. He closed his eyes. Counted to ten.

"Open your eyes," she husked. "Touch yourself."

He did both.

She watched his hands. Licked her lips—slowly. "I don't have any panties on."

"You don't?" His voice was deep and laden with yearning. Ten years worth of yearning. Ten years of imagining this scene.

"Do you want me to prove it?" She opened her lips, and he could see the tip of her tongue between her teeth.

He nodded.

She slowly turned. Spread her legs past shoulder-width. Leaned forward. Very…very…slowly.

Ian watched the skirt inch its way up until he could see her ass. It was the sexiest thing he'd ever watched a woman do in his life. He wanted to film her so he could watch it over and over again.

She reached a hand behind and lifted her skirt all the way up.

Unable to resist, with her legs wide apart, dressed in white stockings, and her skirt flipped up, he grabbed his phone and took a picture. For his eyes only.

"Put your hands on the floor and balance yourself," he ordered.

Their eyes locked. She blinked several times. Then she nodded.

He walked up behind her. Placed one hand on the small of her back. Placed the other between her legs. "Are you sure you want me to be your first?" His finger caressed her clitoris as he spoke.

She moaned. "I've always wanted you to be my first."

He went down on his knees. Kissed the cheeks of her ass. "I can smell your arousal."

"I've been wet all week for you."

"Hearing that is intoxicating. Tell me what you're feeling right now."

"I feel like I'm back in time and something wonderful is about to happen."

"Touch yourself."

She left one hand on the floor and brought the other between her legs.

God, she was flexible. "When a girl loses her virginity. She should choose a man who is worthy of the gift."

"How does she know who is worthy?"

"He'll be a man who will respect her. Who won't brag to his friends about what they did."

She put her fingers between her legs. "I like it when I rub up and down right here. Is that normal?"

"It's completely normal. In fact, a man who is preparing

to deflower you, will rub you there himself. He'll rub you there with his fingers. Or his cock. Or his tongue."

She groaned.

"Slip your finger inside yourself and tell me what happens?"

She did. Slowly. Very slowly. "I'm so wet. And tight. Very, very tight. How big is a man's aroused cock?"

"I could tell you. But it would be better if I showed you." Ian kicked off his shoes and unbuttoned his slacks. He pushed them down and kicked them out of the way.

She raised and turned around.

He stood there completely naked from the waist down. He was still wearing a jacket and shirt and tie.

"Wow. That is so big. I don't think it will fit."

"That's why a guy makes sure you're very wet before he slips inside of you."

"Can I touch you?"

"I'm hoping you will."

Her hand reached out, and she gently slid her palm up and down. "You feel hot. Why is the tip wet?"

"It's because you excite me."

"If you took my virginity would you brag about it to your friends tomorrow?"

"No."

"Would you respect me in the morning?"

"Absolutely."

Kinley grabbed his tie and lead him to the bed. She slipped off her blouse. Unbuttoned and dropped her skirt. Left her stockings on and climbed into the center of the bed.

He came to her. Climbed on top. "In the morning, if I forget to say you were wonderful. That our fantasy week together was the best I've ever—"

She leaned up and kissed him, silencing his words, frying his brain.

Chapter Thirty-Four

Kinley stood in the middle of Ian's hotel suite wearing her chucks, her jeans and her new *What Happens in Vegas Stays in Vegas* T-shirt. Her party dress was stuffed inside her suitcase. Her Catholic school girl uniform was on the bedroom floor.

She blew her nose and checked her mascara in the mirror hanging over the couch. Damn tears.

They'd enjoyed hot sex. Incredibly hot breakup/good-bye sex.

But not once, during or after the sex, did he repeat his declaration of love.

It was as if the words had never crossed his lips while they were standing in the headlights of a cab.

They'd probably been blurted because his pride wouldn't allow him to lose his woman to another man, and that was the only thing he could think to say that might keep her by his side.

Charlie's words came back to her.

Keep leaving until he stops chasing you or catches you.

Truth be told, that was the real reason she'd left the sex

party: to see if he'd chase. But that wasn't why she was leaving this time. Or, at least, that's what she kept telling herself. This time she was leaving because they'd made a no-strings-attached deal. And like Ian, she kept her promises. She had no real illusions that he'd be chasing after her.

She wrote a short note. Her hand was shaking. This may be the last time she saw him. Fresh tears fell.

> *Ian, I didn't want to wake you. You look so tuckered out from our sexual escapades. :) But I did want to say thanks for this week. I've learned far more than I could have ever imagined. You upheld your end of our bet to teach me about sex.*

Her hand hovered over the paper. Should she leave a hint that she'd be open to a new ending? But what if he wasn't, and he didn't come after her? Then her greed in wanting more would take their memory of this week and give it a negative spin. She didn't want that. They had their story. It was a short story, and it was complete.

> *I've given last night a considerable amount of thought. We said at the beginning of the week, what happens in Vegas stays in Vegas. No strings attached. But strings or no strings, you told me upfront you didn't think you could watch me with another man, and I pushed you. Not because I really wanted to be with another man, but I think I did it to make you jealous. Not to learn more about sex. Which was a very immature thing to do on my part. So let me just say, I'm sorry.*

> *This week has given me a lot of information and experiences that will strengthen me as a writer. But more importantly than that, it's given me a new us memory. One that makes me smile. One that has a*

beginning and a middle…and an end.

Again, her hand hovered over the paper. Her heart was pushing her to write on-the-nose dialogue. Like something about maybe next time they could try it with a few strings attached? But her brain told her no. That would put him on the spot. If he really was in love with her, he'd decipher the subtext in her letter. And if he wasn't…

I'll send you my revised manuscript, or the new one I'm working on, by the end of the month. Not because I want you to be my agent, but because I want you to see how much you've helped me.

A tear splashed on the paper. Damn it. She blotted the paper with her sleeve.

P.S. You're not a bad kisser. Not a great one…but not bad either. Maybe with some practice… All joking aside, this week has made me realize how much I've missed having my big brother's best friend in my life. As such, I've decided to add an addendum to my New Year's Resolution List. I won't bore you with the details…

She wanted to leave him with a smile. Love or no love, what they'd done had been incredible. And maybe, just maybe, he'd call and push for details about her New Year's Resolution Addendum. That's what authors did, right? Leave the reader wanting to know what happens next.

She grabbed her travel pillow, her laptop, her suitcase, and her carry-on. She left her room key on the bed next to her note.

"I love you, Ian Thompson," she whispered.

Chapter Thirty-Five

Ian picked up his coffee cup, walked to the large window in his living room, and glanced out at the Apple Store. Normally, he loved the view from his New York apartment. Not today, though. Not yesterday. Not since he returned from Vegas.

After a month of hearing nothing from Kinley, he'd learned not to get his hopes up when he woke each morning—not to get his hopes up that there'd be an email from her. But every morning he'd check his email, and when there was nothing from her, his hopes that weren't up took a nosedive off the Brooklyn Bridge.

If only she'd send her manuscript, he could contact her without breaking the promise he'd made to her that what happens in Vegas stays in Vegas. He could convince her that the sex they'd experienced was too good to have such a short shelf life. That they could have some sort of relationship beyond the conference.

But the manuscript never came, and he wouldn't break a promise. He didn't lie.

He sat down at his desk and pulled up a manuscript from

one of his favorite authors and started editing.

Two hours later, there was a knock at his door.

When he answered, the UPS man was standing there with a package. "Please sign."

Ian did. It looked like a manuscript package. What the hell? He had a strict policy about how to query him. First, he didn't accept snail mail. He believed in saving the trees. Second, if you were querying him, he just wanted the query and the first ten pages of your manuscript—not the entire manuscript. Any author he'd requested a full from would have been given his private email address to send it to.

He glanced at the address. A P.O. Box. He dropped it in the to-be-shredded bin.

Probably some author trying to get his attention. An author who couldn't be bothered to read his guidelines before querying him.

An hour later, unable to concentrate on the manuscript he was reading, he got up and walked back to the kitchen for a coffee refill.

The manuscript in the trash called to him. The tree had already been killed to send it. Perhaps he should at least glance at the first few pages so the tree didn't die for nothing.

He pulled it out, opened the envelope and tugged out the bound pages. He flipped it over and read the title.

THE SEDUCTION OF I. HARTLEY. A novella by Kinley Foster.

A rush of excitement swamped his heart, sending it floundering for dry ground. She'd finished her novella. She'd actually sent it to him. Would it have the tragic ending she promised?

He poured himself another coffee and topped it off with Bailey's, then sat down in his favorite chair to read. Had their experiment worked?

Two hours later he set the manuscript aside. He poured

himself another drink, this time without the coffee and Bailey's. This time all scotch. And, no, he didn't give a damn that it was barely half past noon.

Was he reading between the lines something that wasn't there? Was it wishful thinking? Did she feel anything for him other than desire?

He reread the last line of her manuscript.

Downed his drink.

Poured another. "This is going to get interesting." The seduction of Kinley Foster wasn't over.

Chapter Thirty-Six

Kinley sat in the back of the Karaoke Lounge. Alone. She kept watching the doors for Ian—which was stupid. Just like spending money on a weekend hop to Vegas over her three-day, President's birthday weekend from school. At least her room had been comped due to the conference hotel-room fiasco.

She also didn't need to be spending money on a new pair of silver, sparkly Chucks, skinny jeans, and a sexy black top that made the most of her 34C's.

She didn't really expect him to show up. Happily ever afters only happened in novels and Hallmark movies.

If he'd loved her—really loved her—he would have come for her when she left Vegas. When she went back home. He wouldn't have allowed all of this time to go by. He would have rented a private jet and been at the airport when she landed. That would have been a romance-novel worthy ending to her novella.

"May I get you another Red Zin?" the waitress asked.

Kinley glanced at her empty wine glass. "Sure."

According to Charlie, a woman keeps leaving until the man stops following or stops allowing you to leave.

Ian allowed her to leave.

He stopped following.

He didn't love her.

The fact that she was sitting in the Vegas lounge hoping otherwise was really pathetic. But love, she'd discovered, didn't allow common sense to take root in your brain. Love swelled up so large, other thoughts were crowded out. Pride didn't have a chance.

Which is why, despite common sense, Kinley was sitting in Vegas, betting her heart that Charlie was right.

Kinley was betting that sometimes when a man fails to follow, he simply needs a cattle prod to his ass to get him moving again.

"Here you go, doll," the waitress said, setting her drink down.

"Thanks." Kinley totally blamed the soft side of her brain on the same genetics that inspired her to write romances instead of espionage thrillers.

She'd sent her novella to Ian a week ago. Short a scene. The ending.

In her novella, she'd left her heroine in the Karaoke Lounge over the President's birthday weekend, waiting for the hero to show up.

In her novella, the hero walked up on stage and started singing.

That's when the heroine first noticed he'd arrived.

The song he sings is his answer to the heroine. It's a song that tells the heroine if her love story is going to have a tragic ending or a happy ending. Happy ending—as in love everlasting.

Her phone vibrated. She tensed and pulled it out. Hope twirled like a windstorm around her heart.

She glanced at the phone number and sighed. A text from her brother. What did he want?

Where are you?

She took another drink of her wine. Turned her back to the stage. *I got a wild hair and decided to get out of town for the weekend.*

I wanted to talk to you about something.

Kinley propped her feet up in the empty chair across from her. *What?*

It's about Ian.

Sweat popped out on Kinley's upper lip. *What about him?*

I heard something today that concerns me.

She gulped back the desire to come clean. Spill her guts. She'd had sex with Ian, and she liked it. *What?*

About you and him in Vegas.

She downed the rest of her wine. "Shit." *What about us?* There was a short pause. Kinley nibbled her thumbnail.

Did seeing him rekindle the love you've felt for him forever?

The question brought her up short. She didn't want to lie. She believed in telling the truth. Truth was the backbone of trust. A brother should be able to trust his sister. *Why would you ask me that?*

"This song is for Bossy Pants," a male voice said over a microphone.

Kinley dropped her phone. Her gaze jerked to the stage. There stood Ian...in jeans and a cowboy hat. A black T-shirt hugged his muscles. When had he come in? And since when did he dress like a cowboy? God, he was freaking hot. Hot-coals-in-a-volcano hot.

Had her brother texted her to distract her? Were they in on this together? That was some coincidence if not.

The music started.

Kinley turned her chair around.

Oh, God. He was really going to sing...in front of a crowd. She blushed for him. What was he going to sing? Maybe something simple. Something anyone could sing. Like... She came up blank on a song he might be able to sing.

Ian couldn't sing.

The comment he'd made to her in the bathroom about not being able to sing all those years ago had been her own words twisted and thrown back at her. Words she'd spoken to him hours earlier.

As payback, he'd snuck in while she was taking a shower to steal her clothes. And it had been her bad luck that she'd been singing at the time.

Giving him perfect ammunition.

Was he really going to sing her a song? Humiliate himself in that way? A guy would only do that for someone he...

The music started. A country song. A George Strait song.

She grinned. That explained the cowboy hat. He'd always liked country music. She preferred rock.

He placed the microphone to his lips.

She stood up—too quickly, because the room spun. She grabbed the back of her chair for support. Was there a shortage of oxygen in the room?

Their gazes met. He dipped his head in her direction. His cowboy hat shadowed his face. Maybe that's why he wore it, so no one would know who he was.

"*Dear Kinley, you left your tears on your story,*" he sang, in a country twang.

She smiled. She knew that tune, but like her karaoke debut, he was changing the lyrics. He'd gone to the trouble to make the song theirs. They had a song. She wiped her palms on her jeans.

"*And, damn you girl, they got mixed up with mine.*"

Did he cry tears over her? No way.

As if reading her mind, he nodded.

She felt a tear roll down her cheek. She wiped it away. She bit her lip to stop crying.

"*…there are pieces of my heart I can't find.*"

She swallowed. If only he knew. She hadn't been able to think straight in a month. Her students noticed when she failed to enforce the one-week checkout rule. Her peers noticed when she wore the same outfit to school two days in a row.

"*We're two lonely hearts of a kind.*"

Had he been feeling as discombobulated as her?

"*Let's fall into bed together. Why should we both sleep apart?*"

Despite her watery eyes, she smiled. Shook her head at him. His singing sucked. His changing of the song's words sucked. But God, he had a body that made a woman dream of inappropriate behavior.

"*Tonight, you and me,*" he crooned.

She walked toward the stage. People whispered.

"*Come on up here, darling,*" he said using a slight drawl, his cornflower blue-eyed gaze beckoning.

Her heart skipped a beat. Damn, she had a weakness for smooth talking cowboys. She walked to the end of the stage and stared at him like a groupie.

"*Kinley and Ian are much better together.*"

She nodded. Was it her imagination or was his voice

getting better?

He continued singing.

"*Kinley—why should we go insane alone?*" He held out a hand to her.

She walked up on the stage. He pulled her into his side. He placed the microphone so they could both sing. She rolled her eyes.

He winked at her, causing her knees to feel like the branches of a willow tree.

"*Let's fall…*" they both belted out the song's iconic verse, not caring that they sucked.

When the song ended, he went down on one knee.

She gasped and went down on her knees in front of him. Mainly because her legs refused to hold her up. Her heart spun in her chest like a Vegas roulette wheel. Could this really be happening?

Ian took off his hat and laid it on the floor. Took her hands in his. "Kinley Foster, I've spent the last month thinking you don't like me nor love me. And as a former football player, let me just say loving someone you think doesn't love you back hurts worse than getting slammed by a 250-pound linebacker."

"Awwwww," the crowd said.

Kinley didn't say anything. She was afraid she was misinterpreting his words. Was he asking for her love or her body?

He closed his eyes briefly and then reopened them. "Then I received a novel with no ending. And my heart soared. Kinley Foster, I need to know—do you love me?"

The crowd was so quiet you could hear the slot machines in the casino outside the walls.

Kinley moistened her lips. Her heart squeezed and fainted. She gave him a big, goofy smile. "Ian Thompson—"

"Use the microphone, we can't hear," someone in the crowd yelled.

Kinley laughed, and took the microphone. "Ian Thompson—I'm not supposed to like you. But I do... I'm not supposed to love you, but I do."

The crowd erupted.

She bit her bottom lip. She glanced out into the crowd. Was that Charlie and Dan in the front row?

Ian took the microphone. "Kinley Foster, when you were little, you made me your prince charming." He gently touched the scar on her forehead. "But like an idiot, I let you down. I can't promise there won't be any more scars."

She leaned in and whispered "I can't believe you're really here" in his ear.

"Say it in the microphone," someone in the crowd shouted. She was pretty sure it was Charlie.

"Some things are just for my ears," Ian told the crowd, sitting down the microphone. He kissed her fingertips. "Do you want to marry me?"

She grinned. Nodded. Threw herself in his arms, knocking him over and they both tumbled to the floor, her on top of him. "...I do," she said, with her hands on his chest, gazing into his beautiful eyes.

Chapter Thirty-Seven

"If I die tonight, I'll be a very happy man," Ian said, spooning with Kinley. His cock was finally sated. They were staying in the same hotel room they'd shared during the conference. He'd paid double for the hotel personnel to move the couple assigned the room to a new room and sent the couple champagne as a thank you for their trouble.

She wiggled her ass against him—gasped. "Wow, Mr. Boner's asleep." Her voice was full of a type of wonder that stroked his ego as cleverly as her hand had earlier stroked his cock.

He chuckled and pulled her in tighter. "That's your nickname for my dick?"

"I think it's cute." They were laying sideways on the king-sized bed. The pillows and comforter were on the floor. Their clothes were on the floor. And a lamp from the bedside table was also on the floor.

"Cute?" He groaned. "A man never wants his cock thought of as cute." He tried to sound gruff but didn't succeed.

He spoke the words into her neck where he breathed in

the lavender scent of her, mixed with the more earthy scents of their hours of passion.

She scooted away slightly and rolled over so they were staring into each other's eyes.

"You're beautiful, soon-to-be Mrs. Thompson." He splayed his hand over her hip.

She swatted his arm. "Soon-to-be Mrs. Kinley Foster-Thompson," she corrected. "There's one thing I need to tell you."

"What's that?"

She paused and took a deep breath. "I do remember our conversation about you and Stacy. The one we had when I was drunk."

As clichéd as it sounded, his heart felt like it stopped beating. "And?"

She sat up in bed. "And, I believe you. I'm sorry I took her explanation so easily and never pushed you for a more believable account."

Her words were like medicine, reviving his heart and healing him in places that he didn't even know were broken. "Thank you for believing me. That's the best gift you'll ever give me."

Her mouth fell open, but her eyes twinkled—a tell she couldn't control. "You're not mad at me?"

He'd seen that gleam in her eyes before. Knew that sparkle in her eyes from years of playing Three Card Poker. She thought she was about to get away with something. "No. But...you definitely deserve a spanking for keeping the information from me."

She gave him a what-the-hell look. "In your dreams. Whatever we talk about tonight is off-limits to spanking punishment."

He chuckled, stretching his hand. Anticipation warmed his palm. "Why would I agree to that?"

She didn't look the least bit concerned by his posturing. "Because if it's not, I'll do to you what women do to men when they want to punish them."

"And what might that be?" His gut told him to brace for her reply. That she was about to school him in the ways of a relationship.

She lifted her arms above her head and stretched from side-to-side. "I'll withhold sex," she said mid-stretch.

"You think so? You think you can resist my charm if I want to have sex with you?" He reached out and cupped her breast, rubbing her nipple between his thumb and finger.

She lowered her arms, reached out, and stroked his cock.

He gave her a lazy *so what* look.

She leaned down, her mouth hovered over his cock, and her hair fell down around him.

The stroke of her tongue along the underside of his dick caused him to hiss out a breath.

"Checkmate," she said in smug confidence, quickly moving and getting away from him.

He grinned like an idiot. His brain was a bowl of happy mush. Ian was pretty sure his cheeks might even be pink. "Well played," he said, his voice rough. "Very well played." The vixen knew exactly how much power she had over him.

She frowned. "Wait, just one minute. You agreed way too easily. Why? You've got something to say that I'm not going to like—don't you?"

He sat up, twisted around, and leaned against the bed's headboard.

She turned so she was facing him.

Ian didn't want to introduce anything into their evening that might mar the memory. But he had to. Their relationship had two more hurdles to clear. He hoped she would see them as low hurdles. "Even though we're getting married, I can't be your agent. Nothing has changed there."

She blanched. The color drained out of her face like an IV blood drip with a fat tube. "Do you think my sex writing still sucks?"

He leaned forward and kissed her swollen lips. "You have it down to perfection. I was hard the whole time I read your novella."

"Then why? I know I said I didn't want you to, but I was lying. I want you to represent me."

He cleared his throat. His heart punched against his chest, trying to escape like a racehorse about to be released from the gates at the Belmont. "I can't be clear-headed when I'm reading what you write. I can't give you the type of brutal honesty you'll need, because I won't see the problems."

The color that had drained from her face earlier flamed back into her cheeks. She fanned herself with her hand. "I'm going to be married to the hottest romance agent in the business, and I don't even get to call you my agent?"

Ian hesitated but nodded. "Is that a deal breaker? That's not why you said yes to my proposal, is it?" Although he said it in a joking tone, there was a part of him that needed to hear her say it wasn't: the part that still couldn't believe she'd said yes.

She growled. "You're an ass. Of course it's not why I said yes. But I did think it was a bonus of saying yes."

He leaned toward her and kissed her trembling lips. "I did a little digging into your Twitter history and discovered there's an agent you really wanted more than you wanted me."

She touched her lips. "What? Who?"

"I read one of your tweets where you told Ann Collette that if she ever decided to represent romance authors, you would be the first to send her a manuscript."

Her eyes darkened. "But she doesn't represent romance."

He smiled, feeling pretty full of himself. "You're wrong."

"What? When? Did she make an announcement? Oh my

God."

"I just happen to be friends with her. We had lunch, and she mentioned that she's been toying with the idea of taking on a romance author."

"You're kidding. Has she already opened to submissions? Do you think I have a shot at getting her to represent me?"

"It just so happened that I had your novella with me at our most recent luncheon. I told her who you were on Twitter, and she remembered you because you always retweet her slush pile tweets and leave comments."

Kinley grabbed both of his cheeks in her hands. "Did you give her my manuscript?"

"Yes."

She let go. Squealed. "When do you think I'll hear back? Oh God. I should have been being nervous. And I didn't even know I should have been being nervous. How long has she had it? Is it too late to send out pleas to the universe for some help?"

He could almost see her brain about to explode from all of the questions filtering through it at one time. "She's had it for forty-eight hours."

Kinley fanned herself. "Then she probably hasn't read it yet."

"She's read it," he inserted.

Her eyes rounded. "How do you know? Do you have her on speed dial? Did you ask her?"

He chuckled. This was fun. "I didn't ask her."

"Then how do you know? Did she tweet about it in her slush pile tweets?"

"As a matter of fact she did."

Kinley scampered off the bed.

"Where are you going?"

"To get my Mac. I need to read what she said."

He took a good look at her backside. God, she had a

beautiful ass. "Or you could come back to bed with me, and I can tell you what she said when she called me to talk about your manuscript."

She jumped back on the bed. Straddled him. Straddled Mr. Boner. "Spill it. What did she say?"

"She said I'm an idiot for not signing you."

"She said that?" Kinley squealed.

"And a lot more. She told me I could tell you that she wants to represent you, and she'll be giving you a call after our romantic weekend is over."

"I have to wait until Monday?" She glanced down at Mr. Boner, which was up and about, then gave Ian a coy smile.

"You're all mine until then."

She wiggled up, grabbed his cheeks and kissed his lips. "You're the best fiancé ever."

Although he'd loved where she'd been straddling originally, he gave a sigh of relief. There was more to be said, and he wasn't sure it would have been said, had she stayed in that particular spot. "I have one more confession."

She wrinkled her nose. "What else have you done?"

"I've spoken to your mom and your brother. I told them the truth. And I asked them both for permission to ask for your hand in marriage."

She started to move off him. He slid his hands down to cup the top of her ass and held her in place. "You did? What did they say?"

"They said yes—of course. How else did I get your brother to text you and distract you long enough for me to come up on stage and surprise you?"

She plopped a noisy kiss on his lips. "I knew that was too coincidental."

"By the way, how was my singing?"

"You stunk up the joint," she said in a nasally voice.

He grimaced. "I got the best looking girl in the room to

come up on stage. I couldn't have been that bad."

"Have I ever told you I love a man in a cowboy hat?"

He looped his arms around her waist. "Have I ever told you I love a woman with a smart mouth and an ass made for spanking?"

She leaned back into his hands. "Do I ever get to spank you?"

"If I ever lie to you, you can spank me."

She laughed. A soft, feminine sound. Full of confidence and sass. "Says the man who's never been married and never had a wife ask him 'do these jeans make my ass look fat?'"

And so that was her laugh—the one his dad warned him about. The one he told Ian to learn and commit to memory. The one that would warn him in the future to tread very carefully, because his woman was about to trump his full house with a royal flush. "Love, your ass will always look beautiful in my eyes."

"By the way?" she said.

He raised an eyebrow and cocked his head. "What?"

"We're going to need a new safe phrase."

Acknowledgments

Mark Twain once said, "Writing is easy. All you have to do is cross out the wrong words." I'd like to thank my incredible mentor, Margie Lawson, and my brilliant editor, Vanessa Mitchell, for helping me to cross out the wrong words and fill in the void with the right words.

Thank you to everyone at Entangled Publishing for breathing life into this book. It takes a village to get a book to market. I'm glad all of you are in my village.

A special thank you to author, Megan Ryder, for posting on Facebook about an opportunity to be one of the authors chosen to write a book as part of Entangled Publishing's *What Happens in Vegas* continuity series. Her post started my journey to writing this book. And I'd like to thank Liz Pelletier for choosing me to be one of the authors for this series. Thank you, thank you, thank you.

Thank you to Connie W. who invited me to a Passion Parties event. An event that sparked my imagination for this story.

A huge thank you to my family for believing in me and for

making excuses for me when I failed to show up at functions because I was too busy writing. I love you all to the moon and back.

I'd like to thank my agent, Tish Beaty, for validating me as a writer the day she took me on as one of her select few authors.

And most of all, thank *you*, for purchasing this book. I hope you fall in love with my characters as much as I did.

About the Author

Lisa Wells always knew there would come a time in her life when she'd pursue her dream career as a romance author. This is that time.

Before this moment, she's enjoyed a rollercoaster journey called—The Middle School Counselor—Dramas, Dreams, and Destinies.

After many years of working with teenage girls, she knows when one comes in baffled because another girl hates her, the first question to ask is, "Did you steal her boyfriend?" Nine times out of ten the answer is some form of yes but…

While Lisa enjoys working with adolescents, she writes for adults. Her books contain: Sex, Scowls & Sass.

Discover the **What Happens in Vegas** *series…*

TEMPTING HER BEST FRIEND
a *What Happens in Vegas* novel by Gina L. Maxwell

Tired of waiting for her best friend to see her as more, Alyssa Miller heads to Las Vegas for a romance book convention. But when Dillon Alexander realizes his best friend plans to have a one-night stand on her vacation, he hauls ass after her to make sure he's the one to scratch her itch—commitment issues be damned. Neither of them expects their chemistry to be so explosive, but with a little help, what happens in Vegas might not stay in Vegas…

THE MAKEOVER MISTAKE
a *What Happens in Vegas* novella by Kathy Lyons

A CHANGE OF PLANS
a *What Happens in Vegas* novella by Robyn Thomas

MASQUERADING WITH THE CEO
a *What Happens in Vegas* novella by Dawn Chartier

JUST ONE REASON
a *What Happens in Vegas* novella by Brooklyn Skye

TAMED BY THE OUTLAW
a *What Happens in Vegas* novel by Michelle Sharp

TEMPTED BY MR. WRITE
a *What Happens in Vegas* novella by Sara Hantz

GAMBLING ON THE BODYGUARD
a *What Happens in Vegas* novel by Sarah Ballance

SEDUCING SEVEN
a *What Happens in Vegas* novella by MK Meredith

CALLING HER BLUFF
a *What Happens in Vegas* novella by Kaia Danielle

HER SECRET LOVER
a *What Happens in Vegas* story by Robin Covington

ACCIDENTALLY IN LOVE WITH THE BIKER
a *What Happens in Vegas* story by Teri Ann Stanley

BETTING ON THE WRONG BROTHER
a *What Happens in Vegas* story by Cathryn Fox

LOVING THE ODDS
a *What Happens in Vegas* novella by Stefanie London

Find love in unexpected places with these satisfying Lovestruck reads...

HER SECRET LOVER
a *What Happens in Vegas* story by Robin Covington

Kelsey Kyle was just handed the opportunity of a lifetime. If she arranges a one-on-one fan experience with a VIP client's favorite author, tall-dark-and-intense Micah Holmes, and she'll be a shoo in for the casino's management program. She's not expecting the immediate attraction between her and Micah...or how tempted she is to act on it. Soon, their game of "undercover lover" quickly escalates to something more. But when Micah discovers her secret agenda, all bets are off.

HOW TO SAVE A SURGEON
a *Gambling Hearts* novel by C.M. Stone

When he lost the girl he loved, Dr. Jackson DeMatteo shut down his heart and became a perfectionist surgeon. Now he has a coveted promotion dangling before him, but it comes with a price—working with adorably nerdy first-year resident Darla Morales. But while they don't exactly see eye to eye—ever—there is some serious heat happening between them. And Jackson's tempted to cross the line he swore *never* to cross again...

TEXT ME, BABY
a novel by Jolyse Barnett

New to the Big Apple, the last thing Lexie Bloom needs is to fall for two guys at once. Especially when she can't have either. One is her personal trainer, an Adonis way out of her league. The other? A Brit Lit professor her svelte boss insists she woo for her—via text message, no less. Little does she know, the two are the same man...

BRIDESMAID BLUES
a *Wedding Favors* novel by Boone Brux

Maid-of-Honor Dani Brown can handle anything that comes her way when it comes to her best friend's wedding. That is, until the bride asks for a huge favor—Dani needs to distract the best man, Jamie Kingsland…who happens to be Dani's ex. Even though Jamie knows he broke Dani's heart last year, she's being way too nice. And it scares him. Something is up with his favorite bridesmaid, and he's determined to find out what.

Made in the USA
Charleston, SC
24 October 2016